MW01258927

WHAT PEOPLE HAVE SAID ABOUT OTHER RELATED PUBLICATIONS BY JERRY SEARS:

"I have, over many years, had the opportunity to meet hundreds of lawyers who have solicited our legal business. Many of theses lawyers had good substantive skills, but were not prepared to meet the challenge of rainmaking. This is the focus of Jerry Sears' *How to be a Great Rain Maker* ... It is a 'how to' of becoming a rainmaker." —*Howard Aibel, Esq.*
Partner, LeBoeuf, Lamb, Greene & MacRae, New York, NY
formerly Senior Vice President and General Counsel, ITT Corporation

"Jerry Sears has done an outstanding job of analyzing the rainmaking process and of giving constructive suggestions that will benefit both new lawyers and experienced practitioners." —*Merton Marks, Esq.*
Partner, Lewis & Roca
Phoenix, AZ

"Rainmaking is like having your mother reward you with cookies for getting an 'A' in history. It is a sign of approval and acceptance. Jerry Sears illustrates the way to obtain this talent in this wonderful "how to" book. *How to be a Great Rain Maker* reveals the secret mysteries of client development, and the success it brings." —*Jo Reasor, Esq.*
Partner, Jenkins & Gilchrist
San Antonio, TX

"In *How to be a Great Rain Maker*, Jerry Sears shows how our inaccurate self-perceptions create obstacles in the way of relating positively to other people." —Alan Reed, Q.C.
Partner, Tannis, Leclair, Reid
Ottawa, Ontario, Canada

"It is not about manipulating clients, but rather about changing yourself so that you don't have to manipulate anyone. Jerry Sears has captured how to get one's head on straight enough to do that."
—*Ronald Rose, Esq.*
Partner, Dykema Gossett, Detroit, MI

"*How to be a Great Rain Maker* will help lawyers overcome the biggest obstacle to rainmaking—themselves." —*Greg Theis, Esq.*
Managing Counsel - Litigation
Dow Corning Corporation, Midland, MI

"It is the most successful way of advancing a person, a company, and a country." —*Thomas Hobbs*
Senior Vice President, Human Resources (prior), First Interstate Bank

"Career Miracles is superbly crafted, skillfully written, and has excellent self-measuring … completion exhibits enabling the reader to act on this analysis." —*Franklyn Thomas*
Executive Vice President (prior), J. Walter Thompson Co.

There is no other book like it. It should be required reading for everyone who is serious about their career." —*Robert Roskind*
Author of In the Spirit of Business

"This is tough career love at its most principled. People who apply these principles would be far less likely to have come before me as debtors."
—*Stanley Bernstein, Esq.*
Chairman - Bankruptcy Dept., Foley, Hoag & Eliot, Boston, MA (prior);
United States Bankruptcy Judge

MAKING RAIN

MAKING
RAIN

AN ADVENTURE IN THE LAW

JERRY SEARS

Associates Publishers
Delray Beach, Florida

Cover and book design by Pete Masterson,
Aeonix Publishing Group, www.aeonix.com

This is a work of fiction. With the exception of historic facts, places and persons, all names, places, characters, and incidents are entirely imaginary, and any resemblance to actual events or to persons living or dead, is coincidental. The opinions expressed are those of the characters and should not be confused with those of the author.

Publisher's Cataloging-in-Publication
(Provided by Quality Books, Inc.)

Sears, Jerry
    Making Rain : an Adventure in Law / by Jerry Sears. -- 1st ed.
      p. cm.
      ISBN: 1-887597-00-X
      LCCN: 00-104312
      1. Lawyers--Fiction.   2. Ethics--Fiction
    I. title
    PS3569.E185M35 2000   816.3
                    QBI00-508

Published by
Associates Publishers
7491 N. Federal Highway, Suite C-5
Boca Raton, FL 33487 USA

Voice and Fax: (561) 865-2155 (Available 24/7)
Web site: www.mentoringpros.com
e-mail: info@mentoringpros.com

First Edition, January, 2001
10 9 8 7 6 5 4 3 2 1

Printed in the United States of America

To my wife Ellen, whose own role is that of Janet in this book, without my needing to be Brad; and who is, in equal measure, loving and aggressive in her quest for our perfection, both for us individually and together.

"Nothing can work me damage except myself. The harm that I sustain I carry about with me, and never am a real sufferer but by my own fault."

—*St. Bernard, circa 1100*

CHAPTER 1

The two men watched the waterfront across the street from their comfortable fifth floor hotel suite. In this early dawn they could look down at the small public dock and see the motorized junk as it slowly approached. The lights were out in their suite so they could see, but not be seen from the outside. Both in their early 50's, they were dressed in the open shirt and slacks of newly emerged businessmen in newly emerging tropical China.

The tension between them reflected their different backgrounds. The American Harvard educated lawyer, George Chambers, was six feet tall and looked the part of the ivy league lawyer … white hair, well padded body and strong features all supported his hourly billing rate of $350. The Taiwanese "businessman" Sen Moto, stood almost a foot shorter than the lawyer and was so thin he made George seem enormous by comparison. Sen had never seen Harvard. He got his training in rough business deals on the backstreets of the Orient. He was now "respectable," if rich buys respectability.

It was the scene on the waterfront street below that caused the tension. They watched in silence. The Taiwanese taking rapid, nervous puffs on his cigarette.

The American lawyer spoke first. "Is that the guy's boat?"

"It must be." Sen said in only slightly accented English, "Nobody else is going to dock a junk here at six in the morning with eight coolies on board."

"There sure are a lot of people on the street for this time of morning" George said.

The man from Taiwan didn't take his eyes from the scene below, as the junk began to tie up to the dock he said, "I know it. All those people are the reason why I set it up here in the center of the city. Xiamen's one of the most miserable places in August on the southeast China coast. Early morning's the only time this heat and humidity are bearable, so people crowd the waterfront for some relief."

George looked over the crowd. "I sure don't see anyone who looks like a cop, Sen."

"The cops are there, George. They're in with the crowd. I paid enough to make sure."

"We've got a lot riding on this. If it doesn't go right, we could be in big trouble."

Just watch George, there's going to be a whole lot more people there in a few minutes."

George said, "Two coolies just jumped onto the dock and they're tying up the junk. The other six are putting their carrying poles and baskets over the side of the junk onto the dock. But I still don't see our boy."

Sen laughed. "And you won't see him. His style is to stay on the junk 'til the last minute, to be sure it isn't a trap."

As the two men watched, the coolies crouched under their bamboo carrying poles and slowly stood up, bringing their balanced load of the two baskets each into the air. They had walked about half way up the steep hundred-foot gangway from the dock to land when about thirty plain clothes policemen broke from the crowd on the street and rushed down onto the gangway.

Some of them grabbed the coolies and others kept on running down toward the junk, whose powerful engine had never been shut off. In the same instant the police started their raid, the junk sped away from the dock.

George slammed on the windowsill with his fist. "Son of a bitch; he got away."

Sen sat impassively with a tight smile. "Just wait. As you say in America 'It's not over 'til the fat lady sings.'"

They watched the wake of the junk as it quickly moved to higher speeds. This was clearly no ordinary junk. As they watched, a Chinese Navy gunboat came roaring out from the nearby opposite shore of Gulangyu island, less than half a mile away. But the junk was faster than the gunboat. It was pulling away as the first cannon shells from the gunboat hit it. The junk became a ball of fire, which was followed by the sound of an explosion, and the junk was replaced by floating splinters.

Sen stubbed out his cigarette, poured George some tea and smiled as he said, "My friend, that explosion was the sound of the fat lady singing. Our blackmailer's remains are now being eaten by the fish in Xiamen harbor."

George shook his head. "You planned this whole thing? No ... wait." George held up his hands palms out. "Don't tell me if you planned it. I don't want to know. I don't want to be an accessory. I just don't want to know ... so don't tell me. Just tell me if something like this could be planned in China."

"Sure, I planned it. Chinese police don't carry weapons. They're illegal in China, but the military does. It was the only way to kill him."

"Sen, damn it. I told you not to tell me."

"Well, you're an accessory anyway, George. Where the hell do you think I got the money to pay for all this? From you, my friend and I've got every transaction documented. I even have a tape of your instructions. Remember? 'Sen, do whatever's necessary to make sure he's not a problem ... I mean 'whatever.' So, I did 'whatever' and what you just saw was 'whatever.'"

"But I didn't mean to ... "

"Save it for the Judge." Sen said as he reached up, putting his arm on George's shoulder and looked in his eyes with about three inches between them. "But there better not be a judge, George, or you may not be around to tell it to him." And then, more ominously said, "My friend."

George hadn't taken any courses at Harvard in how to deal with this situation. He wasn't even sure there were any. He sighed, pulled himself free from Sen's not so friendly embrace and picked up the phone. Sen looked at him with the obvious question of who he was calling at six thirty in the morning. George said, "I'm calling the junior partner who works for me in Washington. I want him to get the ball rolling right now. Our dead blackmailer's held it up too long. We need to file those papers immediately. The deadline's tomorrow."

Sen said, "I know it's important to move fast, but how are you going to reach him? It's early Monday morning here, which means it's early Sunday morning there. The office will be closed."

"The office, my friend" ... [George put the emphasis on the "friend,"] "is never closed for people who work for me. I make them all carry a portable phone everywhere, even in the bathroom, even in bed, theirs or someone else's. They know that if I can't reach them, they're in trouble ... period."

"Can you do that? We've got wage slaves in the Orient, but I thought you had laws about that in the states."

"We do. They just aren't applied to professionals moving up the ladder. If they don't have any business of their own, they do what I say. I provide their daily bread, every day, and I expect them to butter it with lots of their own sweat … every day."

"Can he file the papers when the Courts open tomorrow morning?"

George dialed the number. "Sure, all he has to do is stay up all night to draft them … and believe me he'll do it, or else."

Sen gave George a look of genuine admiration. "What a man. I like your style, George. We'll get on just fine."

George held up his hand for silence and spoke into the phone. "Brad … George … look, I'm calling you from Xiamen, China … What? … Xiamen … it's on the coast between Shanghai and Hong Kong … What? … Of course you can't find it on a map. It's pronounced 'Shaman' you know, like the Indian medicine man, but it begins with an "X" … got it? … good. Look, we're now clear to file that petition for injunctive relief … I know the deadline's tomorrow. I want it filed when the court opens, not when it closes… your daughter's birthday is today? … well that's the breaks … so have the party next week … . Listen, Brad I want that petition on my desk when I get back, time stamped when the Court opens tomorrow … that's it … if there are any real problems you can reach me at the Lujiang Hotel … 2022922 … but they better be real problems … Goodbye." He hung up.

Sen, showing his new respect for George's superb human relations skills, asked in a deferential way, "Does this guy Brad know anything about what's really going on?"

"Are you kidding? The guy's so out of it he doesn't even have the guts to ask a client for business. He's just a great grinder and that's all I use him for. I bring it in and he grinds it out. We're a great team. Only I make five times what he does."

Sen said, "Look George, now that I've seen you in action I know that you're not just another Harvard … how do you say it in America … you know … Harvard jerk. I only found out last week that it wasn't one word. Let's have breakfast … make sure we're okay on this one and I want to talk to you about some other possible business."

The hotel had the best Dim Sum breakfast in town. As George and Sen picked their snacks from the rolling carts, they also reviewed and picked out each step in their plan.

As he nibbled his Dim Sum, George thought, *well I'm in this now, so I may as well find out how Sen set all this up ... maybe I'll need it to protect myself from him if I need to.*

He said, "Look, Sen I sure would be interested to know how you set up that scene in the harbor."

"I thought you didn't want to know."

George said, "I changed my mind."

Sen said, "I understand. That's a right reserved to lawyers and women. Until I heard you on the phone this morning I thought they were the same thing."

George laughed. "There are some women lawyers in our firm you wouldn't want to tangle with. Even I'm afraid of them. Anyway how did you do that?"

"Well, all it took was a few thousand dollars and a money-oriented Chinese police official. I paid him six thousand yuan... what he makes in a year ... about ten thousand American ... and he's a captain ... "

"Why didn't he just shoot the guy?"

"'Cause even he doesn't carry a gun and there were too many people around to kill him anyway."

George was amazed. "The police don't carry guns?"

"Nope, but I think that's going to change. Crime is picking up in China, just like in Russia – I mean a whole lot. You know, it happens when these countries become capitalistic. People see the big cars, fancy houses and sexy women and they want some. They don't know how to get it so they steal it. They aren't willing to work for it like you and me, George."

George chewed on his Dim Sum and nodded his head reflectively. "I guess the work ethic's a problem all over the world. The sad truth is there just aren't many people willing to work as hard as we do. I hope you don't have the same problem we do in the States, trying to get anyone to put in an honest day's work. Anyway, did the Navy cost another six thousand?"

"Nope. They were free. The police captain set it up with the Navy. My worry was that the junk might not escape from the police. He made sure it did. He told the Navy they were armed, desperate killers. That's probably true anyway ... and so the gunboat just blasted them."

"That's real clever Sen. You got the Chinese to kill our main problem guy. But how were you able to set him up?"

"I made him think his blackmail was working. He wanted a bigger cut, so I told him okay, if he delivered and picked up the stuff himself. But I figured he'd be careful, and he was. He stayed on the junk, just like I thought he would ... that's why the Chinese Navy could do its thing."

When Brad put the cellular phone back on the dresser and turned to face her, his wife Janet lay in bed and silently looked at the signs of crisis. She could see his face dripping perspiration. His fists were clenched and his jaw locked. It was that defiant silence she had known since their marriage began six years earlier. She thought, *I have to be fair to him.* Eight years ago was when the practice of law changed and getting business started to count as much as being a good lawyer ... sometimes more.

How different he had been in law school. She was sure then. She knew him so well. They both graduated in the same law school class. Janet asked herself the question, wasn't three years of the same classes, and two years of living together, enough time to really know someone?

She knew what the problem was. If only she could give him a transfusion of self-confidence in dealing with people. But she wasn't sure how much she had herself. Janet often pictured herself lying next to Brad with tubes connecting them and carrying some of her self-confidence, as it flowed into him. He would get up from the cot - the same Brad she met and loved in law school. He would be full of optimism about the future ... ready to meet the world.

Janet pictured the Brad she used to know, that six foot athletic bookworm, she saw his sandy hair and strong body. She loved to watch him play pick up games of basketball on weekends. She would sit on the bench beside the basketball court and pretend she was a cheerleader. Then after the game they would go back to their apartment to "clean up" but they did a lot more than that. She got so turned on by his body on the basketball court, she practically raped him each time. She looked at his back as he went into the bathroom. She actually thought he might be shrinking. He didn't seem six feet tall anymore.

As she watched him moving to the shower, she knew this wasn't the time to say anything ... not yet. That would come after he went through his thoughtful, analytic time alone. She knew he was a kind, loving man, but so analytic. He had such a difficult time making small talk.

Janet got up, immediately lay down on the floor and pushed her sleepy five foot six inch body into fifty sit-ups and one hundred crunches. She knew it was either exercise or cut her appetite. She chose exercise as the only real way to keep her one hundred twenty pounds trim. She kept her blond hair short so a few brush strokes after the sit-ups did it. She slipped on her robe and went downstairs to make breakfast so they could talk while the children were still sleeping.

When Brad came into the kitchen he said, "You know who that was – George Chambers."

"Do I dare asked what he wanted?"

Brad sat down with a sigh. "What he always wants ... the impossible. I don't really understand what's going on. He's still over there in China. For some reason he didn't want me to file a really important petition, but I couldn't figure out why and he wouldn't tell me. In fact he told me not to discuss the matter with the client. Now tomorrow's the final filing date and he wants it filed in the morning when the court opens."

"Oh, Brad, Jenny's so excited about her birthday. She told me she has five kisses ready for you ... one for each year ... even Tommy knows it's something special ... you can't fool a two year old ... don't tell me ..."

"Maybe I can be there for a little while, but I have to go to the office right away. I didn't draft it 'cause as far as I knew, we weren't going to file it at all."

Janet poured some coffee. "Brad, how long are you going to put up with this? Aren't there other firms who'd like to have you? You graduated in the top ten percent of your class from a good law school. You were magna undergrad. You're a good lawyer. You work hard. You're smart- "

Brad cut her off. "We've been through all this before Janet. I'm not a fungible commodity anymore. I had six or seven years as an associate when everybody wanted me. Now I'm a partner without any business. Nobody wants me. I'm a high priced slave. Firms can get kids to do what I do – a hell of a lot cheaper and without any political problems from bringing in this high priced grinder."

"Then why doesn't George replace you with a kid?"

"'Cause the kids have mobility, so they don't have to take his crap. I do."

"Brad, you've got to do something. It just gets worse every year."

As he thought about his predicament, Brad could feel his stomach muscles tightening. He thought, *those same damn symptoms ... always the same ... but I don't do anything about it. I just want to stop thinking about it. I always feel terrible when I think about it.*

Then he thought back to his childhood ... to the town where his family lived ... the town where his relatives found him a bastard embarrassment ... the town where he was sent to far away private schools ... those schools where he never was part of the crowd of boys ... where his lack of pocket money and cheap clothes marked him as an outsider ... to his mother who he longed for but seldom saw ... to his father who he never met ... where he was abandoned ... to the school where other boys' parents would come ... but never his ... where he was abandoned ... to his unsuccessful attempts to make friends … where he was so lonely … where he was abandoned …

Through his pain he felt Janet's arms around his shoulders, hugging him. He felt her tears on his face. He heard her whisper. "Are you thinking about it again? Don't do it to yourself. Get some help Brad. I can tell when you do it. I can feel your body getting tense."

Brad said, "I know it and I can feel the tears, yours and mine too. I don't even cry, Janet. The tears just start flowing whenever I think about it."

"Get help Brad, now."

He said, "You've lived through all the other times I tried … three different therapy groups and two therapists. But it's so hard for me. My record with these guys sucks. I've quit them all. I know why I quit, and I know I shouldn't quit, but I can't seem to do anything about it."

Janet said, "It's time to drop the same lame excuse. Don't blame it on the pressure of work. Damn it Brad, either do it or stop trying. You're tearing yourself apart."

He lowered his head into his hands and spoke in a low husky voice. "It's the worst when … when I'm with a client. I watch George in action. George who doesn't give a damn about anyone except himself. He's so fucking affable, it makes me sick. If the clients only knew … it makes me sick. I try Janet, I really try, but it won't come off."

"You try what, darling?"

"I try to be like George."

Janet didn't understand. "What's the point of imitating a snake?"

"He's a very successful snake."

"That doesn't change his slippery skin."

"He manipulates people, Janet. And he does it by playing up to their ego. He promises them anything … no matter we can't deliver."

"Don't the clients know or even guess he's bullshitting them?"

"No, they want to believe him. Everybody's looking for a savior. It's like this petition filing tomorrow. I know why he wants it filed when the Court opens. He can bullshit the client into believing that George, the futurist, could predict what would happen; so he had the petition ready all the time."

Since Janet was a lawyer too, she understood. "Don't the clients ask you about stuff like that?"

"Sure, but if I cross George it's my job."

"Aren't you ever alone with clients, so they can see how wonderful you are and that you do all the work? George doesn't know shit."

Brad said, "He knows how to kiss ass."

Janet hugged him again and said, "Maybe you could talk to Miles Dean."

"I've tried to before. But I always chicken out at the last minute 'cause I feel intimidated. It's like if I complain, something terrible will happen."

"It's the same old thing about complaining, isn't it darling?"

Bruce silently shook his head, yes.

She asked, "The beatings when you complained to the headmaster about being abandoned?"

"Miles reminds me of the headmaster. He's one of the most important partners in the firm and he's Chairman of our department. His client base is a hell of a lot bigger than George's. I think he likes me and I like him too. I do some work for him sometimes. What a class act he is. But I still get scared when I think of telling him. It isn't rational Janet and I know it. But there's something else."

She said, "Something else?"

He slowly nodded his head. "I can't figure it out. But there's something wrong with this China thing. It's like I'm down in the engine room and George is up on the bridge. He sends down commands. But I never get to see the direction we're heading. This petition's an example. I don't know what was holding it up. It should have been filed two months ago, but George kept stalling on it."

"Does the client know what's going on?"

"I don't think so. The client trusts him, so George is basically out there on his own, doing his thing – whatever the hell that is."

Janet said, "The client can't be that dumb."

"They aren't dumb, Janet – they're just really busy and George always comes through. He bills them up the kazoo, but they don't care. He performs … sometimes almost impossible results. That's why he's in China now. It's for them. But I feel like he never tells me the whole story."

A child climbing into Brad's lap interrupted them. "Daddy, Daddy, Jennifer fife years old today, so fife kisses for Daddy."

"Daddy loves Jennifer." Brad said as he wrapped his daughter in his arms. He savored the joyful sweetness of her love, but it was sadly flavored by the salty taste of his uncontrollable tears.

CHAPTER 2

George and Sen were just going back into the Lujiang Hotel lobby from the hotel's main dining room after their breakfast. Suddenly George grabbed Sen by the arm and pulled him back into the dining room. He pushed Sen into an empty small dining alcove and closed the doors.

Sen pushed him back and said, "Hey George, take it easy. I didn't think you Harvard boys went in for the rough stuff."

"This isn't funny, Sen. I just saw David Gold at the registration desk. He represents Magnotech, my client's main competitor. We paid you to set this up so there was no competition for this contract. What the hell is he doing here?"

"Maybe he's on vacation."

"In Xiamen, China in August? He could get the same effect staying at home, sitting in his club's steam bath and ordering fried noodles. When's the big meeting with the government people?"

Sen said, "Let's see, today's Monday. We meet first in Beijing on Wednesday then again in two days on Friday at nine in the morning, here in the Xiamen University offices. Then we all have a luncheon meeting, right here at the hotel, in a private dining room. I arranged to use the time in between for us to sort of ... how do you say it in America ... sort of ... grease the skids."

"Well, someone screwed up, Sen, and it's you. I paid you to be sure there wasn't gonna be competition. David Gold didn't just get on the wrong plane and wind up in Xiamen, China. So you fix it" and then added in a much slower tone, while staring hard at Sen, "My friend."

Sen thought for a minute then said, "Wait here. Have a cup of tea on me. What's he look like?"

"What's he look like? What the hell kind of question is that in this part of China? There's about six people waiting to register. All the rest are Orientals, about a foot shorter than him and if you still can't figure out who he is, he's the only one who's bald, wearing a tie and last in line. If that doesn't do it, I could ask my office to fax a picture from our law school year book. We were in the same class, so as a last resort I could come out and finger him for you."

"Very funny George, but even I might be able to identify him."

He left George, walked into the lobby, motioned to two men sitting on the couch and stepped into an open elevator. They both entered quickly and the door closed, but the elevator didn't go up. The three of them just stood inside while Sen quickly spoke for a minute. When the elevator doors opened both of the men walked out briskly, the first to the registration desk and the second one out the front door. The first one stood behind Dave.

The second one crossed the street, joined a group of three young men playing cards at the land side of the dock where the police had been only two hours earlier. They listened while he spoke, then nodded in agreement.

The man behind David in line said, "It take long time ... register in small China provincial hotel ... only take people one at time ... too many formalities in China ... you make arrangements with Bank of China?"

David said, "What arrangements?"

"For passport and documents."

"I was just going to put them in the hotel vault."

"Would not advise in China, sir ... country has big crime problem ... very dangerous ... hotel staff steal from vaults to sell passports ... very valuable ... sell for ten thousand Chinese yuan, about one thousand America dollar ... take one year to make that much for Chinese ... Bank of China like American Federal Reserve Bank ... only safe place ... I already registered and on line to get information ... I go to put own passport in Bank of China right after information ... " He paused and waited.

David thought for a minute, before saying, "Hey, I really appreciate knowing that. Is the Bank of China far?"

"Only few blocks."

"Could I join you after we take care of our business here and deposit mine there too?"

"Sure ... happy to help."

They were only a block from the hotel, cutting through a side street, when the three card players came out from a side alley. Two of them held knives at Dave's throat, while the third took everything of value. When David took a quick look, his Chinese friend from the hotel was gone.

David stumbled back to the hotel without his wallet, money, passport, documents, glasses, watch, traveler's checks or credit cards. But he had acquired two bleeding wounds where knives had been held to his throat.

Sen waited in the lobby until he got a thumbs up signal from one of his men. He returned to the dining alcove where George waited and motioned to him to leave.

They went up to Sen's suite without saying a word.

As soon as the door to the suite was closed Sen said, "Well, my friend, the problem is taken care of."

"You didn't kill him, did you?"

"George, I thought you didn't want to know about these things. Besides, what do you care? Is it 'cause you don't like killing or 'cause he's an American, maybe 'cause he's a classmate, how about 'cause he's a lawyer? No, it's gotta be 'cause he's a Harvard man."

"You smart ass, it isn't any of those. When I was in law school I always thought about how great it would be if my classmates who ranked ahead of me would be killed. But that was for a good reason. Then I could be first in my class. The problem was that would be just about everybody in my class. I don't care if he's an American, a lawyer or went to Harvard. I just don't like to see a good mind go to waste."

"George, you're a real sensitive guy. I'm proud to know you."

"So, did you kill him or not?"

"We didn't have to. We have a better system in China. We took his passport. Killing him would bring lots of heat. But passports are stolen all the time in China … thousands of them. There's a whole Chinese industry built around it. The beauty is it's a crime where the thief is seldom caught, so the frustrated authorities punish the victim. Without passport or identity card in China you're a non-person. You can't do anything."

"I don't understand, Sen. How the hell is just losing a passport going to put him out of business? He'll just get another one."

"Not so easy in China. It'll take him a week of hard work just to do the paperwork with Chinese officials in Xiamen. Then he has to go to Guangzhou to the American consulate for a new passport."

"Guangzhou? What the hell is that?"

"It's the communist name for Canton."

And he can't do that 'til he has a certificate of lost passport from the Chinese officials. Your own American government is the best we could hope for. They're out to punish Americans who lose a passport. So they make it real tough on them. Then when the American government finally does issue him a new passport, he'll have to start all over again with the Chinese to get a new visa. Without that exit visa, he'll be stopped from leaving by the Chinese frontier police at every border station. He's a prisoner in China. They will … how do you say it … drive him crazy."

George said, "Come on, you're exaggerating. When a country has real crime problems, the State Department puts out an Advisory for American travelers."

"Not for China, when they're trying to be buddies with the government. Anyway, chances are you have a couple of messages from your classmate already. Why don't you check your room. It's only across the hall. Nobody will see us together."

When George returned, he said, "You're right. He left two messages on my hotel voice mail. I left them on the machine. What should I do if he reaches me?"

"Be a good sympathetic friend. Give him lots of sympathy, but not much else."

"What if he asks for money?"

"Give him money, too. Maybe he'll figure it's like … where did you say he was from?… I remember, Chicago … and so maybe he'll do it like they do in Chicago and bribe a Chinese official. Some of them are straight arrows, so he'll end up in a Chinese jail. That'd be even better. Then he definitely won't be going to any meetings."

"Will he be making it to our Beijing meeting, day after tomorrow?"

"Not a chance, even if he doesn't try a bribe. Don't return his calls for at least another two hours and watch what happens."

When George returned to his room three hours later, his message light was blinking. Sen had come with him to hear any messages.

Sen said, "I don't want to spoil it for you, George. So I won't tell you what he's going to say. But before you play his messages you'd better go into the bathroom and get a big wad of tissue to dry your tears."

George ignored him and pushed the play button. The machine made an announcement in Chinese.

Sen said, "Its telling you there's five messages, and here's the first one."

"George, this is David Gold. The most god-awful thing happened. I was mugged. They took everything, including my passport. I don't have any credit cards and only the little bit of money that I left in my room, and the hotel says they can't advance anything. Please call right away. I'm in room 305."

"George, this is David again. I tried to reach my office in Chicago, but they're closed. The police have interviewed me. They used the manager here at the hotel as a translator. Jesus, nobody here speaks English, nobody. I called the American Embassy in Beijing. The guy was real helpful. He called back a number of times and called the Chinese officials here. I'm sure this can all be taken care of quickly. Call me, room 305."

The next message was a little testier. "George, I assume you didn't get my other two messages. I'm calling you from the Public Security Bureau. It's somewhere in this city of winding alleys and milling people. I don't even know where the hell I am. First they told me to come here. Our hotel's been great. They even sent someone with me. Then when I got here they said I came to the wrong place. First I have to get a police report. I'm running out of cash for taxis. Please call when you get this message."

Then there was a message in a plaintive voice that was starting to crack. "George, I'm at the police station. They say they won't have their report until tomorrow afternoon. Then I have to bring it to the Public Security Office. But they tell me I can't leave here without a passport. Is there anything you can do so I can make the Beijing meeting on Wednesday? I know we're on opposite sides on this one George, but we're classmates. Please call me ... room 305."

The next message was the most heart breaking of all. "George, this is David. I'm back here at the hotel. The front desk tells me you've been out all afternoon. That makes me feel better. I must confess I was beginning to have dark thoughts about my Harvard classmate. I know they aren't warranted and I can count on you George. Please call whenever you return, no matter what time ... Room 305."

George turned and smiled. "I've got to congratulate you, Sen ... that's excellent. What do you suggest I do now?"

"Get some sleep. Leave a call for midnight at the front desk. Call him then when you're rested and he's been up worrying all night. Tell him you just got in ... then spend at least a couple of hours with him. Wear him out so he's more likely to break and start shouting at the Chinese ... a thing they hate. Give him some money and suggest a Chicago style bribe. Tell him you'll do everything you can. You can't really do anything anyway. He's had it."

"But won't the police give him the report tomorrow? Then won't

Public Security give him something so he can go to Beijing?"

Sen laughed. "If the police do have a report by tomorrow, he'll have to go to the police station again and wait a couple of hours for it. And if that happens, when he goes back to Public Security, he'll find that's only the beginning. I could walk to Beijing faster than he'll get there. Goodnight. Get some sleep so you can counsel and support your good friend ... your classmate."

The next morning George had breakfast in Sen's suite, so they wouldn't be seen together.

George was beaming. "Sen, you're the best. I called him a little after midnight and went down to see him. His room is two floors down but it may as well be in the basement ... 'cause that's where his spirits are. You couldn't have done a better job. He's been going back and forth to Chinese authorities all day, waiting hours at each one."

"And it's just started. We call it the Chinese passport torture. Wait 'til you see what happens tomorrow, or better yet what doesn't happen."

"He asked me, as a fellow attorney, to either delay the Beijing meeting or to ask the Beijing Chinese officials to consider our applications equally."

"What did you say?"

"I agreed, as a fellow attorney."

"Does that bind you to anything?"

George laughed. "Are you kidding? There's no transcript in these meetings. In Beijing I'm going to strongly imply since there's no one else present, there must be no other companies interested. So what's on my agenda for today, Mr. Tour Guide?"

"We've got you lined up with three guys at the University. One of them is like their chief legal officer, you're on with him at ten this morning. One is like your university Vice President of business. You'll have lunch with him. Then at three is a courtesy call on the Chairman of what they call, 'The State Key Laboratory for Physical Chemistry of Solid Surfaces'. That's the group that developed the technology. He runs one of the best solid surface chemistry departments in the world."

"What am I supposed to do with these guys?"

Sen said, "I arranged for a translator. Can you just stay friendly all day?"

"Are you kidding? In China they'll remember me as the great schmoozer."

"I don't think that word's Chinese. Anyway, avoid your classmate."

"Won't David be doing the same thing?"

Sen said, "Mr. David Gold will be a victim of the Chinese passport torture. He'll spend his day waiting endlessly in Chinese government offices, and the wonderful thing is he must do it in person. Only he can fill out the reports, sign the documents and endlessly explain what happened."

At the end of the day George played his messages. There were two.

"George, are you free for dinner? I've had a hell of a day, going from one office to another, filling out forms and waiting, but I still don't have the document I need to go to Beijing. Please call me … it's now five P.M. … room 305."

The second message was much shorter, in Sen's clipped Chinese accent. "Come for a drink when you get back."

As soon as they were settled in Sen's suite looking over the beautiful harbor, George asked, "How do you think I should play it with David?"

"Have dinner with him. He's not going anywhere. He can't even register in a hotel in Beijing without his passport. So be his friend. Just make sure you're on that early morning plane. The translator knows where to go. He'll meet you at the gate in the Beijing airport."

George and David had barely sat down for dinner when David started telling George about how terrible the situation was. "I can't get any kind of temporary document so I can get on a plane to Beijing. I spent half the day waiting at the Public Security Office. Then I had to go all the way out to the airport and get the frontier police to certify my arrival in Xiamen. Then I had to go back to the Public Security Office and present that certification. At the end of the day they told me 'Come back tomorrow … maybe we have document, but maybe we have to contact Beijing for permission … may take a week.'"

"Gee, I'm awfully sorry, David. Is there anything I can do to help?"

"How about the meeting in Beijing, are you going?"

George said, "Sure."

"Can you reset it, while you're there?"

"I don't know, but I'll try for you."

"Well, even if I get my Public Security Clearance, all I can do with it is go to Canton and get my new passport."

"How long will that take?"

"Who knows. I called and spoke to the American Counsel who handles these things. I gave her my passport number, but she tells me the government isn't that efficient. They can't fax a copy from Washington, even with the number. All she would give me was their office hours and an endless speech about being more careful with my passport. She was about as helpful and sympathetic as a cockroach."

George put on his best sympathetic look. "Have you called your office?"

David said, "Two or three times. They tell me they contacted the State Department in Washington, but only got the runaround."

"Are you okay on money?"

"I think so. I've got enough to get taxis in Canton and a little extra."

George gave David his most sincere look, rested his hand on his shoulder and said, "My friend, this has got to be hell for you. You know you can count on me. Just let me know what I can do."

"I won't forget this, George. You've been great."

Sen, watching and listening from a nearby table, thought, *he's perfect, that warmth, that ability to project absolute sincerity but no scruples. I could be sitting here watching someone who could be high up in government someday, maybe in Congress, or maybe even President.*

When George returned from Beijing on Friday morning, he immediately went to his room in the Lujiang Hotel and listened to his messages.

The first one was in the familiar clipped Chinese accent. "George, I've got news, call me."

The rest of them were from David.

"George, I got my Public Security clearance and am leaving on the next plane for Canton. It's in about an hour. Thanks for all your help. I'll be back and ready for our meeting on Friday. You've been a real buddy."

The next message was, "George, this is David. I've been to the American Consulate in Canton. They didn't tell me that I have to start all over like a new passport application. Our own government is as bad as the Chinese. I've been filling out their forms and having pictures taken all morning. But, I've run out of money and, of course, I can't get any without a passport, but they won't issue the passport without paying a whole new round of fees, up front. I can't even check into a hotel, 'cause I don't have a Passport. I finally got into the White Swan Hotel, next door to the Consulate. The manager took pity on me and let me stay using the credit card I found in my suitcase. Please call 02008300 room 1387."

"George, this is David again. I finally got a temporary passport. I found some Hong Kong dollars I had put in my suitcase. It only took money, a full day, lots of begging and listening to the same pedantic speech at our Consulate three times, about how I should be more careful with my passport. Is this what we pay taxes for? There isn't an ounce of sympathy in these people. I'm leaving the White Swan and am on my way to the Chinese Visa Department. It's in another part of the city. I'll be back tonight."

"George ... David ... I'm at the China Hotel in Canton. The Chinese Visa Department won't issue the visa until tomorrow. They don't know when. Lucky for me, with my new passport I can now get some money to pay their whole round of fees. I'm going to miss the meeting in Xiamen. But I know I can count on you to do the right thing. Call me please 0207680 room 726."

George didn't erase the messages. He called Sen who came over to listen. Then they had a drink to celebrate.

CHAPTER 3

I t was Janet who woke up first in their suburban Alexandria home. The ringing sound was constant.

She shook Brad lying in bed next to her. "Brad, your cellular phone's ringing."

He didn't even raise his head. "What time is it?"

She looked at the lighted dial across the dark bedroom. "Two thirty."

"Then it's George calling from China or, if I'm lucky, it's a wrong number."

Janet turned on the bedroom light while Brad mostly listened to George. After he put the phone back on the bedside table, she asked, "Well?"

"The good news is he's been delayed, probably another week. The bad news is he's coming back at all. He says to work with Miles."

By now Janet was as awake as Brad. She said, "Well that's helpful. You like Miles, don't you?"

"Like him? Hell, I almost love him. He's a great guy. Compared to George he's Jesus, Moses and Buddha, all in one."

"Why don't you ask for a transfer to him?"

"'Cause it doesn't work like that. Rainmakers are careful not to rip off other partner's grinders. They all know George probably couldn't get anyone else to work for him. Before I came, George went through about six people."

"Brad, darling, why don't you talk to Miles. Tell him about your problems with George. After all he's the Chairman of the Department. Maybe he can help."

"Miles isn't going to directly confront him. George just brings in too much business."

Brad saw that Janet was getting her angry look. He thought, *I better head this off before we really get into it.* "Look, Janet, tell me what you'd like me to do and if it's humanly possible, I'll do it."

He was relieved to see Janet become less tense. "Isn't there some kind of support group? You know, 'Attorneys Anonymous' ... like a twelve step group for lawyers who can't build their own book of business?"

"It's a great idea, Janet, but most attorneys wouldn't join, 'cause they don't want others to know their problems. So I'm pretty sure there isn't such a group."

"Well, then maybe there's therapy groups for shy people who can't ask for business. That's what you are Bradley Talbert, you're shy. It's no sin to be shy."

"Lawyers aren't supposed to be shy, Janet."

"Well they're not supposed to be pricks either, but George is."

"Given a choice most lawyers would opt to be a prick rather than to be shy. A shy lawyer is almost a contradiction. Clients don't hire shy lawyers. They mostly hire lawyers to be aggressive ... and prick is closer to aggressive than shy is."

"I want your promise, Brad. If I can find a group, will you promise to join it?"

"That depends on ..."

"Don't give me that lawyer 'that depends' stuff. I want your promise, Brad. I've given this a lot of thought. If you can't promise, then I think you should stay home with the kids and I'll go back and practice law. We wouldn't be the first couple who's done that."

Brad found himself speechless at the suggestion. He started to say something a couple of times, but even though his jaw moved no words came out.

Then he said, "Do you really mean that?"

By now Janet was out of their bed and pacing the floor. She stopped beside him looking down on him as he lay in bed and said, "Look at this face and tell me you don't think I'm serious. I mean every word of it."

Brad blinked his eyes a couple of times. He was so uncomfortable. Janet just stood there and stared at him.

Finally he said, "Can I answer you in the morning?"

She put her hands on her hips and said, "It is morning. It's three o'clock in the morning."

"I mean in the morning – morning ... when we get up."

Janet stood there for a minute more. Then said, "Yes."

The alarm went off three hours later at six. Janet rolled over and faced Brad. She lifted his eyelid and said, "Are you in there?"

He mumbled "Yes."

Well which is it? Should we find a suitable dress for you to wear to the Children's Church Society Luncheon today, or are you going to the office?"

"Very funny."

"It's not funny. It's sad. We're all suffering and you the most, because you won't take care of yourself. Either do it or don't, but stop pussyfooting around the issue."

"I wouldn't exactly define it as pussyfooting. I'd tend to say it's more like … "

Janet was up again standing over Brad. "We're not going to get into another one of these sophomoric debates. You made a promise. It was to give me an answer when we get up. Well, we're up, or at least I am. So answer."

"Alright, I promise. You find the group and I'll join it."

"No more lawyer debates, right?"

"Right, I promised. I'll do it."

When he arrived at the office, Brad always listened to his voice mail first. There were a number of messages, but one that caused his pulse rate to increase. "Brad, this Jack Mann from Tensitron. I had to make a quick trip to DC for a meeting. Since George is still in China, I wondered if you're free for lunch or sometime during the day. Don't worry Brad, I realize a lawyer is never really free. I expect to pay … hope you can make it. Please leave word with my secretary in San Diego as to where and when. Thanks … look forward to seeing you."

Brad could feel the perspiration on his forehead, as he thought, *I like Jack. He's a great guy … almost too great. But I never know what to say. Once we've covered the business, I always feel like I want to escape back to the office. I could force it into a quick phone conversation the way I usually do, but I know that's not the right thing to do. I can't really tell him I don't have any time all day. Maybe I could make it a short lunch by having sandwiches brought into our conference room. I'll get my secretary to interrupt after about thirty minutes with an urgent message.*

It was only six A.M. in San Diego and Tensitron wasn't open yet, so Brad left word on Jack's voice mail. "This is Brad Talbert, noon would be okay for lunch here at the office. It may have to be short 'cause I have a conference call scheduled about twelve thirty."

Brad thought about what George would do if he got that same call. He had been in George's office lots of times when those client calls came in and he patiently sat through George's side of the conversation. He pictured George on the phone. "Jack, what a pleasure to hear from you. You're in Washington. That's great. Are you free for dinner? Oh, too bad. Can you make it for lunch? Good. I'll have to cancel something, but I'm sure it'll be okay. There's nothing I'd like to do more than have lunch with you. Why don't we meet at the Cosmos club at noon? Wonderful … I'll look forward to it … see you then."

Brad thought, *Why do I think that's such bull? Is it just 'cause I can't do it or 'cause I know how insincere George is? Janet's right. People are sensitive. How different our two styles are … I'm so damn sincere, but I always screw up Jack's calls compared to the way George, who didn't give a shit about anybody, handles them.*

His Secretary's buzz interrupted his thoughts. He picked up the phone. "Mr. Dean on the line." It was Miles Dean, his Department Chairman.

Brad picked up the phone and said, "Brad Talbert."

Miles said, "Brad, did your secretary tell you who this is?"

"Sure she did, Miles."

"Then I don't understand. Why don't you say something except 'Brad Talbert'? I don't mean to be negative, Brad. But, I know who you are. I called you. So unless we're paying an imposter to occupy your office, I assume it's you in your own office … particularly after I asked your secretary and she told me you're in. I don't need you to confirm that it's you. Brad, this is the kind of stuff I've mentioned to you so many times before. Did you go to that interpersonal relations course I suggested?"

Brad felt nauseous. "I've been so busy- "

Miles didn't wait for Brad's usual excuse. "I've covered this a number of times in departmental meetings, Brad. Try to look at it from the client's perspective. He calls the main number. He gets the switchboard. He asks for you. They ask him whose calling, 'cause you want your calls screened. God forbid a mere client should get right through to you. Then he gets your secretary, who intercepts all your calls at your request. Then he asks for you again. She won't even give him the courtesy of answering his question, again at your request … 'cause you want to have another personal screen of your calls. So instead of answering him, she asks him again who's calling. Then he gives his name again. Then she still doesn't tell him whether you're in, she puts him on hold while she waits for you to answer on the intercom. Then he waits until you're finished with whatever you're doing. Then finally he gets through to the great Brad Talbert. And what greeting does he get after all that? The great Brad Talbert doesn't even say hello. All he says is 'Brad Talbert'. By this time he's really pissed. Only the fact that he's temporarily dependent on this firm keeps him from telling you to shove it."

Brad didn't say anything.

Finally, Miles said, "Hello, Brad are you there?"

"Yes."

"Then say something."

"I'm not sure what to say."

"How about something like, 'Hi, Miles or good morning Miles or it's good to hear from you, Miles'. Any one of those would be fine."

"I'll try- "

Miles cut him off. "I sure hope you don't treat clients like that on the phone. It may be one reason why you don't have any, Brad. But that's not why I'm calling. George left word. He'll be in China another week, on that Tensitron matter. He asked if I could keep you billable. Although, there's sure never a billing problem with you … you're amazing in cranking out the hours. If anything you work too hard. Could you stop by my office around two this afternoon? We'll talk about what you've got on for this week then … Good, I'll look forward to it … and Brad would you please bring the Tensitron – China file with you?"

Brad was both recovering from Miles' rebuke and wondering why he wanted to see the Tensitron file, when his secretary handed him a call slip. "Brad, can you be home at six tonight? It's important. Janet." His secretary had scribbled on the bottom, "Told her you were on the phone with Mr. Dean – she said not to interrupt and you don't have to call back unless you can't make it."

At noon, while Brad and Jack Mann sat in the conference room having their roast beef sandwiches, Brad thought, *I sure do admire this guy. He's built Tensitron from nothing in five years. Now he's got over a hundred million in profitable sales and he's a decent guy, too. But how the hell can he be fooled by phonies like George? Is it possible even self-confident people like Jack need reassurance?*

Jack asked him, "Are you on top of what's going on in China?"

Instead of answering directly and saying either "Only certain parts" or "With George's clients nobody's on top of anything except George." Brad chose to take the coward's way out and said, "It depends on what part of the operation you're referring to."

Brad always tried to answer a question with another question as he had been taught in law school. He didn't understand how much that antagonized clients.

Jack said, "I'm referring to this joint venture with Xiamen University. I don't understand why there aren't others in there competing with us … at least Magnotech. I don't want to talk directly to them about it 'cause of antitrust. Have you gotten any calls or correspondence from any other law firms about the possibility of joining their clients in a three way joint venture with the University?"

Brad said, "Not a word from anyone."

They talked on about other Tensitron matters. At twelve thirty Brad's secretary interrupted with his "conference call." Brad was relieved at ending the lunch, but he sensed that Jack wasn't done.

When he went up the three floors to Miles' office at two that afternoon, Brad thought about how great it would be to work for Miles. He had a book of business probably three times larger than George's and he was decent as well.

Miles was on the phone. He smiled and made a broad sweeping motion for Brad to make himself comfortable, then said, "May I call you back? One of my most industrious partners has just come in for a two o'clock meeting and since I made the date I want to keep it."

"Brad, I'm sorry for what must have seemed like an attack on you this morning. But I find you frustrating. You're one of the very best junior partners in this firm. You've got everything going for you, except your personality is doing you real damage. You're smart as hell, do good work, are a great lawyer, but your interpersonal skills, as my kids would say, 'suck.'"

"You're not the first one to tell me that. Janet tells me all the time." Brad usually felt at ease because Miles was so open with him.

"Then why the hell don't you do something about it?"

"I've tried, Miles. But it's a lot easier to say than to do it. Janet's got me on a whole new program."

"Well keep at it … now about Tensitron in China. I routinely got a copy of the petition you filed on Monday. It looks as though it should have been filed three months ago. Why wasn't it?"

"I don't know. George just kept telling me to hold off."

"Brad, how much do you know about what's going on in China?"

"Not much … just what George tells me."

"Why is George there at his billing rate? That strikes me as the kind of matter that you or an associate should be handling."

Brad was embarrassed how little he knew about what was really happening with Tensitron. He should be able to answer Miles' questions.

"I've suggested that to him a couple of times, but he always insists on doing it himself."

Miles sat for a moment thinking, then said "There's nothing you and I can do about it now, the person with the answers isn't here. So let's go on to what you're planning to do this week."

"Well, actually, George gives me stuff to do ... sort of ... well, day by day. He keeps his clients' plans pretty much to himself. So, I don't have that much to do for the balance of the week."

"Okay, finish up George's stuff today and then you and I will be working together for the rest of the week. God knows, I can use the help."

When Brad came home at six thirty, there was a baby sitter waiting and Janet was dressed to go out. "I've done the spoiled housewife thing and made reservations for dinner ... just you and me, baby. If this doesn't work out and we swap roles, I'll show you how to sweet talk me into doing it when I come home from the office."

"Janet, do we have to? I'm whipped."

"I did the research on groups for you and we're going to decide ... tonight."

Brad chuckled. "Have you ever thought of getting a black leather outfit?"

"If that'll motivate you, we can pick it up on the way home."

"I don't know if it'll motivate me, but it might be fun."

"It'd give you a complete twenty four hours. George beats you up during the day and I could take over at night. We could enter you as Masochist of the Year."

"Very funny. Do I have time to say goodnight to the kids?"

"Sure. I told them to expect you."

As soon as they were seated in the restaurant's most remote corner booth, Janet began. "I know you can't wait, so I won't keep you in suspense."

"Right. This is all I've thought about all day – I didn't have anything else to do."

Janet said, "Good, 'cause then it'll be easier for you to make decisions tonight. I made about twelve calls ... "

Brad started to interrupt, but Janet cut him off. "Don't worry. Nobody knows who you are. I described the situation accurately, but used a phony name. Here's what I found ... "

Brad said, "Should I take notes?"

"I know you're trying to be funny, but actually it's a pretty good idea." She reached for her purse and fished out pen and paper.

"First, there's three or four different kinds of groups. You're right. There's no group for lawyers who can't get clients."

Brad started to interrupt. Janet held up her hand and said, loudly, "BUT, there are groups for non-salesmen, sales challenged people and that certainly includes you. They come in a broad range. At one extreme is Dale Carnegie, which is sort of a fake it while you make it course. There's nothing wrong with that, except for you. 'cause you're not making it so you can't fake it. Besides, I checked them out and they won't give feedback. That means they won't keep me in the loop, even with your permission, and I want to do it that way to be sure you're coming along. "

"Is this gonna be an 'attack Brad' dinner?"

"Nope, it's gonna be a 'let's be realistic about Brad dinner.'"

Brad shook his head. "Okay, proceed."

Janet got up from the table, curtseyed, batted her eyes and said, "Oh, thank you, your honor. With your honor's permission, I'll continue my comments."

Brad glanced at her with unbounded love. "Very well counselor."

Janet returned his loving glance. "Maybe your honor would like me to get under his robes later. Is your honor wearing clean undies?"

"Come on, Janet. This is hard enough as it is."

"Well if it's that hard, it'll be even better when I lift your honor's robes."

"Please, Janet ... get on with it."

"Okay, but if your honor isn't hard, I'm going to report your honor to the Judicial Commission on Performance."

But she saw his reaction and quickly said. "At the other extreme is something called the Sandler System. It's good. It's meant to toughen people up. But it's best for people who are so afraid of not getting the sale they give the store away. Since you're not even in the store, I don't think either one can help you yet."

"What do you mean, I'm not even in the store?"

"You have such low self esteem, you can't even relate to clients when they come after you."

"That's not true. Anyway, how would you know?"

"I know 'cause you've told me ... lots of times ... tonight too."

"Tonight ... I told you tonight?"

"You did. When we were in the car coming here you told me about you and Jack Mann today at lunch in the conference room."

Brad shook his head and sighed. "Oh yea, I forgot that."

"Well, I didn't. And I don't forget all the others Brad, 'cause every one hurts me."

"Anyway, remember I was a Psychology major, undergrad. You only majored in whatever they do in Political Science classes."

"We spent all our time figuring out how to get female psychology students into bed."

Janet said "See, it worked. But now you've got to deal with her out of bed, too. I don't think you'd be any good in a one on one with a therapist. You'd be engaging in your sophomoric debates all the time. Unless he was awfully tough, you'd be wasting your time and money."

"Well, that's a positive thought."

"It is, if you want to see it positively. Let's go on to the other option, and that's groups."

"What's an example?"

"You know, like the Alcoholics Anonymous 12 Step Groups."

"Sure, Janet. I can see it now. 'Hi, I'm Brad and I'm a recovering grinder.'"

"No, you're not recovering. You're still a confirmed grinder. We're trying to get you into recovery, so you can say that."

"Are there 12 Step Groups for sales challenged people?"

"I don't think so, but there are other groups."

"Like what?"

"Now Brad when I say this, I want you to promise to consider it before speaking."

"Okay"

"Co-dependent survivors groups."

"Oh yeah, that's even better. 'Hi, I'm Brad. When I was a child I was abandoned ... so I'm a recovering co-dependee.'"

They were interrupted by Brad's cellular phone ringing in his breast pocket. He was embarrassed, but answered it.

He heard, "Brad ... George ..." Then the voice became very dim.

"George, can you speak a little louder? I can barely hear you."

"It must be the connection. Can you hear me now?"

Brad could just hear him by pressing the cellular phone hard against his ear. "It's a little better."

"You know that draft of the agreement between Tensitron and the Chinese government and all the related papers? Well, I can't find a copy. Fax me a copy. I need them for a meeting ... When? Now, that's when. I need it now. Just drive into the office and fax it to the Lujiang Hotel in Xiamen. Mark it for my immediate attention with my room number, 506. I'm at the hotel now waiting for it. You've got the number. Goodbye."

Brad hung up and said. "Guess who and guess what."

"So do you want to make fun of my suggestions, or are you interested in fixing the problem, so you don't have to keep carrying that damn phone everywhere in the world?"

Brad said, "You're right. It's serious business. But I don't see how a bunch of people who are crying on each other's shoulders about being co-dependent will help me."

"If you don't like that, there's also just plain old vanilla self esteem groups. The problem is they try to treat the symptom of poor self esteem rather than the cause."

"I admit my self esteem is pretty bad to put up with all the crap from George. But, it seems to me, I've got to deal with the reasons why it's bad. Otherwise it's going to be like one of those motivational talks. They're great, but the feeling only lasts for a few days."

"There's a lot of "higher power" groups around. They're more spiritual."

Brad said, "I don't want to get into some kind of religious thing. 'Come to the rail, brother, and get baptized. Then give us your money'."

"You can blemish every group, Brad, but you've got to try something."

"You're talking to a boy who grew up in a religious family. My parents and relatives are a bunch of narrow-minded religious bigots. I don't even want to think that way."

Janet said, "For a smart guy, you can be pretty dumb. These groups aren't religious. They're spiritual. There's a big difference."

"Oh yeah, a big difference. Their slogan is 'It's our way or the highway'. I chose the highway and I'm not going back to their bigotry."

"They're not at all like that, Brad. There's Course in Miracles groups, and there's probably a dozen descendants of the EST movement. Their whole idea is equality."

"I know how they think. They're okay, but everybody else is going to hell."

Janet put her hand in his. "Brad, they don't think that way. But your life is already hell."

"So, what do I get out of going to a group?"

"What you get out of it is the one thing you don't have now, the ability to be open. You're so closed you can't even relate to people who love you and want to be with you."

Brad stuck out his chin. "Give me one example, just one."

Janet looked up at him with wet eyes and said, "Me."

CHAPTER 4

Brad started to knock on the door to Miles' office the next morning, when he saw the office was empty and heard the paging system, "Mr. Dean, Miles Dean, call waiting."

Miles' secretary said, "I'm sorry Mr. Talbert, I know you had an appointment at nine, but Mr. Dean just left for an urgent meeting with Mr. Long. I tried to call you."

Brad said, "That's alright Sheila. A meeting with the firm's Managing Partner takes precedence over me any day. Did Miles say when he'd be back?"

"No, about ten minutes ago Mr. Dean asked me to call Mr. Long's secretary and ask when he was available. She talked to him and said, 'If it's important let's do it now'. Mr. Dean left immediately and has been with him since. I don't know what it's about, so I don't have any idea how long it'll take. Can I reschedule you?"

They had just pulled up Mile's schedule on the computer, when the paging system announced, "Mr. Talbert, Brad Talbert, please pick up."

Brad knew the 'please pick up' was an internal way of saying urgent, in the way police use "Code nine." He quickly picked up the phone on Shelia's desk, pushed "0," and said, "This is Mr. Talbert."

The operator said, "One moment Mr. Talbert."

Brad waited for some time. Then another voice said, "One moment Mr. Talbert for Mr. Long and Mr. Dean."

Brad thought, the Managing Partner and my Department Chairman … I wonder what I screwed up. He waited for what seemed like another five minutes. Then he heard Miles' voice on a speakerphone. "Brad, this is

Miles. I'm in Tim Long's office. There's only the two of us here and the door is closed, so feel free to be open. When did you last talk to George?"

"Last night. He called me about eight our time."

"Do you know where he was calling from?"

"He said he was in his room at the hotel in Xiamen."

"Hold on a minute, Brad." There was a pause. Brad knew, from the total silence, the mute function had been activated, so he couldn't hear what they were saying. While waiting, he thought, *I should have wondered more about that conversation with George. I was so wrapped up in what Janet was saying. I didn't think much about it at the time, but that call was abrupt even for George. I wonder why he couldn't find any of the Tensitron papers. That's strange.*

Then Miles came back on the line. "Brad, where are you now?"

"At Sheila's desk."

"Could you please come to Tim Long's office right now?"

"Sure."

"The door's closed, but just tell his secretary we asked you to join us."

When Brad entered the office, he knew there was something wrong. Neither man greeted him, other than Miles saying, "Sit down Brad, and tell us in detail what happened in that phone call last night from George."

Brad described the call. They asked him some questions. Then Tim Long said, "Thank you, Brad. We'd like to talk about this for a couple of minutes. Then we may get back to you."

There was some long delayed research which Brad was doing in the law library about fifteen minutes later when he heard. "Mr. Talbert, Mr. Brad Talbert, please pick up." He went to the wall phone.

"Mr. Talbert, Mr. Long would like you to come to his office, immediately."

As soon as Brad entered, Miles said, "What we're going to tell you is in absolute confidence, Brad. We don't want any partners who don't have to know, to be aware of this."

"You have my word."

Tim said, "We know we do and we also know you couldn't possibly know about this, Brad. I returned an urgent call first thing this morning from the American Embassy in Beijing. It was their Duty Officer telling me that George had been admitted to a hospital in Xiamen, unconscious from loss of blood. He apparently had a minor stab wound which he tried to doctor himself … I guess to avoid publicity."

"A stab wound … you mean from a knife?"

"Exactly … anyway, the hospital called George's hotel, the hotel called the American Embassy, got the Duty Officer, who happens to speak Chinese. The hotel gave him the name of this firm. The Embassy Duty Officer called here and asked to speak to the head guy and the answering service referred the call to me."

Brad had mixed emotions about George's problem. Still, he thought, *I shouldn't think this, but I hope the guy is shipped back in a box. But I guess I better be polite.*

"Is George Okay?'

Tim said, "Maybe … we don't really know. I've had four phone calls with that Duty Officer … Bill … I can't remember his last name. Anyway, this Bill even acted as interpreter with the hotel on a three-way call. Bill asked the hotel to send a security man to George's room. This is the strange thing, and the one on which we don't want you to say anything. Hotel security saw George get picked up last night by a prostitute in the hotel coffee shop and he took her up to his room."

All three men shifted uncomfortably when Tim said this. Brad thought, *Well, even if we don't talk about that in stuffy law firms, it's good to know that George has at least one organ that's normal, in spite of the rest of him being screwed up.*

Tim continued. "Anyway, hotel security said there's a real problem with prostitution now in China and even in their hotel, which is a pretty nice one. The girls sit in the coffee shops and solicit, 'cause they know the guys with the big bucks are in the good hotels. But a lot of the girls aren't in it just for the payment. They plan to rip the guy off. If they can't steal while he's sleeping, they do it by using a weapon or by letting their pimp into the room."

Miles interrupted, "Do you remember this morning, you told us he just asked for a fax of the Tensitron documents? Well, that confirmed what hotel security said. His money, credit cards, passport and traveler's checks were all right there in his room, and easily taken. Only the documents were stolen. Either the girl is retarded, or there's something else going on. Can you help us out?"

"Gee, I'm sorry. I can't. I don't know that much about what he does in China."

Miles said, "Bill, the Embassy Duty Officer, arranged for the hotel to put George's valuables in their vault and asked the hospital to contact him as soon as George regains consciousness. He'll let us know immediately so we can call George. The State Department should give that guy a medal."

Tim, in good Managing Partner fashion, said, "Well, I guess that's all we can do for the moment. Let's get back to work."

As Brad walked down the hall, Miles said, "Remember Brad, no word of this to anyone. Now, let's get you started on some other matters. Given what happened, George may not be able to return for awhile. First, I have a client coming in for lunch today. Can you join us?"

Brad was so surprised he could hardly get out his "Sure." In six years George had hardly ever invited him to have lunch with a client. It was almost always: prepare the paperwork and then make yourself scarce.

When they got back to the office, Miles gave Brad the file and said, "I'd like you to review this, ask any questions you think are pertinent at lunch and then draft the acquisition agreement we're going to talk about. I'm going to be gone tomorrow, and it's a rush, so just call the company with any questions. Okay?"

"You mean call them directly?"

"Sure, how else would you call them?" Miles looked puzzled. "Are you okay?"

"Fine … I'm fine, Miles. It's just that you operate so differently than George."

"Maybe someday we can talk about that. But for now let's get this acquisition agreement done."

After lunch, Miles said, "I like the way you handled that. Your questions were right on target. It was clear you read the file and understood the issues. I could tell the client was impressed, too. There's only one thing Brad … "

Brad waited, dreading the usual cutting comments he got from George. "Yes… "

"You don't seem very sociable. I mean if you're not talking business or law, you just sit there. You should do something about that. It makes people uncomfortable, Brad. They think you don't want to relate to them as human beings, only as a source of billing hours."

"It's hard for me, Miles. I was always told as a kid to be seen not heard and I don't have much experience with clients, 'cause George handles all that stuff himself. Besides, it always seems so phony to me." Then he quickly added. "I don't mean you seem phony Miles."

"My own experience is to relate to clients depending on how I feel about them. I can tell how you feel about me by how you relate to me. I know you don't think I'm phony with clients, just by how you act toward me."

Brad said, "I don't understand."

"Either you like me or you put up a great front. You aren't silent with me. I'm your boss, but we're friends. You talk to me, but you don't talk to clients. You're just a pleasant computer with them, but still a computer. And you don't seem programmed for anything but law or business."

"I think of a hundred things to say, but I don't say them. I know I should, but I just can't get it out."

Miles said, "Maybe you'd feel easier about being sociable, if I told you how I feel about clients."

"I'm sure I would."

"Okay, here it is. We're lucky. You and I both have lives that most of the rest of the world only dreams about. We get to meet and deal with the best of the best. The only people who can afford this firm's billing rates are those who are themselves successful. They're bright, articulate, positive ambitious and have chosen us. Remember, we can't choose them."

Brad thought about that a moment and said, "That's true Miles, but there's a lot of slime buckets with money and I guess we get our share."

"The firm may get its share, but that doesn't mean you and I will get any."

"I don't understand."

"We tend to draw that which we are. Understand?"

"But what about, and I've got to say this, people like George? The Tensitron management are good people. I know them."

"Most laymen don't understand the law. Most of our clients are too busy to take the time to understand it. So, the Georges of the practice can take advantage of that and schmooze them. Sometimes it can go on for a whole career. But that doesn't change the basic rule. You'll draw the same kind of clients as you are as a person."

CHAPTER 5

When George regained consciousness in the hospital, he didn't know where he was. He still felt light-headed from his loss of blood. As his vision came into focus he saw five other beds, each with an Oriental in it, two men and three women. He was in the bed in the corner farthest from the window of this small plain white room with six single plain white beds.

He thought, *I must be dreaming. I remember those books on dream interpretation my wife made me read, when I was having those awful dreams. This has to be some important dream message. What does it mean to be dreaming you're in a white bed in a white room with five other white beds, each of them having an Oriental in it? One book said every element of every dream had meaning.*

I better figure out the meaning before I forget the dream. Lets see ... white room, white beds ... five Orientals ... six beds ... farthest from the window; ... maybe I'm guilty about being white ... Shit, that can't be it. I'm never guilty about anything. Maybe the Orientals in my life are blocking my view of the world. Maybe that's why I'm dreaming I'm so far from the window.

I sure feel weak. I wonder why I'm dreaming that I feel so weak. I never feel weak. Maybe I read an article on the power of the Orient ... 1.5 billion people and all that.

He dozed off again, but after awhile felt his bed moving. It was actually three hours later. He felt pressure on his leg. He opened his eyes and saw an Oriental sitting on his bed, right up against his leg. He looked at the man and thought, *This man looks familiar. Who is he? Wait ... wait ... it's coming back. I know this guy, but from where?*

"Sen, are you Sen?"

"Sure, George who else is gonna be visiting you in a Xiamen hospital?"

"Hospital?"

"George, you're in the best hospital in Xiamen. You're in the best room. I arranged it myself."

"This is the best room? What the hell are the others like? There are six people in here.

"This is a private room in China, comrade."

"How'd I get here?"

"Don't you remember?"

George thought about it. "Sort of … some woman in my room. She pulled a knife on me. I fucked her then she pulled a knife on me."

"You must not have been very good, George. You know how women are when you don't satisfy them. Have you tried Viagra?"

George answered in a weak voice. "That's not funny. This was serious … strange thing was she didn't go for my money. She was going through my briefcase, going after my papers. I don't think she could even read English. She sure couldn't speak it."

"I know she couldn't read English."

"How do you know?"

Sen leaned over George and said, "I hired her."

George tried to sit up, but fell back and weakly said, "You what?"

"You heard me. I hired her."

"Well, if you hired her for me, she ripped us both off. I paid her too."

"I didn't hire her only to fuck you, George. That was just part of her job. The other part was to rip off your papers."

"You told her to rip me off? Did you tell her to stab me too?"

"Nope, just to rip off your papers."

"You're admitting that. That's conspiracy to commit a felony, and you're admitting it in front of all these witnesses."

"See how smart a Harvard law degree makes you? I hope you won't charge me for that opinion, counselor.

George managed a weak smile.

But you're not so smart, George. First, no one here except the two of us speaks English. Second, as opposed to your fancy position in the States as a lawyer in a big firm, so you can bullshit the courts … here you'd be a liar going in … 'cause of that same fancy position."

"Sen, we're partners. Is this how you treat a partner? I could've been killed."

"So call the police."

George sank back into his pillow, completely baffled. "Why, Sen ... why?

"For the same reason I'm telling you I did it. You're too big for your britches, counselor. I wanted to teach you a lesson. You can bullshit your clients and your partners, but not me."

"I bullshitted you?"

"Yep, and that question means you're still doing it ... 'cause you know what I'm talking about."

"Honest, Sen ... I don't."

"My friend, I don't believe you. But if you want to play games, I'll go along with it. Remember when I asked you how important this was to your client? Well, George, you lied to me ... big time. You told me it was a marginal deal and so if my rates were too high, you'd just drop it. Remember?"

George still didn't understand. "Sure, I remember. It was at the beginning of this deal."

"So, my friend" ... Sen said as he smiled, "I set my rates low to do the business, but you didn't tell me what was really involved ... did you?"

"What was really involved?"

Sen reached over and pushed his finger hard at the stitches repairing the knife wound in George's arm. George winced in pain as Sen held his finger there and said, "Don't keep on bullshitting me, George. I've found out about the 'marginal' Xiamen University technology that we're after and what it really is."

"Really is?"

Sen pushed harder on the wound. George said, "Okay, I got the message."

"The message, George, is don't bullshit me. This isn't Washington where you control things and you can bullshit the courts too, when you get caught. Here, you'd just be another dead foreign devil, and nobody would care. For a very few yuan more, I could have you on a cold slab, instead of this ... " Sen punctuated each of the next four words by jabbing at the stitches in George's wound. "This ... nice ... warm ... bed."

George drew back in pain. "Okay, I got the message. But I don't know what the hell you're so pissed about. I didn't tell you anything I wouldn't tell someone in the States. I don't ever pass on the real importance of a project. It's just not good negotiating."

"That's the only reason you're alive George. I figured you were just lying to me the way you would to anyone. My message is: I'm not just anyone – got it?"

"What'd you expect me tell you?"

"Something closer to the truth … that the technology developed by The Xiamen University Lab for Physical Chemistry of Solid Surfaces" Sen said each word slowly and carefully, while looking George right in the eye "… is a revolutionary breakthrough in nano-technology. They can build molecular structures."

George looked at Sen in astonishment. "How the hell did you find that out?"

"What difference does it make? How much is that technology worth, George?"

"Who knows?"

Sen pushed his finger into the wound again and said. "You know."

"Okay … probably millions."

"How many millions?" Sen asked, punctuating each word with a push on the wound, which was now inflamed.

"Jesus, Sen, you're gonna open the wound again."

That's only if you're lucky George … otherwise I've paid someone here to kill you. So, let's cut out the bullshit."

George began to understand his danger and blurted out, "Not millions … billions."

"Billions of what, George?"

"Dollars … billions of dollars."

Sen leaned back with a satisfied smile. "Exactly, my friend. And so, wouldn't you agree my fees are way too low?"

"This is extortion."

"Nope, it's a renegotiation, with both parties having the facts."

George thought for a moment, recovered some of his composure and said, "Are you willing to have any increase on the come?"

"Sure, George, part of it … as long as I'm sure of the payment. But I want fifty grand more up front, now."

"Jesus, Sen, fifty grand more?"

"Jesus doesn't rule here … Buddha does. Besides, neither one of them cares about money. George, who can put a price on a life?"

George said, "I guess I'm beginning to see your viewpoint. I'll do what I can to get it."

Sen smiled. "I thought you'd see my viewpoint. But what's this stuff about 'you'll do what you can'?"

"Okay, I'll do it."

"When?"

"Quickly."

"How quickly?"

George didn't answer.

"You've got five days. I've arranged for you to make one telephone call to the States, today. Other than that, nobody will be put through to you. After that call, you stay in this hospital. The guards have orders to kill you if you try to leave … understand?"

"George sighed and nodded yes. "I understand."

"So, tell me about this billion dollar technology, George and don't bullshit me."

George knew he was forced into the unusual position of having to tell the truth.

Scuffling in the hallway interrupted George's thoughts. He couldn't see who was shouting, nor could he understand the Chinese. But he did understand his name even when it was spoken with a thick Chinese accent.

Suddenly two men squeezed through the door, one built like a Japanese sumo wrestler. He was practically carrying the other, a tiny thin man, into the room. Sen sat passively on the bed and quietly spoke a sharp command. Both men immediately stopped struggling. The big one bowed toward the bed, while the little one lay limp in his arms. George assumed the bowing was paying respects to Sen, not him.

The big wrestler dropped the little man on the floor and waddled out of the room. Sen spoke again in Chinese. The little man got up, rearranged his clothes and bowed. George thought, *wait a minute, I know this guy … from where? … where? … I saw him just recently … where? …*

George was still trying to remember when Sen said, "George, this is Dr. Chang, but I don't think I have to introduce him. You've already met. Isn't that so, Chang?"

Chang said, in clear but heavily accented English, "Yes, I've met Mr. Chambers."

George said, "I remember meeting you, but where?"

"Mr. Chambers, I was but a minor functionary in the large group you met at Xiamen University. You don't remember me because I didn't say anything, but - "

Sen interrupted, "Now, that we're done with the formalities, George, Chang is here to help you remember what Tensitron's gonna do with this technology. In China, every department has a … a … a certain secret representative from the government. Chang is that person in the Xiamen

University Chemistry Department. But he also receives, let's say, certain income supplements from us."

George asked, "So why does he visit hospitals and bring his own wrestler with him?"

Sen laughed. "I'm sure Chang didn't choose to wrestle with anyone that far out of his class. The wrestler is on our payroll, George, or more specifically my payroll. He's guarding you … right outside your door … Chang must have tried to come into your room without getting permission."

Sen turned to Chang. "Pushing into this room wasn't smart, Chang. I mean for a guy with a Ph.D. in Chemistry, you should know better than to take on a guy twice your size, and three times your weight."

Chang said, "Believe me, I didn't take him on. I tried to avoid him. He just lifted me up in the air, right in the hallway, as soon as I headed for this door, before I could say anything."

Sen said, "See, there's a good example. This little talk is all about how size does count. You understand what I mean about size, don't you George?"

George didn't answer. Suddenly he felt a sharp pain in his arm. He looked down to see Sen's finger poking at his wound. "George, you didn't answer. You know about size don't you … nano size … right George, nano size?"

George said, "Right."

Sen said, "So, Chang's here to talk to you about nano technology and I'm here to listen. You know all about nano technology … right George?"

"I don't know all about it."

"Your answer is so lawyer-like, George. But, you're not taking a deposition here. I am. As he said this, Sen moved his hand toward George's wound.

George watched the hand and quickly said, "I know enough about the principals to talk about it."

Sen pulled back his hand and said, "Good. So, talk. I'll listen. But I hope I don't have to ask too many pointed questions, George." He wiggled his pointing finger in George's face as he said, "Go ahead Chang."

It seemed to George that Chang was embarrassed about his role as interrogator. "Mr. Chambers, I understand the steps our Xiamen lab used to build the nano devices. But I don't understand why Tensitron is willing to put up so much money to develop that technology. Perhaps you could clarify that."

Sen interrupted. "Chang, first tell me what the hell this nano is."

"It's so small the untrained human mind can't even visualize it … down to molecular size. You know how huge computer hard drives are measured in gigabytes? Well, nano is the exact opposite. Giga is one billion bytes. Nano is one billionth of a byte. At this size we can actually manipulate the molecules. We make up molecules that replicate themselves. It's done chemically."

Sen said, "Okay, so what's the big deal?"

"The big deal is when they self-organize, they become their own factory. Like if you have a bad heart, we design one molecule of a good new heart, install it in you, and it builds a new heart for you, by itself."

Sen asked, "Is that what Tensitron is after, George?'"

George said, "That's privileged."

"I don't even know what 'privileged' means." Sen said, as he wiggled his finger at George, "But if it means you're not gonna answer, I'll make my question more pointed." He wiggled his finger an inch under George's nose.

George looked at the finger, paused a moment, then said, "Yes, that's what they're after … medical applications."

"Why?"

"Why?" George asked.

Sen said, "George, I'm warning you, don't answer one more question with a question or you'll be part of tomorrow's chow mein."

George quickly said, "Because they think that's the most immediate market."

"So, why do they think that?"

"Sen, I'm a lawyer. I just take their word for a lot of this stuff. Ask Chang. He's the scientist."

Chang looked puzzled and said, "I don't know either, Sen. There's all kinds of applications … life extension, conquering space, making diamonds … "

"Making diamonds!" Sen shouted. "So why are we screwing around with this life saving stuff? Let's just make diamonds."

Chang said, "Look Sen, all this is theoretically possible, but it takes a company like Tensitron to force practical applied applications out of the University's technology. Tensitron doesn't make diamonds. They make medical devices, but I don't know what specific devices they have in mind."

Sen turned to George. "Do you?"

George said, "Even if they told me, I wouldn't understand." Then, as

Sen started to move his finger, George quickly added. "But, they didn't tell me."

Sen asked, "So, what are the possibilities?"

Chang said, "You wouldn't believe it."

"Try me."

Chang said, "Well, in the medical field they could make up a sort of immune patrol, install it in your body. It goes on … sort of search and destroy missions. It could give immunity from most anything."

"Very impressive. If all this is possible, why hasn't someone done it before?"

Chang said, "Nobody figured out how, 'til the guys at the Xiamen lab did it, about six months ago. Scientists have known about the technology for decades. But, until now, nobody understood how to work in an environment that small."

Sen asked, "How did Tensitron hear about Xiamen solving the problem, George?"

George was reflective for a minute. "I'm not sure, but I understand some Chinese chemists in the states who work for Tensitron told them. I don't know how they knew."

Sen asked, "So how'd you get involved?"

"Tensitron's President asked me to get them an exclusive."

Chang said, "I understand why he'd want an exclusive, but I can't figure out how he got one. The Chinese government is opposed to non bid deals."

Sen said, "Don't worry your Ph.D. head about that one. That's my department. Just tell me more about the technology."

Chang said, I've just scratched the surface. These little nano molecules can do structural repairs or change the body, in all the ways surgeons do, without surgery or pain. This applies even to the most extreme. For example, they can perform sex changes in days. Men could have babies."

Sen said, "Who the hell would want to? Maybe that's what we could do to you George, if you don't cooperate.

George thought, *the firm has law searches out for women partners. I wonder if they'd pay me more money as a woman?*

Sen said, "What else, Chang?"

"They can change DNA to give people basically endless life … sort of age reversal."

Sen said, "Our friend, George, may need that pretty quick, if he doesn't start cooperating. So, George, are you gonna cooperate and tell me what Tensitron's planning to do?"

"Look Sen. I don't know about specific products. That's proprietary and secret. But I can find out. I'll just tell them I need to know for some obscure legal reason. They'll tell me. They trust me."

Sen said, "They must not be very smart. I'm not even paying you and I don't trust you."

CHAPTER 6

While George was unavailable in the hospital in Xiamen, Brad had a number of telephone calls with Jack Mann, the President of Tensitron. Jack would usually call with a question. Sometimes Brad had to go to other partners to get the answers, particularly for complex tax or litigation questions. The issues were usually so different from Brad's own transactional practice that he thought it better if each partner talked to Jack directly.

Brad felt closer to Miles after working with him directly. On the third day he was in Miles' office and asked, "Is it okay to answer questions from the Export Control Board about Tensitron? The Company referred their inquiry to us. I called Jack Mann, but he said George always handles that directly."

"When is George due back?"

"I don't know. Not for awhile."

"Can we reach him?"

"I think he's still unavailable in the hospital. Should I have our partners talking directly to Jack Mann at Tensitron? George usually handles any conversation with Jack himself."

Miles took off his glasses, wiped them clean, sat back and said, "It sounds like you don't talk to the senior management at Tensitron and neither does any other partner at the firm. Who's backing up George?"

"I guess I am."

Miles thought for a moment, then said, "Who, besides George, knows the most about Tensitron?"

"Probably me."

"With all respect, Brad, it doesn't sound like you know a whole hell of a lot. How much do you know about their technology and the reason for this joint venture in China?"

"Hardly anything."

"Have you ever asked George about it?"

"I used to try, but I got the brush off so often that I haven't asked him anything for years."

Miles said, "Supposing something happened to George?"

Brad thought, *I couldn't be that lucky.* But he said, "You've got a good point."

"How can you help them if you don't know what they do?"

"Miles, I'm embarrassed to admit it. But I only know the company is involved in making medical devices, I don't know what the reason is for the Chinese JV."

"Who at this firm does?"

Brad said, "I don't think anyone does, except George. Tensitron uses a separate patent firm, and that lawyer just about reports to George. I've never even talked to the patent lawyer. George acts like he's the inside General Counsel of the Company, and everybody, including that patent lawyer reports to him. Since I've worked only for George, I always thought it wasn't that unusual."

"It could be considered extreme, Brad."

"Well, George does let specific partners talk to more junior people. The tax guys talk directly to Tensitron's Controller and our real estate guys did their new plant deal directly with the Plant Manager. But nobody except George talks to the senior management or the Directors."

"Brad, it would help me if you'd clarify the nature of your relationship with Tensitron. Tell me how it compares to what you've done with my clients in the last three days."

Brad thought, *What an opening. Can I be straight with this guy? I may never get another chance like this. I better take advantage of it, but carefully.*

"Do you really want to know the details?"

"I do."

Brad gulped nervously and thought, *Okay here goes nothing, except maybe my job.*

But even then he couldn't escape being Brad and answered Mile's question with a question. "Could you be a little more specific."

Miles surveyed him, saying, "I think you know exactly what I mean, Brad. But, I'll spell it out if you feel like you need the protection of answering specific questions. First, has Tensitron even filed an Officer's and

Director's statement with us, either in connection with an audit or a securities offering?"

"They're still private, so they've never had a securities offering and, yes, we have the Company's signed statements in connection with their audit every year. We provide one to their auditors, too."

"Who signs it for us?"

"George."

"What due diligence is done before he signs it?"

"None, that I'm aware of."

"Brad, what is it that makes you feel comfortable about operating in the dark?"

"I don't understand."

Miles said, "Okay, I'll ask it differently. What do you get out of being so unaware of what's going on?"

"Get out of it?"

"That's my question."

"I don't understand."

Miles said, "I believe you. You really don't understand, Brad. How much of a price are you willing to pay in order to avoid putting your emotional house in order?"

They were interrupted by the interoffice buzzer. Miles pushed the speaker button. "Yes, Sheila?"

"Mr. Chambers is on the line from China."

"Put him on."

"George, I'm glad you called. I'm sitting here with Brad talking about Tensitron. You couldn't have called at a better time. Are you Okay?"

"Yeah, I'm fine, thanks, Miles. Look, I need a wire transfer for fifty thousand dollars."

Miles looked at Brad, but said, "George, I didn't realize hospital bills were that high in China."

"It isn't for the hospital. It's to buy local talent for Tensitron."

"Local talent?"

"Yeah, you know. Professional talent like Chinese lawyers and accountants."

Miles was mystified. "Don't they bill the Company?"

George said, with Sen both watching and listening on a silent extension. "It isn't done that way in China. We pay them up front. I called Jack Mann. He's already agreed to cover it. You'll have a wire transfer today from him. When it comes in, just arrange to have a wire transfer from the firm to me here in Xiamen. Originate it in any bank you want. Have it pay out through the Bank of China. Tell the Bank to give me notice here at the hotel."

Miles said, "George, are you sure this is okay?"

"Sure, it's okay. You'll have the money up front. What's not okay?"

Miles thought for a minute, then said, "George, I want this in writing from you. Send me a telegram."

George looked at Sen, who nodded yes. Then he said, "You'll have it today."

Miles said, "Take care of yourself, George."

"Sure … talk to you later. Goodbye." Then the line went back to dial tone.

Miles sat back reflectively and looked at Brad. "What thoughts do you have?"

Brad made a supreme effort and resisted asking his usual antagonizing question: "About what?" He asked that question even when it was obvious what the other person meant. It was his way of protecting himself from being wrong.

Instead, he forced himself to be more open and said, "I thought I was getting paid not to think about that kind of stuff from George."

Miles smiled. "I can see how six years of it could harden anyone. The reception's in an hour" he said, looking at his watch.

"Reception?"

"Our reception for potential clients, aren't you going?"

"I don't have any reason to go. I don't have any potential clients coming to it."

Miles said, "Look, Brad, you're supposed to go anyway and you're supposed to bring Janet. Even if you don't have any clients there, it's a way to see how it's done. We've paid a bundle to have a Senator from the Banking Committee give a talk on the economy."

"I suppose I could ask Janet, but I don't know … it'd be at the last minute."

"Would you think I'm sarcastic if I say I've never known anyone with more enthusiasm for the firm's social events than you, Brad?"

Brad had a faint smile. "I would, but it's understandable."

Miles was abrupt. "You're going, Brad. Lincoln may have freed the slaves, but he didn't free lawyers from going to receptions. At least he didn't free lawyers who want to have a practice of their own. So you're going."

Brad thought, *I hate these things. I never know what to say. They're just a bunch of people, bullshitting each other and I always end up eating too much, 'cause I get so nervous.* But he said, "I appreciate what you're trying to do for me Miles, but there's no way I can get Janet to go at this late hour. She'd have to get dressed, find a baby-sitter and get into the city. It's impossible." With a sigh of relief, he thought, *thank God for wife excuses.*

Miles said, "Do you know where the reception is?"

"No."

"It's at the Army-Navy Club, a few blocks from here."

"Oh, well that's a good place for it. Yep, it's first class."

"Do you know where Janet is?"

Brad looked puzzled. "Not precisely at this very minute."

"Would it surprise you if I told you I do?"

"Do what?"

"I do know where Janet is."

"It would surprise the hell out of me."

"She's there, Brad."

"Where?"

"At the Army-Navy Club, you klutz."

"What's she doing there?"

Miles said, "For someone who graduated near the top of his class, you aren't very swift. Since she isn't in the military, hasn't been in the military and this happens to be the night of our reception there, why do you think she's at The Army-Navy Club?"

"But I didn't tell her about the reception. How'd she even know?"

"I asked Sheila to tell her, over a month ago. That's a thing good secretaries do."

Brad said, "I don't think Sheila told her. Janet never said a word to me about it."

Miles got up, walked around his desk and sat in the chair facing Brad. "We all decided not to tell you."

"Decided not to tell me … Janet too?"

"Mostly Janet … she made me promise not to tell you 'till tonight. She said otherwise you'd spend the month driving her crazy with lame excuses."

"This one isn't lame, Miles. George doesn't like me to go to these receptions. He doesn't want me talking to his clients."

"Isn't it handy, Brad, that you picked a boss who would give you another excuse?"

"I didn't pick George. He picked me."

"That's debatable, Brad. I think you picked each other. Anyway, George is in a hospital in China."

Brad didn't answer, so Miles sat in silence looking at him. Finally, Brad said, "I need to go home and change, if I'm going to go."

Miles put his arm on Brad's shoulder and said, "Janet was right."

"Right about what?"

"Right about your resisting to the last minute. She said you'd want to go home or you'd get your period or some other dumb reason. So she said she'd bring a fresh change of clothes and a box of Kotex. There are showers at the Club."

Brad had delayed as long as possible during his shower and could have been even later, only if he actually had a period. By the time he arrived, there were over a hundred people already in the Grand Ballroom at the Army-Navy Club. Tim Long, Miles and a number of other senior partners stood at the entrance greeting people.

As Brad waited in line for his turn, he felt the nausea rising. He thought, *I hate this stupid, goddamn small talk, these phony people, and the same idiots who populate all these parties. Damn Janet, why does she get me into these things?* Then he saw her, wearing a strapless brilliant blue evening gown, in a group of about three men and two women. He thought, *God, she's beautiful.*

He was staring at her when he heard Tim say, "Well, Brad Talbert, this is an occasion. Didn't you have anything else on your schedule Brad, or were you just in the neighborhood? Come on in and see how the other half lives."

Brad headed straight for Janet's comforting presence. He whispered "You sure set me up."

She whispered back, "It's about time somebody did. Now go do your thing."

"My thing?"

"Sure, go get some clients."

"That's easy for you to say."

"If I were in practice, I'd be picking up clients all over this room."

"I bet you would, particularly in that dress."

"Do you want to borrow it?"

Brad laughed. "Sure, should we change here or retire to a bathroom? I don't know if it should be the men's or the ladies."

"I mean it Brad. I'm not going to talk to you. Go talk to clients, not to me. I can't give you any business."

Brad shrugged and wandered off. Janet watched him as he moved around the room. She thought, *he seems like a marshmallow floating on the water. He just wanders from group to group ... he never joins in ... he doesn't smile ... he just stands there nervously eating ... eating ... well, I guess it's better than drinking ... now he's ended up with two of his other wallflower buddies from the firm ... the three of them talking to each other ... what a waste ... they hardly have a client between them ...*

Janet said, "Would you excuse me? I see a lonely man, my husband."

She walked across the large ballroom to the corner with the three wallflowers, including her own, and said, "Brad, I wonder if you have a moment."

As they walked away she said, "Those two guys aren't clients and neither one of them knows how to get clients. So, what are you doing with them?"

"Well, they're good friends."

"So's our dog, but he can't get you any business either. Do you want me to show you how to do it?"

"Sure, but I already know more than I can use. It's the doing it that's the problem for me, Janet. I always choke up."

"Okay, pick out a potential client."

"That group over there. There are three people there, all running techie companies near Washington."

She grabbed his arm. "Let's go."

Brad hung back. "We can't just break in. It's too obvious."

"Do you know them?"

Brad grudgingly admitted, "Well, I've met two of them before. In fact one's an important supplier to Tensitron. He came to the office once with Jack Mann."

"That's more than enough." Janet said and took Brad's arm, forcing him toward the group.

When they walked up, one of the men shook hands and said, "Brad, Brad Talbert ... how are you ... seen Jack recently?"

Brad said, "No, not for awhile."

Janet broke in. "I thought you told me you had lunch with him this week."

The man said, "Is this Mrs. Talbert?"

"It is. But please call me Janet."

"Well, Janet, how does it feel to be married to the lawyer in Washington, who's at the top of Jack Mann's favorite list?"

"I think it feels better for me than it does for Brad. He never believes people feel that way about him."

"Hell, I'd give him business, except he'd have a conflict, 'cause he already represents Jack."

Janet poked Brad. "See, that's what I've been telling you."

She turned to the man and said, "Would you please tell Brad that again. He has self-image problems."

Brad said, "You're embarrassing me, Janet."

The man said, "Hey, Brad, I wish I had a wife who embarrassed me like that. You're a lucky guy."

After awhile Brad and Janet moved on, mostly because Janet insisted. As they passed the food table, Brad stopped to get some. Janet dragged him by. "No more food. You've eaten most of it already. You looked like you'd just come in on a refugee ship and were starving, the way you wolfed it down."

"It's a nervous habit."

"So's picking your nose or grabbing your nuts, but I'm sure glad you stopped doing those."

Brad came to a dead halt. "What'd you mean 'stopped'? I never did them to begin with."

"Yes you did. I have pictures of you as a little boy. In some you're picking your nose and in some others you're grabbing your nuts."

"Maybe I had to go to the bathroom."

"Sure, that's the only time your family took your picture … when you had to go to the bathroom … or maybe your family had a nut fetish, or a booger fetish, and so they only took your picture when you were grabbin' or pickin'. Did they ever get any close-ups … you know, of a big booger dangling from your picking finger?"

"Janet, you're gross."

"My point is they're nervous habits … just like wolfing down food is. If you've stopped grabbing your nuts and picking your nose you can stop anything else. You're not mining for buggers, or massaging your nuts, here 'cause your partners would be in a state of shock. At some level you know they'll put up with the other marginal stuff you do."

"What other marginal stuff?"

"Look sweetie, I love you. But I watched you. In ten minutes you ate three big plates of food. I counted twelve egg rolls, ten meatballs with gooey sauce that you wiped off on the tablecloth, a mountain of carrot sticks, six deviled eggs, and endless shrimp with more sauce, the remains of which now adorn the tablecloth as well."

"Well, it's just a nervous habit. I get nervous in big crowds."

"Maybe you'd be better off pickin' and grabbin'. At least you wouldn't gain weight. In fact if you got enough boogers, you might even lose weight. You certainly have enough experience with tablecloths, so you could get rid of them."

"Don't hold back, Janet. Just say what you think."

"I haven't even started on interpersonal skills, of which you, Brad Talbert, have got a serious deficiency."

"I guess that's why I love you. You're always so ladylike in your comments."

Janet got as far as saying, "It doesn't have to be this way, Brad. How long do you want to keep suffering?" when a man walked up to them.

"Brad, I've been looking for you. In fact you're the reason I'm late for this reception."

"I'm the reason? How could I make you late? I haven't talked to you all day."

The man laughed, turned to Janet and said, "Hi, I remember you, we met at the annual firm outing. You're … Jane … no, wait a minute Jennet … Jennifer?

"Janet."

"Right … see I was close and it's been six months since we met. I'm Brad's partner, Dale Quinn. Brad can I talk to you alone for a minute?"

Brad said, "If it really has to be alone, okay. But Janet's an attorney too. Feel free to talk in front of her."

"Okay, Brad, but it's about you and it isn't good."

"Let 'er rip, Dale. This is Janet's night to pick me apart anyway."

"I'm not picking you apart, darling. I'm trying to put you back together, only differently."

Dale said, "Okay, stay right here while I get a drink. You may need one too when you hear this. Janet, Brad … how about it? What'd you like?"

He went to the bar pointing at the floor. "Right here, don't move. I'll be back in a minute, and believe me this is worth waiting for."

Janet said, "See Brad … see how smooth Dale was. He didn't remember my name but he didn't have any trauma about it. He introduced himself and then tried to guess my name and when he couldn't, he congratulated himself for coming close. That's a positive self-image."

"He's a good guy. I've always liked him."

"I can tell he likes you, too."

As they were talking, Dale returned. "Brad, do you know Dave Gold in Chicago?"

Brad thought for a minute. "Oh yeah, he's counsel for Magnotech. I met him on that joint venture negotiation for Tensitron."

"Well, I got a call from him late this afternoon. He's just returned from China and he had a whole lot of things to say, but first I want to tell you about what he covered last. It was like this was the reason for the call but … well, you know how with lots of people they never come out with the real reason 'till the end … that's what he did ... I suspect."

Brad said, "If he was calling about Tensitron, I don't know why he wouldn't call me."

"That's the strange thing. All I ever did with him was the limited real estate issues on that same joint venture. Based on what he had to say, I could swear he was asking me to keep an eye on you, so you didn't grab any of George's clients."

Brad asked, "You mean George is worried that I'm gonna … be picking up his clients while he's gone?"

"Exactly. And it sounded like George put him up to it."

Janet said, "Oh, I don't think George has to worry about that. Brad hasn't done any pickin' since he was a little kid and the only grabbin' he does is personal and then only sometimes early in the morning, just after he gets up."

Brad said, "Ignore her, Dale. What else did Dave say?"

"He said he finally got to see George in the hospital in Xiamen about two days ago, after a lot of trying. But, it was a strange visit. It was like they didn't want to let him in. George had a hard time talking 'cause there was a big open wound on his arm. It was raw and red and looked like it had just been stitched together. There was a little Oriental guy sitting there the whole time. Even though he never said a word, Dave had the impression he spoke English."

Janet asked, "Did Dave say why he was calling, other than to protect George from Brad, the fantastic, pickin' and grabbin', rainmaker?"

Dale looked at Janet quizzically, but continued. "He told me the most extraordinary story about his passport being stolen. He said George had been very helpful and he wanted to return the favor by calling me."

"Stolen?"

"He saw George when he got back to Xiamen from getting a new passport at the American Consulate in Canton. But, by then the University agreement had been wrapped up with Tensitron."

Brad said, "Well, aren't you the wrong guy to call with a complaint. After all Tensitron is our client."

Dale said, "He wasn't calling to complain. In fact, it was just the reverse. He said George had done all he could to make it competitive. I had the impression he was making the call mostly about you, Brad and only 'cause George asked him to."

Brad said, "I don't understand, George has always had client paranoia, but not like this."

"I know. Dave beat around the bush so long, the call took over an hour. Most of it was story telling, but he did say one interesting thing about the Chinese deal."

Janet asked, "You mean about how helpful 'George the Wonderful' is?"

"He did say that. But he still thinks the Xiamen deal should be competitive. He's gonna' file a complaint with State, Commerce and the International Trade Commission. In short, he's gonna raise hell. He's gonna' ask for a full formal hearing on what's going on in China. He wants a full investigation, witnesses, subpoenas, an administrative law judge, the whole shot."

CHAPTER 7

The next day, as they were having dinner, Brad said, "I got a call today from Jack Mann at Tensitron. They're in the final stages of their initial public offering and I have to go to San Diego tomorrow to spend a day … maybe two … going through documentation."

Janet asked, "When do you have to leave?"

"At the end of the day."

"Tomorrow?" She stuck out her lower lip, pouting. "I'll miss you sweetie."

Brad nodded and sort of mumbled, "Me too." But Janet was used to his shy behavior.

Janet said, "Brad, I've given what happened at the reception last night a lot of thought. It just reinforced my belief you need help. I've done my homework, but I'll be damned if I can figure out where to suggest you go. It's all so complex."

Brad nodded. "Unfortunately, George has to return sometime, and when he does my life won't be my own anymore."

"I thought of one possibility." Janet said, "It's a long shot, but it might tie in with your trip to San Diego."

"Well, long or short … tell me."

"Do you remember my Uncle Art? I don't know why I didn't think of him sooner."

"Who could forget him? But isn't he living somewhere out of the country now?"

"He lives in Tecate."

"Is that a country or a city?"

"It's a real small city in Mexico, right on the border, near San Diego.

The only thing there people have heard about is the brewery. He moved there after he got home-towned. It was the only way he could escape that crooked Judgement … 'not dischargeable in bankruptcy' all because of his so called 'fraud'. That's what judges do to you when they want to impress neighbors or they don't like you. Remember, after that Art's wife divorced him, and he married a Mexican woman."

Brad said, "I remember … they really skinned him. How much was that judgement … maybe a million bucks? Too bad … your hero … a psychologist who went to law school. I remember when he practiced law. He did mostly 'med-mal', defending therapists. Then he quit the law, and opened that residential clinic where he got home-towned. Where was it?"

"I don't remember the name of the town, but it was one of those pretty little historic towns up in the California gold country. The kind of place where most psychologists dream of opening a clinic, and where most local residents object to it. They told Uncle Art, 'We don't want a bunch of nuts in this town.' He told them 'stuff it'. I remember when he had trouble meeting debt service. The residents got the bank to foreclose and sue him for fraud. It wasn't much different than a lynch mob and the judge was happy to yank the noose for his neighbors."

Janet said, "He struggled for some time, but then felt the only way to overcome the pain was to look for the gift. Can you imagine finding a gift in that mess? But he did. I talk to him once in a while. I just love him."

"Are you thinking I should talk to him?"

"I can't think of anyone better, and you're going to be in San Diego. He's a straight shooter, knowledgeable, positive and a relative."

Janet expected Brad to think about it for the next millennium, but he surprised her by saying, "Let's call him."

She was beaming. "You mean it … right now?"

"Yep, right now … got the number?"

They each got on a phone extension. When Art answered, Janet said, "Is this Pancho Art, the famous American fugitive?"

Art answered in a strong fake Spanish accent. "Si, Senora Talbert. Et es Pancho Art himself. In de flesh. Whaaat is de problem, dat you call me at siesta time?"

Janet said, "The problem, Senor, et es Brad, de silent. He's having beeeg problems 'cause he is souch a wallflower."

"I remember hiem, Senora. Is he not de one who does not speak and when he does, only in mumbles and grunts?"

Brad said, "Look you two, you're very funny. Maybe you could do a comedy thing at one of the clubs …"

Janet said, "You're right, Brad, we shouldn't be making fun of you. It's just that Uncle Art and I are soulmates from way back." Then she quickly told Art the problem.

Art said, "It's a complex subject. Yes, I could meet you in San Diego. But I need to be careful in the States. I'm sort of a fugitive."

"You, Uncle Art, you've never done a criminal thing in your life."

"You don't have to do anything criminal any more, you only have to cross the wrong people. The bankers had my ex wife get an order saying that I owed her back support. They filed that with The Border Patrol, which now enforces support orders."

"Are you serious?"

"I am. It's like turning over bad checks to the assassination team at the CIA."

"How do you get into the country?"

I cross the border on a fake passport, which is a crime. They could trace my car license plate. But it's Mexican, so they don't have it in the U.S. computers. But some day they could … "

Janet said, "Why doesn't Brad meet you in Tecate? He can take a bus or something."

Art laughed. "You haven't been to Tecate. There aren't any busses from San Diego. He'd have to go to Tijuana and take a bus from there. It'd take all day. He can rent a car and drive here from San Diego. But the road is a terror. I'll meet him in San Diego."

"Isn't that dangerous, Uncle Art?"

"I'm doing it because there's someone I need to see there. And I want Brad to meet him too. He's in San Diego. He's sort of a refugee too."

Brad said, "Are you going to tell me about him?"

"Nope, not 'till you get here. I want to make sure you get fixed up, so you can support my niece."

Brad said, "I'm coming Art. I have to spend a day or two with a client in San Diego."

Art asked. "Why don't you bring Janet with you?"

Janet said, "Oh, Uncle Art, I'd love to come but I can't leave the children without making a lot of arrangements and there isn't enough time."

Two days later, when Brad came down into his hotel lobby in San Diego, he recognized Art. He was the same: tall, thin, although somewhat older.

Brad shook hands and said, "Good morning, Art."

Art looked at him for a moment, then said, "I'm glad you're here. I sensed how introverted you were at your wedding and wondered if it would 'cause you problems. Brad, are you happy to see me?"

Brad was flustered, "Of course ... sure ... I am, Art."

"Then why don't we go into breakfast and talk about why you don't say so? It'd make me feel better after risking a border crossing and coming to San Diego."

As they were walking into the hotel dining room Brad said, "I have to stay the weekend and go back to the client on Monday."

"Why don't you come home with me and stay with us in Tecate? There are some commuters from Tecate to San Diego. I can get you a ride back Monday morning."

"I'd like that. The only place I've been in Mexico is Acapulco."

Art laughed. "Well, Tecate ain't quite Acapulco. But other than the ocean, the harbor, the climate, stores, hotels, money and people, it's the same."

"Sounds terrific. Is that why I haven't seen any tourist brochures?"

"I don't think there are any."

After they were sitting in the dining room for awhile, Art said again, "Brad, once again, the question is are you glad to see me?"

Brad smiled uncomfortably. "Why wouldn't I be?"

"Look Brad, those kind of questions answering questions may be cute and show how cagey you are in depositions, but in normal conversations, with people who care about you, they cut you off from mankind."

Then Art waited, he thought, *Can this decent man be brought back from the living dead? He's so far gone ... he's bright, presentable ... he's got it all ... except the most important thing ... the ability to deal with people ... maybe I'm jumping on him too soon ... after all we just got together.*

Finally Brad said, "I don't understand."

Art reached across the breakfast table and touched Brad's hand. "I believe you, Brad. You really don't understand. When you're truly happy to see someone, how about saying something like "I can't tell you how good it is to see you. I've spent two grueling days at my client's, reviewing documents. Art, you're a breath of fresh air."

Brad shifted uneasily, "You always did get to the point. But I don't do bubbling effervescence very well. As a matter of fact, I don't do it at all."

"If you label it 'bubbling effervescence', you'll never do it. What about thinking of it as being honest about your feelings?"

Brad said, "That's a thought."

"What does that mean, Brad? 'That's a thought'. Is it a good thought, a crappy thought or a crazy thought?"

Brad said, "I can tell you and Janet are related. Is this psychological inquisition something only the two of you do or is it a genetic family trait?"

Art said, "Worse, it's a genetic family disease, and we're the principal carriers. You should have caught it by now. It's sexually transmitted. But, you didn't answer my question. Do you feel the way I described?"

"It's almost exactly how I feel."

"Then why don't you say so? No one's going to be offended 'cause you tell them you're happy to see them."

Brad said, "That's a thought."

Art shook his finger at him and waited.

Finally, Brad said, "I get the point. I'll try to remove 'That's a thought' from my vocabulary."

Art said, "Just don't replace it with anything similar."

Brad hesitated and said, "Can I change the subject? There is one thing." And then he paused.

Art waited and then said, "Yes, what thing?"

"Well, it's a problem I have at the firm."

"Yes?"

Brad said, "Okay, Art, I didn't even tell Janet this. But I'm really worried about stuff my boss is doing in China. It smells. But I can't find the source of the aroma. If something goes wrong, his style is to blame it on me and I don't even know what's going on."

"Do you think it's illegal?"

"Knowing him, if it is, it's probably big time."

"If it were me, I'd write my feelings and then seal that paper with a clear statement, that you know it sounds self-serving. Include the specific reasons why you aren't blowing the whistle now. Seal it and I'll sign and date the envelope. But, maybe we better have Jim Ward do it too. He has a vault here. I don't anymore, since I'm not in practice. You could deposit it with him."

"Would he do that? He doesn't even know me."

"No, but he knows me and I've told him you're Okay for an uptight WASP with a big Washington law firm. Sure, we'll do it. Neither one of us will know the contents of the envelope. We just witnessed its being sealed. So don't discuss the issues with us, if you want to do this."

After they talked for awhile, Art winked and said, "We've got to move on so I don't get arrested ... and I wish I was kidding."

Brad said, "Will you wait, while I do that statement and envelope you mentioned?"

"Sure."

They left as soon as Art signed the sealed envelope. While they were driving in Art's car, he said, "The man we're gonna' visit is a long time friend. Before he was a lawyer, he was a banker. Before he was a banker he did lots of other things. I won't tell you more than that 'cause I don't want to spoil it for you."

About fifteen minutes later they pulled up in front of a small house overlooking the Pacific. Art said, "This is it. His name's Jim Ward and he's got a thriving practice."

Brad asked. "What kind of practice?"

"You'll see."

Jim came to the door while he was talking on a phone with a long cord. He smiled and waved them into seats. There was a table set with coffee ready for them.

Jim kept talking on the phone, "Okay, I understand. What did you do then?" … And then what happened? … What did he say? … Then what did you do?"

He listened carefully after each question. He was so concentrated on the call that it was almost as though he was with the person on the phone, rather than in the same room with Brad and Art.

The call took almost thirty minutes. While they waited, Brad listened and thought, *he never interrupts and he doesn't tell the caller what to do. He asks questions. "Have you thought about …?" or "Does it seem to you that perhaps … ?" and he spends most of his time asking questions. Man, does he ask questions. Yet, they're all directed questions.*

Brad was jolted out of his thoughts by Jim saying, "I'm not sure I share your view, but that's a whole complex conversation. May I call you back? I have some people waiting. … Okay, great, I'll get back to you. Thanks for being patient."

Then Jim turned to Brad, and said, "It's a pleasure to meet you Brad. Art tells me you've got people problems. He asked me to help. I've known Art a long time. The help's simple, but it isn't easy. If you've come this far in your life and you've still got serious people problems, it's gonna take a lot of work on your part. Do you want help?"

"What kind of work?"

"Work on how you react to people … like right now. The way you asked that defensive question, instead of answering my question, pisses people off. I asked you a question. Do you want to hear it again?"

Brad felt his anxiety increasing. This guy was tough. He said, "Yes."

Jim said, "Does that mean you don't remember the question I asked less than a minute ago?"

Brad looked around. Art just sat there without an expression. Brad wondered how he could get out of this gracefully. He thought, *Whatever I do I don't want Uncle Art reporting back to Janet that I was an uncooperative jerk.*

He said, "No, I remember the question."

Jim laughed. "So if you remember it, why the games? That's not a good habit, Brad."

Brad felt trapped. He'd like to punch this guy out, even though he hadn't done that to anyone since high school. He pictured himself decking Jim, then walking out. But, he said, "Sure I want help. That's why I'm here."

"So, I'll ask my second question again. If you want help, why the games?"

Brad just sat. An uncomfortable silence filled the room. Brad looked down at the Pacific shore. Jim looked at Brad and Art looked at Jim.

None of them said anything for a very long three minutes. Finally Brad said,

"You call them games. I call them techniques. I've used them since I was a child. They protected me from being verbally or physically attacked after my parents abandoned me. They worked then, so I still use them."

Jim asked, "Do you understand why they keep people, particularly clients, from trusting you?"

Brad thought, *I hate this. I Goddamn hate this. If Janet weren't looking over my shoulder through Art's eyes, I'd tell this guy to stuff it. Who needs this shit? But, I better be careful. If I do that, I'll never hear the end of it.*

Brad sat without saying a word for another five minutes.

Finally Jim said, "Take a look down there at the seals and the pelicans. What do you see?"

"I see them in two separate groups, ignoring each other."

"What else are they ignoring?"

"I don't understand."

"See the one seal and one pelican, off by themselves? I mean the ones that aren't part of their group. The pelican's about two hundred feet away from the others on a rock and the seal's lying on a buoy, about five hundred feet out, by himself."

"Yeah, I see them now. Are they antisocial or do they have bad breath?"

"I'm sure that seal has bad breath, but so do all the other seals. Do they remind you of anyone?"

"I suppose you're going to say me, right?"

"You got it. Now what are you gonna do with it?"

"Look Jim, I have to do whatever it takes. I don't think my alternatives are attractive. If I don't change, my wife will probably divorce me and my boss will devour me."

Jim laughed and said, "From what I understand of your boss, it's too bad it isn't the other way around."

Finally Art said something. "I don't know anyone who doesn't say they want to change, but most people aren't willing to put in the work."

Brad said, "Look, Art, you didn't want to tell me about Jim's practice. Don't you think it would've helped if I knew something about it before I got here?"

"Nope. I don't Brad. 'Cause Janet told me that if I told you how it really was, you'd get your cramps and have to go back to the hotel."

"Terrific … just what I need, a Janet substitute three thousand miles away from home."

Jim said, "To give Art credit, he didn't tell you 'cause he probably couldn't. I'm not sure my practice is describable. Even though I practice law, I really practice people."

"People?"

"Yep, a lot of my clients are quite successful people. They need a friend more than anything else. I do legal work for them, but sometimes much of their legal work is done by someone else."

"Then what else do you do for them?"

"Mostly I talk to them about their personal concerns. It does tend to revolve around the law, but sometimes their personal issues are much broader than just their business."

"Isn't that expensive for them?"

"Not really, much of the time the company pays. People tend to be the forgotten equation in this society, at every level. But particularly the high level people."

Brad said, "I don't talk to my clients about personal problems, hardly ever."

Jim said, "I believe you. Yet that's where their biggest problems are. Most people in personal services like law, banking or accounting … they're just afraid to open that personal door."

"I just don't think it's any of my business."

"I don't understand. You're in a business where the client has selected you in large part 'cause of who you are. Yet you don't feel free to be open with them about who you are."

Brad said, "They don't select me. They select the firm.

"That belief is one reason why you have the problem. Big law firms, banks, accounting firms, all want to institutionalize client relationships, but it goes against human nature. People pick people."

Brad said, "I sure feel that people pressure."

Jim said, "When I was in banking I saw the same thing. Good people who were fired or quit because they couldn't generate loans. They just didn't have the people skills."

Art said, "It's just as competitive when you're trying to establish a psychology practice. You'd think being a banker and having money available, or being a psychologist, would reduce the need to sell, but it's all the same."

Jim said, "Look Brad, being a lawyer, on average, is one of the handful of highest paying jobs in the country. People think it's because of the education or the legalistic nature of our society, but that average is misleading. There are lots of lawyers who are barely making it, but the good ones make it big and so the average is big."

Art said, "As far as the public is concerned, all lawyers' education is the same. They just aren't all created equal when it comes to dealing with people."

Jim said, "Yep, that's what makes the difference. The other extreme is something like a prison guard. Their average earnings are about one fourth that of lawyers. That's the price for being able to club people into submission.

Art said, "The price is high when you aren't willing to face your own issues."

Brad said, "I still don't understand what kind of law you practice."

Jim said, "I practice 'Heart Law'. It has to do with people's hurting hearts. And, incidentally, I throw in a few legal opinions."

"I've never heard of that practice area."

"That's 'cause the American Bar Association doesn't recognize it as a practice area."

Art said, "What Jim does is to come from his heart. So, he's able to touch the heart of the other person."

Brad said, "I've been listening to you on the phone. I'd be worried I'd offend someone with all those personal questions."

"I know you'd be worried, Brad, but do you know why?"

"'Cause I'd offend them?"

"That's one possibility. What's the other one?"

"Beats me."

"How about that they might get equally personal with you."

"I wouldn't like that. Besides, it none of their business."

Jim asked, "Which? You wouldn't like it, or it's none of their business?"

Brad didn't even smile when he quickly blurted out, "Both."

"How about you wouldn't like it 'cause you're afraid to look at yourself?"

Brad squared his shoulders. "My personal life is just no one's business."

"Including you?"

"Sure, my personal life is my business."

Jim asked, "Then why don't you take care of your business and do something about it?"

"Like what?"

"Like fix it." Jim said as he filled Brad's coffee cup.

Brad bluntly asked. "Have you fixed yours?"

Jim thought ... *so defensive ... he's so defensive ... why can't he just ask the same questions without being abrasive?* But he said, "Not entirely, Brad. But I'm willing to be open about myself. Are you?"

"It's no one's business."

"Do you think maybe it is, if they're gonna trust you with their legal matters?"

Brad said, "I'm a good lawyer, I don't have to pour my heart out, too."

"When you look at their interest as a gift rather than an intrusion, you'll be happier."

"What am I supposed to do, tell them my life story?"

Jim said, "Sure, why not? If they want to know it, they're entitled and they're doing you a favor."

"I sure don't see the favor."

Jim thought, *how can I get him to see the favor? He's such a good guy, but so defensive. Can this guy be saved?*

He said, "The favor is they're forcing you to look at it."

"If that's a favor, then I prefer a tooth extraction."

Jim laughed and said, "You can't get the tooth back. But you can get yourself back."

"I haven't lost myself."

"From what Art tells me, you lost yourself about age six, when your parents deserted."

There was a long silence. Finally Brad said, "Look, I know you're trying to help and I appreciate it, but ... "

"Do you really appreciate it, Brad, or do you just want to go back to your hotel and watch TV?"

There was another long silence. The three of them just sat. Jim and Art looked at Brad who was looking at the ocean.

Finally Jim said, "Brad, do you think you could start to look at people's interest in you as a gift rather than an intrusion?"

Brad wiped his mouth with a napkin while quickly wiping his eyes at the same time. "Maybe."

"Can't ask for more than that." Jim said as he got up to answer the phone.

Brad said, "Before you pick up the phone, I want to say that I think even I'm beginning to get the point."

Jim said, "I hope so. You don't want to end up like your Uncle Art here, who's really not part of this society anymore 'cause he didn't pay attention to people's hearts."

While Jim was on the phone Art said, "I don't consider Jim's comment an attack on me, 'cause it's true. Do you understand why I feel that way? You should understand. Janet told me you were real smart."

"I think … maybe I do … sort of … but it's not all that clear."

They stayed for a long time. Jim's phone rang all the time while they were talking. He always took the calls personally and spent about a half-hour on many, except for a few quickies. Art seemed to be letting Brad listen to Jim's phone conversations.

Later that afternoon Art said, "Brad, before we go, let's get Jim to witness and hold that envelope. We need to shuffle off to Tecate, 'cause the road through the mountains is tiny, winding and dangerous, particularly after dark."

They drove south to the border. After about an hour, as it started to get dark, they turned off onto a narrow mountain road leading to the small border crossing at Tecate.

Art said, "When we get to the border don't say anything unless the Mexican Police ask you a question. There's usually only a couple of Mexican police. They hardly look up … just wave people through … Mexico's glad to have the gringo dollars."

"It sounds like intrigue."

"Nope, it's just the way you cross the border when you're a fugitive."

"I can't imagine what that's like to be a fugitive. It must be terrible."

Art said, "You should know what it feels like. You live your whole work life as a fugitive."

"I don't even know what you're talking about."

"I'm talking about being a fugitive from the mainstream of practice … just like I'm a fugitive from the U.S."

Brad thought about the connection as the car climbed the steep, deserted narrow road into the dark mountains near the border. But all he said was, "Where the hell are we? There's been no people and damn few cars or houses for miles. All I can see are mountains towering over us on both sides."

"Yep, it's desolate. I wouldn't want to break down. About the only people on this road regularly are the U.S. Border Patrol and I sure don't want to meet them. Now will you answer my question?"

"I didn't know it was a question."

"Janet told me you love a sophomoric debate. Okay, you win. Will you respond to my comment?"

"Comment?"

"Brad, please don't do that ... just respond. The key word for you elderly Alzheimer's memory loss sufferers, is 'fugitive'."

"Okay, I'll try not to play those word games with you anymore. They're dumb anyway. The answer is, I thought about it, but I don't see the connection."

Art said, "Want me to spell it out?"

Brad said, "As Jim Ward would say, I'd be most appreciative if you would take a moment to do that."

"See, you did get something out of going there."

"I got a lot out of it. He's great. But I still don't see the connection."

Art said, "One connection is that I have to spend a lot of energy avoiding the Border Patrol and you have to spend a lot of energy avoiding clients."

"I avoid clients?"

"You said you weren't gonna play those word games with me anymore."

Brad said, "Well, okay, I suppose there's the faintest possibility that I might, on those occasions when I'm really busy, seek to avoid clients."

"Did you learn that double talk in law school or does it just come naturally?"

Art couldn't see Brad's smile in the darkened car, when he said "Both."

"Want to know another way you're a fugitive?"

"Can I avoid it?"

Art said, "Well, you can get out and walk. But these mountains are full of wildcats and coyotes, animal and human."

"Human coyotes?"

"That's what they call the guys who lead the illegal Mexicans across the border. Sometimes they kill unarmed gringos."

Brad said, "Charming, I'll stay and listen or maybe you could drop me at the next gas station with a phone."

"There aren't any."

"Restaurants?"

"None of them either."

"Grocery stores?"

"Nope, none of those."

"What the hell is there?"

"Wildcats and coyotes."

"Art, you didn't have to take the most desolate road."

"It's the only road."

"Then I'm sure I'll stay and listen."

"I'm really glad to hear you're so dedicated to learning."

Brad asked, "How far do we have to go?"

"We're about ten miles from the border, as the crow flies. But the crows can't fly here. The mountains are too high. We're maybe twenty-five miles away, going through these winding canyons. But we can't go over thirty on this road anyway, so it'll be a little while."

"Great."

Art said, "In addition to enjoying the pitch-black scenery, I'd appreciate it if you'd help me keep an eye out for rock slides ahead on the road. Rocks get shaken loose from above by the constant little earthquakes. If we hit those rocks they can cause us to go off the road into one of those deep canyons you saw."

"I can see why no one lives here."

Art didn't wait for any other comments. "The other way you're like a fugitive is that you're always at risk that your freedom will stop without any notice."

"I don't get it."

"In your case, freedom is money. You don't generate any. You just bill out your time on work originated by others. They get the origination credit, not you. You're like a plumber who doesn't own the business. If your boss, George Chambers the wonderful, decides to quit, fire you, go somewhere else, get sick or die, you've had it."

Brad said, "That's a positive thought."

"That's not all."

Brad laughed, "I was afraid it might not be."

Then Brad shouted. "Wait … stop!"

Art jammed down on the brake. "What … what?"

"Look, up ahead, a big rock on the road."

Art put the car in gear and moved forward slowly. "No, it's only a dead raccoon, but a big one. I wouldn't want to hit it."

"How do they get so big?"

"They eat the rats. Those mountain rats are as big as any rats you've seen."

"I don't want to know."

"Well, you asked."

As they inched past the dead raccoon in the middle of the road, Art said, "That's another thing about being a fugitive. It's like driving this road. It's dangerous and you're always worried."

Brad said, "I'm not always worried."

"Well, if you aren't, you should be. My psychology background tells me that at some level you're worried, no matter what you say."

"Are you always worried?"

Art said, "Sure, it only takes one slip and I'm in big trouble ... same for you. And that's not all."

Brad looked at the dead raccoon as the car passed it, and said, "I'm sure glad there's more. I was concerned this verbal beating might actually end."

"No such luck, Brad. You're like me in another way. Neither one of us can do what we want. I'm stuck in Tecate and you're stuck at your firm ..."

Brad interrupted him. "I'm not stuck."

"When was the last time you tried to go somewhere else?"

"Maybe a year ago."

"Okay, that 'maybe' probably means more like two years."

Art asked, "When was the last time a headhunter, who knew about your lack of a book of business, called you?"

Brad sighed. "That bluntness must be part of your family genetic disease. Janet has the same genetic imbalance. Okay, I got the point."

Art was in the midst of thought, *Maybe I am too blunt. I need to say something nice.*

Suddenly a car turned its headlights on as it came around a sharp curve only a few hundred feet ahead, speeding straight at them in the middle of the narrow road.

Brad braced his arms against the dashboard and shouted, "Jesus, he's gonna hit us."

Art jammed the wheel and brake. But it was too late. The little car spun off the road into a creek bed and hit a tree. The other car roared by.

CHAPTER 8

Brad felt the blood trickling down his face from the cut where his head hit the windshield. He saw Art slumped over the steering wheel. "Art ... Art ... are you okay?"

Art only groaned. Brad tried to turn toward him, but he couldn't move his body. He thought, *God, everything hurts so bad ... so bad.*

Art groaned again and moved, but his head just flopped back on the headrest. He opened his right eye, looked at Brad and croaked in a whisper, "You picked the wrong car, counselor, no insurance and no money." Then he passed out again.

Brad rolled down the window to get some air and rested his head on the dashboard. He looked out the window and thought in slow sequence: *Damn, it's dark out there. How bad am I hurt? Why can't I move? How the hell are we gonna get out of here? Are we gonna die?*

He sat there for a long time. The only sound was the crickets and every once in a while an animal somewhere in the creek bed. There were no cars on the road about thirty feet away and maybe three feet above them.

Art stirred again. This time Brad painfully reached over and put his arm around Art's shoulder, hugging him. "Are you Okay, Art?"

Art held up his hand for Brad to wait. After a few minutes, he slowly said. "I think I'm okay. How about you?"

"I hurt all over, but I seem to be okay.

"Can you get the door open?"

Brad tried his door. It flew open because the car was resting at a steep angle. He tumbled out, rolled over twice and fell into the creek. The cold mountain water shocked him, but it felt wonderful. He just sat in the creek, splashing water on his face.

Art pulled himself out of the car, eased down in the creek opposite Brad and said, "Just what the doctor ordered, ice water for bruised bodies."

The two of them sat there until their bodies began to get numb from the cold water.

As he climbed out of the creek, Brad said, "What're we gonna do?"

"I don't know. It's your turn to make a plan, Ollie."

"Ollie?"

Art said, "It's a generational thing. You'd say Captain Kirk, or something like that."

Brad said, "Okay, Captain Kirk, how do you plan to kick it into warp drive and get us the hell out of here?"

"Before we do warp drive lets see if we can get up and take a look at the damage."

They helped each other out of the creek and limped around the car. Brad said, "I think we went through those big bushes and they slowed us down, so it isn't bad."

Art got in and tried the engine. It started. Art shut it off.

Then they heard a car as it came closer. They reacted slowly. Brad started to move toward the road, when Art said, "Wait."

"Wait? This may be the only car through here all night."

"But it might be the Border Patrol."

"So what?"

"They'll want all kinds of papers I don't have."

Brad said, "Well whoever it was, they're gone now. Look, Art, we can't stay here all night 'cause you're afraid of the Border Patrol. It's cold and I don't mind admitting, it's damn scary too. Supposing some coyotes come around."

"Human or animal?"

"I'm not looking forward to either one."

Art said, "It'll just be worse if I get arrested. We can watch from the side of the road. If it's not the Border Patrol, we'll try to flag them down. Maybe whoever it is will stop and help us. Look for Mexican license plates. They're more likely to help than gringos are."

"How the hell am I gonna tell them apart in this pitch black?"

"Easy, Mexican plates are yellow, usually on old, beat up cars, driving slow and having a good time together. California plates are white, usually on fancy new cars, speeding and arguing or ignoring each other."

Brad asked, "Why would anyone stop on this deserted road in the middle of the night?"

"You're right. The gringos probably won't stop. There are two prisons near here, so they'll think we're convicts."

"Great."

"But the Mexicans will stop anyway. If you're Mexican, your whole country's a prison, so it doesn't make any difference."

"Hey Art, I'm freezing. Can we sit in the car, start the engine, turn up the heat and figure out how to get some help? This is a great place … convicts, rats, coyotes, mountain lions … "

Art mumbled, "I forgot to tell you about the rattlesnakes." But he sat in the driver's seat and started the engine.

Brad took a quick look for rattlesnakes, jumped into the passenger side seat and heavily pulled the door closed against gravity. "Art, do you realize how screwed up your life is? You can't even go to the authorities for help."

"Neither can you."

Brad said, "It's not the same."

"No, you're right. Yours is much sadder, 'cause you create your own prison. You can get out any time you want. But you don't want to bad enough."

Brad said, "I don't mean that and you know it."

Art said, "My problem's real. I would get arrested. Your problem's all in your head. So which of us is worse off … me trapped by the law or you trapped by your fears?"

"Do you think it's easy to change a whole way of thinking?" Brad asked.

"I agree. It's simple, but it's not easy."

Brad said, "It's not even simple."

"Look, Brad, it all has to do with how you feel about yourself … which I gather is crappy. So, you didn't have a mother or father to nurture you. Are you going to let it ruin your life?"

Brad was silent for a long time, then said, "Why am I sitting in a disabled car on a lonely mountain creek listening to someone tell me about my crappy self image?"

"'Cause you want a father figure to recreate a lost childhood?"

Brad laughed. "Isn't there any way to turn off your therapist?"

"Sure, but you'd be indicted for murder. How quickly you change. Wasn't it only this morning you told me how happy you were to see me?"

"That was coerced."

"Maybe so, but that's your problem. It had to be forced out of you. Brad, you're no different than anybody else. Everybody plays to the parents in their mind. You're still trying to please them."

"I don't believe it. That was a long time ago. Why would I do that?"

Art said, "You couldn't face their rejection as a kid. You never came to grips with it. So you won't face client rejection now, 'cause it's the same rejection pain that you stuffed down, only each time it gets worse. You don't want it to come up. But if you faced it, it would be gone."

"That's easy for you to say."

Suddenly Brad said, "… wait … wait … look. There's something moving across the road."

They both looked into the darkness. Art had shut off the engine, so it was quiet. There were about a dozen people quietly crossing the road, following a man.

Brad started to open his door. "Let's ask them for help."

Art put a restraining hand on Brad and put his finger to his lips. "Keep quiet. If you open that door you may be a dead man. It's a human coyote with his pack of loyal followers. They've paid him to sneak them across the border and they'll do what he says. He won't bother us if we don't bother him. Just stay here."

Brad sat and sighed as the group disappeared into the darkness. "Maybe one of us should go up on the road and wait for cars."

Art asked, "Not much point … Border closes at midnight. … not many cars after that."

"How do you close a border?"

"You shut the gates and shoot anyone who tries to cross … just like prison."

"The Border patrol shoots Americans?"

"Americans don't sneak across. It's the Mexicans who are in prison."

"So are we just gonna sit here all night?"

"We might as well, the Border doesn't open again 'till six a.m. But the border to your prison's never closed, Brad. You can get out anytime."

"It's a good thing you don't charge by the hour."

"I would if I thought it would do any good. In spite of what you think, I'm not the best thing in your life, Janet is. Do you know why?"

Brad said, "As amazed as you may be, I wasn't sitting here in your crashed car, freezing in this creek and thinking you're the best thing that ever happened to me and I know why Janet is."

"It's not why you think. It's because your relationship with her shows there's hope for you. It's good. It's healthy. And yet she's your best critic. That's an emotionally healthy intimate relationship."

"Thanks … I think."

"It shows you're able to overcome the lack of any nurturing when you were growing up."

They talked on for awhile and then both dozed off.

A few hours later Art woke up and whispered, "Do you hear a phone ringing?"

Brad stirred a little. "Are you crazy, a phone out here?" Art shrugged and went back to sleep.

A minute later Brad jerked awake, sat straight up, eyes wide open, yelling, "What time is it in China?"

Art woke up and said, "Are you crazy? I don't even know what time it is here."

Brad said, "The phone … the phone … it's my phone. It's my phone ringing."

Art watched amazed as Brad leaped up, hitting his head on the car roof, got on his knees backwards in the front seat, rapidly pawed through the back seat and opened his briefcase. Art could hear the phone clearly now and a moment later he saw it.

Brad grabbed it from the briefcase, pushed the button and said, "Brad Talbert."

He listened for awhile, then said. "… Sorry, George … I know it took a long time to answer. I'm in … "

Then he stopped and listened again. "I'm going there again on Monday, George."

He listened again. "It's a full registration. I've got five boxes of documents to review … "

Then he waited again. "I haven't talked to Jack Mann. He isn't there. I'm working with the Controller."

He listened for awhile, said, "Okay," and then pushed the off button.

Art looked at him and said, "You had a phone … all this time?"

"I forgot about it. The whole idea is so painful."

"We can use it to call Maria in Tecate. They close the Border, not the phones. She can come out here with another car and ropes as soon as they open the Border in the morning. Can I use it?"

Art dialed the number and spoke rapidly in Spanish for a few minutes. Then said, "All set. She'll bring breakfast too. She was up and worried when we hadn't come home, particularly after the Border closed."

"Can she get us out?"

"She'll bring a couple of men along. I hope it'll be okay." Art paused and then asked, "Brad, do you remember what the nightmare was that made you ask me what time it is in China?"

Brad said, "It's both a nightmare and a daymare. I remember doing it and why I did it. But maybe it's better not to talk about it."

"Whatever you want. But will you remember it later?"

Brad shook his head. "Unfortunately, yes I will."

"The reason I'm asking, Brad, isn't to pry. It's that you told Jim Ward you didn't remember your childhood. That's not a good sign. It usually means that you're blocking painful memories. My only concern is that you're continuing to do that as an adult."

Brad asked, "Remember I said, 'It's both a nightmare and a daymare'?"

"Sure."

That call was from my boss in China."

"The aggressive prick?"

Brad said, "The same and he was worse than usual, and usual is bad."

"What's he doing in China, of all places?"

"He's there for a client, but he's been in the hospital and they don't know when he can get out."

"That's another hopeful sign about you, Brad. You're in a passive position, but you don't become more actively aggressive as a result. Most people become tougher when they're forced to be passive and it sounds as though your boss is doing that."

Brad said, "That's true. He's been worse since he's been in China."

"Everybody tends to be the same. We all want to quiet our fears and there's only two ways to do it. You've got one of them in a great intimate relationship with Janet going for you, but the other one, your self image, sucks."

"Thanks."

"You're welcome … no fee either. It's your lucky day."

"You wouldn't think so if you heard that call from China."

"Brad, George is scared. He's got to be afraid of you."

"Afraid of me?"

"Sure, you're here with 'his' client. He's on the other side of the world, in the hospital. The sicker someone's personality is, the more likely they are to act the opposite of how they feel. So the more afraid George is, the tougher he's gonna get."

"So, what do I do about it?"

"Just ride it out for the moment and take care of yourself. That's your gift from George. He's forcing you to take care of yourself. You've kept something good through all this that could be your salvation."

"I don't understand."

Art put his finger to his lips for silence and pointed to the pool in the creek where they had sat a few hours ago. The moon had come out from the clouds. They could see a small mountain lion stalking a coyote drinking in the pool.

As they watched, the cat crept on its belly moving forward slightly. Each time the coyote looked around, the cat lay silent. Suddenly, the cat struck. The night was filled with cat screams, coyote growls and thrashing in the water.

After a moment of silence only the cat was standing. It grabbed the coyote by the neck and dragged it to a clearing beside the creek. Then it sat and waited. In a few minutes a pride of another adult and two small cats came out of the brush. The new adult started eating the coyote while the first cat and the kittens waited.

Art said, "That's what you've got going for you, Brad."

"I should eat coyotes?"

Art ignored the comment. "You have the office pressures, but you don't bring it home. Janet's told me about how loving you are. And that's what it takes. Just think if that female cat killed the coyote and then didn't let her mate have first licks. It's the culture and she conforms. The kittens do too."

"Thanks, Art."

"But it's not all good."

"I suspected that."

"The price you pay is that you don't really compete. As a result, your family, someday, may actually go hungry. The challenge is not to bring a competitive work personality into a loving home relationship. You don't know that challenge 'cause you don't compete."

Brad thought, as he watched the other three cats start to eat the coyote. Then he said, "You're probably right."

Two hours later, about six thirty that morning, Maria found the two men in the car. Brad's head was resting on Art's shoulder. They both were sleeping so peacefully she was reluctant to wake them.

CHAPTER 9

When Brad returned to the office on Wednesday, there were lots of calls from George's clients. His secretary had put a message slip on top of the pile with a red exclamation mark on it. It said, "Brad, please call as soon as you return. Miles Dean."

Brad picked up the phone and dialed. He was idly flipping through his messages, waiting for Miles to come on the line, when Sheila, Miles' secretary, answered the call, "Mr. Talbert, Mr. Dean will be out of town until Monday. He asked if you're available for lunch then."

"Sure, Sheila, should I bring any particular file?"

Sheila paused, as though trying to think of how to answer, then she said, "No, just bring your most positive attitude."

He thought, *What is that all about? I have a good relationship with Sheila. Is she trying to warn him about something?* But he said, "Thanks Sheila. Is the meeting gonna be difficult?"

"Now, Mr. Talbert, you know I can't tell you what it's about. That's up to Mr. Dean, but as a friend I suggest you get some rest before Monday."

"I understand and thanks, Sheila."

"Everyone here likes you Mr. Talbert, myself included."

"Jesus, Sheila, now you've really got me wondering."

"I'm sorry, Mr. Talbert, but I hope you understand I can't say anymore, and I've probably already said too much."

After Brad hung up he didn't have long to worry about Sheila's comments before the phone rang again. "Brad, I'm glad you're back. This is Dinky Moran. The Tensitron registration should go to the printer tonight. Did you get my message?"

"I got it Dinky, but I've only had time to return one call and that was to Miles."

"I've been waiting for you to get back from Tensitron before proceeding. Have you completed your due diligence?"

"I just got back into town, Dinky. I've got a fistful of calls here. Can it wait? Does the whole life of my favorite securities partner revolve around going to the printer with a prospectus?"

"Yep, you got it partner, my life revolves around going to the printer, or getting a break to go to the bathroom while I'm at the printer."

Brad thought, *This must be why I like Dinky so much. I envy him. He makes me laugh. I don't make anybody, except my kids, laugh and, even then, not that often. Those times Janet and I have gone to see Dinky's show at some comedy club ... how does he do it? ... a securities partner in a big fancy firm. Securities partners are usually the most serious ... but then there's Dinky, a stand up comedian. Maybe, it's what gives him the stamina to withstand the pressure.* But what Brad said was, "Very funny, Dinky. Is this part of your comedy act?"

"Hey, Brad, it's no act. The printer's a demanding place. Sometimes it's either hold my water or hold the presses. It's a tough choice. But I'd rather wet my pants before the presses run, than wet 'em 'cause I see a mistake in the prospectus after it's printed."

Brad laughed. "I gather you're still doing your stand up comedy thing."

"Depends on the printer, some have urinals; some you got to sit down."

"For Christ's sake, Dinky ... enough."

"So are you available? ... Or should I just tell Tensitron's hard pressed Controller he can't have the twenty million-dollar proceeds from the offering? I'll just say, 'Sorry, but Brad Talbert couldn't make it.'" He'll understand. The guys at the Bank will understand, too. Tensitron's only into the bank about six million now. But, don't give it another thought. Should I just route the banker's pleading calls to you? I mean, Brad, are you good on responding to pleading, or what?"

"Only yours, Dinky. But I have a fistful of matters on my desk. I'm gone for the weekend to some damn self-improvement thing Janet dreamed up and then I have an important lunch with Miles on Monday. If I do the all night thing at the printer, It'll go into the next day and the next and I'll be wiped out."

"Don't worry about it, partner. My secretary just handed me a message. The banker called and is waiting on my other line. This early in the day is new. It's only seven in the morning out there in California. His first call's usually about eight. Most days, that's followed up by a couple of more calls. I'll tell my secretary to switch them all to you. When you talk to him, remember, Brad, you're a big time Washington lawyer. You don't respond to begging or pleading or anything like that. I'll even tell him myself, before I switch this call, that you're impervious to his groveling too ... "

"Dinky, how the hell did you ever make partner in this firm? Did you do this stuff when you were an associate, too?"

"You forget I wasn't ever an associate in this firm. I came in here as a partner and I stay a partner 'cause I fool so many clients into paying my billings. But, back to the subject, partner. When the banker tells you about how he may lose his job over this and about his wife who can't work, ignore it. I don't know whether to believe his other stories either ... about his retarded child or about his invalid mother in the nursing home. You know how those California guys exaggerate."

Brad said," Alright, I'll be in your office at noon and I'll tell Janet I'll be at the printer, instead of home, tonight. But, Dinky, there's no way short of divorce I can cut out of this weekend retreat."

"Does that mean you don't want to take the banker's calls?"

"That means you know how to deliver a tough message and still keep a good relationship. I'd like to take lessons sometime, Dinky."

"Hey, Brad, anytime. Maybe we could get you on the comedy stand up circuit, too."

"I'm a long way from that."

"You could start right now. Personally I think you're great, Brad. But you'd have to start doing the strong, silent statue thing. I'd ask you questions and you'd just stare into space or grunt."

"That's not a very kind thing to say, Dinky."

"You asked for lessons. That's the first one, partner, and it may be the kindest. See you at noon." He hung up.

Brad looked at the clock and thought, *I've got two hours to do about ten hours work. Where do I start? How would a big rainmaker solve this problem? Would he call his most important client first? No, he'd call his best prospect first. No, he'd tackle the most critical problem first. No, he'd call the one with the biggest immediate fee first. No, he'd ... I don't know what he'd do, but he sure wouldn't sit here wondering what to do.*

What would Jim Ward do? I don't know that either. He's talks about Heart Law. How would Jim come from the heart? For once I'm gonna take care of myself, instead of George's clients.

He picked up the phone, called Art in Tecate and explained the problem.

Art said, "Sure, call Jim. A lot of his clients are on the East Coast, so he's at it about six in the morning. He'll be glad that you called to follow up. Give him my best."

Jim listened carefully to Brad's question. He asked a whole bunch of his own questions. Then he asked, "Brad, if you were gonna do what comes naturally, what would you do?"

"Probably concentrate on the most interesting legal question."

"Why?"

"'Cause I'm practicing law and I like law."

Jim said, "I understand. Does that remind you of the physician who has to work in a hospital setting 'cause the only time he talks to patients is when they're flat on their back and then only in incomplete sentences or monosyllables?"

"Nope, I don't see the connection."

"Are you ready for this? They're both selfish acts."

"Selfish?"

Jim said, "Sure, selfish. The physician won't solve his own interpersonal problems, so he creates patient anxiety in sick people by grunting monosyllables at them. He's selfish. His family suffers 'cause he makes a lot less money and his patients suffer, 'cause he acts like a jerk.

"I don't see how that compares with me."

"You let your personal interests and needs control, rather than client needs controlling. That's selfish. You should be guided by the most important client need … not Brad's needs."

"Jim, those client needs are important, but each one in different ways."

"Can you describe the specific different ways?"

"Well, one has an immediate critical registration statement issue. Another one has a President who's a worrywart even though the problem isn't that real. Another one has a moderately serious problem, but the guy talks forever. I just can't get him off the phone. Another one, I have real problems relating to. He's so damn abrasive. George just bullshits him, but I can't do that. I won't bore you with the rest, but I've got a bunch of others."

Jim laughed. "See, what a gift it is to be in a big firm. You get a real wide range of interesting client types."

"Yeah, interesting."

"Here's how I do it. I decide on the basis of a series of factors. First is the one you mentioned, urgency. Next, I decide how rational the person is. If they're irrational about their need or fear, the conversation's gonna take a lot longer and generally irrational isn't objectively urgent. Now we come to the most important factor: pain. How much pain is the person in? I took your call, Brad, because you're in real pain. Or, if you aren't, someone should check your vital signs."

"That's the second time this morning someone's accused me of not being alive."

"I wonder why, Brad. Do you remember the insurance industry defense limerick? When the claim was presented, benefits were denied. The Company said since he never lived, he couldn't have died."

"That's pretty subtle. Am I that bad?"

"I think so. What do you think?"

"I don't know. If I could see the problem clearly, there probably wouldn't be one. Can I think about it and get back to you?"

"Sure."

"But before I hang up, I've got to ask you one more question, Jim. Why are you doing this? I'm not a client. I'm not even billable. To be blunt, Jim, what's in it for you?"

"That depends on the realm in which you're asking. From a spiritual perspective, you're a child of the universe, struggling with your identity. I want to respond to the energy you're putting into yourself. I don't do this for worldly reasons, but it always pays off."

"Pays off?"

"Sure, I don't have time to go out and get clients, nor do I need any. People like you refer clients to me. But I don't help people for that reason. If I did, I don't think I'd get any clients."

"That's profound metaphysics in a legal environment where people give their left nut for a good client."

It's also pretty radical in a society where there's lot of people walking around who've given both nuts to get clients. Take your time. Think about it and let me know your concussion."

"You mean conclusion."

"Nope, concussion … Think about it. You'll understand. Talk to you later."

"Wait … wait … Jim?"

"Yes?"

"Can I ask you one more thing?"

"Sure."

"My wife lined up some weekend therapy retreat. Have you ever been to one?"

"Here in California? You've got to be kidding. There's not a weekend goes by, without at least one. I've been to a number of them. There are all kinds here. Is this one where you levitate, gyrate or masturbate?"

"I don't know, but I don't do any of them anyway.

"That may be your problem, Brad."

"Did they help you?"

"Which one, levitation, gyration or masturbation?"

"Come on, Jim, the therapy sessions … did they help you?"

Brad heard a knock on his office door. "Hold on Jim. Come in."

It was his secretary. "Guess who's on the phone from guess where?"

Brad thought and said, "Oh, shit."

His secretary said, "Exactly, and even worse he wants to talk to you."

Brad said, "Can you tell him I'm busy?"

"Are you kidding? Do you really want me to tell the great George Chambers that you're too busy to talk to him?"

"Tell him I'll call him right back."

"You know him. He won't wait. He'll just stay on the line 'til you pick it up and if you don't pick up right away, he'll keep calling back. Is it worth it?"

Brad sighed, "Yeah, you're right. Tell him I'm getting off the call I'm on."

As she walked out of the office she said, over her shoulder, "Smart move."

When Brad put the handset back to his ear he heard Jim say, "I've been listening … not such a smart move. But go ahead, take the call and then call me back if you want."

George was calling for an update on the Tensitron prospectus. When he was done, Brad dialed Jim again.

The first thing Jim said was, "I've had time to think about your question. It deserves a better answer. You actually did me a favor by asking, 'cause it reminded me about the process I went through to establish this practice."

"But mostly I wanted to know if those kinds of therapies helped you."

Jim said, "It's impossible to describe how crappy the bad ones are and how great the good ones are. I remember the best one. It was about fifteen years ago. I had been to, maybe, three before that and was getting fed up. A woman ran this one, not a beauty but definitely a presence. She was maybe fifteen years into career counseling. She had been a social worker before that. I was an unhappy banker back then, with an MBA, but no law degree.

She just had a knack for it. Her insight was better than the others. She held her sessions in the evening at her home. But I met her at a sample presentation she did at one of those weekend retreats. It was held in a church camp way up in the mountains between San Diego and LA. I can remember it as though it just happened. Her name was Leona something."

She said, "Jim, tell me about what you've enjoyed most in your life. I mean what I'd like to know is the type of work you've done at which you felt the most joy."

I said, "I'd have to think about that, Leona. But I liked being in the military."

"Why?"

"They give junior officers lots of responsibility in the Coast Guard."

"What else Jim? In what other jobs did you feel like a natural?"

"I like being a banker, 'cause people trust me."

"But you say banking is in trouble."

"It is. Most all the banks have a portfolio full of bad loans. My bank does too. I don't know how long I'll have a job."

"What else, Jim?"

"I like the titles at the bank. It was like the military. I liked being called 'Commander' and in the bank I'm a Vice President. It gives me identification."

"Anything else?"

"I can't think of anything at the moment."

"How about all that power you project?"

"I try to hide it, 'cause it causes problems."

"Problems?"

"People get scared and resentful of me."

Leona talked to me like that for maybe a half-hour, back and forth. Then she said, "If you're going to change careers Jim, look for work that has the attributes at which you're a natural."

"I don't know what that is."

She said, "You've just told both of us. You want to have responsibility, be trusted and do something where your power can show."

I said, "You mean like a policeman?"

"A policeman would do it, but your education gives you the ability to make more money and have more intellectual challenge than that."

"You mean something professional?"

"Right … like a doctor, CPA, therapist or lawyer."

Brad interrupted, "Is that why you became a lawyer?"

"Yep, but only because I was too old to start being a doctor, hated CPA number crunching, and couldn't sit still all day for a therapist's patient load. But I was worried about the adversary nature of law. I don't like fighting."

"But fighting's part of practice."

"Not necessarily, at least not the way I practice. So, Brad, I've answered all your questions. Are you gonna go to it this weekend?"

"I don't know. Maybe not, if I can find a way out of it."

CHAPTER 10

George had worked hard on a plan to sneak out of the Xiamen hospital during the night. But the security guard caught him and forced him back into his room with his five Chinese room-mates. He lay awake most of the night. Now, the morning after his escape attempt, he lay in his bed talking to Sen, whose five feet five inches towered above the bedridden George.

George was getting impatient and said, "Damn it, how can I get you the money if you don't let me out of the hospital? I told you the fifty thousand has been wired to The Bank of China. I've only got to go there to get it. Then it's yours, Sen."

"The problem is that I'm not getting good reports on your attitude, George. You tried to escape last night. I don't think your heart's in the right place … no … it's not in the right place at all. How do I know you won't just take off with the money?"

George thought, *I've got to control myself. I can't let him see how goddamn frustrated I am.* But he said, "For Christ's sake, Sen, go to the Bank with me. I'll give it to you there, inside the Bank."

"How do I know you'll go to the Bank once you're out of here?"

George said, "Look, hold my passport, so I can't leave."

"I already have your passport, George. But maybe you have another one. You Americans are so inscrutable and tricky. Tell you what, George, we'll wait 'til the Bank opens at ten. Then we'll go directly to the Bank together, like the good buddies we are."

"I'll do just what I said, Sen. I want this to work. I have a lot riding on it, too."

"I know you will, George. See that guy standing in the hall, right outside the door? He's with the Chinese Armed Police, but I pay him. They're sort of a cross between the police and the military. It's kind of like your Coast Guard, only on land. He'll follow us. If you make a run for it, he'll shoot you and, if you're lucky, you'll be back here."

"He won't have to do that, Sen. I want this to work and I'm gonna cooperate to make sure it does."

"You're gonna cooperate for another reason, George. You're gonna move up in the organization from being an accessory to being a coconspirator. I've got interesting travel plans for you, my friend."

George could feel the bile, that came with his fear, rising in his throat. "I told you, Sen, I don't even want to be an accessory, let alone have more involvement."

Sen said, "My thinking is you'll be a lot less likely to screw around when you're in the pot, instead of only watching it boil. The nurse will be here in a few minutes to help you get dressed. Sign the receipt for all your stuff, including the false Russian passport. I already have your documents, so don't say anything to the nurse about there being any missing."

George half rose up out of his bed, all his energy would allow. "Now you want me to sign false documents. I'm not going to sign … "

That was as far as he got before Sen put his hand flat on George's chest and pushed him back. "Now George, that's what I mean by cooperating. Almost every document you sign is false. So don't give me that innocence stuff. You'll sign it if you want out of here. This way if our friend out there has to shoot you, he'll have probable cause. You were carrying a false passport and tried to escape. That's a serious crime in a police state, particularly in one where they hate Russians. I hope you like the picture of you we put in it. We did it right here while you were drugged … sorry it isn't studio quality."

"But I've got to have my real passport at the Bank of China."

Sen said, "You will, but only long enough to get the money. Then our friendly policeman will make sure you give it back to me."

"I can't leave the country without my passport."

That's generally true, but you're going to be an exception and leave without your passport."

George thought, *This son of a bitch is crazy. I can't remember feeling so scared in a long time.* He asked, "Are you going to shoot me?"

"You're a client. We don't shoot clients. Besides, that isn't the kind of journey I had in mind, George. More like a sea voyage."

"You're going to drown me?"

"I'm going to drown you in facts, George. But when I'm done, you'll be sunk. Here's the nurse, so get dressed."

George felt incredibly frustrated while they were waiting at the Bank of China. When he got his own passport he wanted to make a break for it, but the policeman stood right behind them.

When they were out of the Bank and back in the car, George said, "Hey, this isn't the way to the Lujiang Hotel."

Sen said, "You're not registered there anymore, George."

"But I didn't check out."

"Yes you did, George. Don't you remember?"

"Come on Sen, what's your point?"

"My point is that you checked out and even gave the front desk a forwarding address."

"What address?"

"It's in another country, George. But it definitely was you who checked out because you even used your own credit card. Are you sure you don't remember? It was this morning, just before you went to the Bank of China."

"I suppose you have a copy of the hotel bill and the credit card receipt too?"

Sen reached into his pocket. "Right here, George. That Lujiang Hotel is the best. They even enrolled you in their 'Honored Guest' program. That's the gold card attached to the papers. Next time you get a twenty percent discount." And then more ominously, "If there is a next time."

George said, "I know I didn't sign this, but it sure looks just like my signature."

Sen asked, "Have you ever tried to write Chinese characters? That skill does amazing things for penmanship. In fact calligraphy was perfected right here in China. It produces some of the world's best forgers."

George said, "If we're not going to the hotel, where are we going?"

"We had a meeting of the Executive Committee, George. Most of the members lived through the Cultural Revolution. They decided you would benefit from a similar experience."

George, feeling increasingly anxious, asked, "What experience?"

"The experience of being with the working man ... in fact, being one of them. It's out to the rice farm for you George, or more specifically in your case, out to sea."

As Sen said this, he turned the car into a small shipyard. George saw maybe thirty fishing boats tied up to the dock and another dozen pulled up on land, in various stages of being worked on. Sen pulled the car into a sort of shed. He motioned to the policeman sitting in the rear seat. The man got out and opened the trunk.

Sen said, "Time to get out George. You really do look out of place here in those western clothes. The policeman has something more comfortable for you to slip into." He handed George a coolie top, pants, sandals and a conical bamboo hat.

George took one look and said, "You've got to be kidding."

Sen said something in Chinese to the policeman; who took his pistol out, pushed it hard into George's crotch and pulled the trigger. There was a loud explosion.

George felt a hot fire tear through his crotch. He stood still in terror, while Sen and the cop watched. Then he grabbed for his nuts in terror. He expected to scream in soprano, but his testicles were still there. How could that be? He was shot. He pulled his hands up and looked at them for blood, but there wasn't any.

Both Sen and the cop started laughing. Sen said, "Don't worry, George, your jewels are still safe, for now. The first round in the chamber is always blank, but the rest are real. Those blanks do produce a lot of heat. Look, George, there's a burn hole in your pants, right up front in a vulnerable place. Now, you'll have to change and you're in luck. We've brought your new wardrobe."

Then, he said, in a tough, commanding voice, "Put them on, now."

George changed clothes.

Sen said, "Looks good, now let's go out in the sun and take some pictures." The policeman waved George out with his pistol. George stood in front of the shed with Sen and the policeman shot a whole roll of film. After that George walked in between them, feeling awkward in his coolie outfit, onto the dock. They stopped at a fishing boat that was a little bigger than the others. Some coolies were unloading fish and loading ice.

"George, this is what the Cultural Revolution group of the Executive Committee decided would be good for you. Join the men and do the same work. I'll bet you haven't worked your big Harvard ass for a long time."

When he thought about the rest of the bullets, George walked over to the men and started loading ice and unloading fish. The other men kept working and just ignored him. After the boat had its fish unloaded and was ready, the men all sat down on the dock waiting for something. Sen had gone off somewhere, but the policeman just leaned against a shed and waited, too. He motioned for George to sit. George sat. The policeman took more pictures.

After about an hour, as it was getting dark, Sen returned with the boat's crew. They started the engines and cast off all the lines except for two. The boat stayed tied up to the dock, engines idling. About ten minutes later a van quickly pulled up to the boat. The men all jumped up and hurried over to the van. The policeman motioned for George to join them and took some more pictures when he did.

The van doors immediately popped opened and each man, including George, Sen and the policeman, was rapidly handed a baby. They each rushed aboard the boat and deposited their babies into one of three big cribs in the main cabin. Then they quickly went back to the van for more babies. George saw the policeman watching him, so he did the same. He estimated there were about ten babies in each crib, thirty in total, but what for?

George didn't have time to think about it. The van turned around and left immediately. The coolies quickly jumped off the boat after each put a second baby in a crib. The policeman pushed George into a deck chair as the last two lines were quickly cast off. The boat gained speed out of the harbor and was in the open water within a few minutes. Sen was up in the pilothouse. George couldn't ask him questions, so he sat while the policeman took his picture again.

It seemed to George that they had just started picking up speed, when the fishing boat's engine slowed. Even though it was now dark, George could see land, a few lights and a dock only a few yards ahead. The boat came into the dock and the process was reversed. Lines were cast over, a smaller group of waiting coolies scrambled aboard even before the boat was made fast. Each coolie took a baby to a waiting van. George and Sen each took a baby to the van. Sen got in the van's front passenger seat.

The policeman motioned to George to sit in the back of the van, then closed and locked the van's back door. George climbed in with the thirty babies, picking up three of them to make room. He had just sat down and put the three on his lap when the van started moving. So many of the babies were crying he couldn't talk or be heard. The van made a number of stops. Each time women reached in and randomly took some babies. George wished they would take his three. One baby had wet and crapped on George's coolie pants and another had thrown up on his coolie shirt. At the fourth stop, six women crawled into the back of the van and took the remaining babies. George smelled the baby shit and vomit, but at least it was quiet.

Sen turned around in the front seat and smiled at George. "Congratulations, comrade, you have helped bring new life to thirty Chinese infants."

George just sat slumped on the floor against the side of the van. He was too bewildered and exhausted to say anything.

Sen said, "Well, George, this IS new ... the first time you've been at a loss for words ... no questions? no sarcastic comments? ... no sparkling conversation? no assurances of trustworthiness? I'm disappointed. No matter ... we've arrived."

The van stopped. The driver got out and opened the back door for George. Sen had already gone inside the attractive house where they had parked. George stumbled in, pushed by the driver. He looked around the modern furnishings and realized this was an expensive house.

Sen was sitting on a couch in the middle of a sunken living room using a telephone. He smiled and motioned George to an adjoining chair. The driver pushed him into it and went back out to the van. George could hear its tires on the gravel as it drove away.

George sat, exhausted and waited. Finally Sen hung up the phone and said, "Well, George, you ARE a world traveler. Here you are in yet another country. Are you excited?"

George barely had the energy to croak out, "What country?"

"Did I forget to tell you? George, you're in Taiwan. Oh, didn't you remember to get your exit visa from China? ... Too bad. That's about five years in prison. You say you also forgot to get an entry visa to Taiwan? What a shame, that's another, maybe three years. You sneaked into this country and you're traveling on a fake Russian passport? My goodness, you may actually be a spy. That might be the death penalty. What a shame. I wonder what they'll say about this in the Harvard alumni magazine?"

George slumped in the couch. "Sen, are you going to tell me what the hell is going on?"

"That's the least I can do." Sen smiled, paused and then said, "... my friend. You're on the island of Quemoy, sometimes called Kinmen. Even though it's over a hundred miles from the main island of Taiwan, and only about a mile from Xiamen, it's owned by Taiwan. Actually, George, even if all your documents were in order, you're not permitted here. It's mostly a military base and you need a special permit. That by itself would probably convince authorities that you're a spy. But don't worry, we're friends. I won't turn you over to the authorities. I have much better plans for you."

"Plans?"

"Oh, George, I'm sorry. I forgot to tell you, I gave you a piece of our baby business, without your even having to make an investment. It's a little gift from me to you. You'll like it. It's very humanitarian, just like you."

George just held his head in his hands, rolled his eyes up to look at Sen and waited.

"This IS a new George ... so silent. But I know you're burning with questions ... just too modest to ask. The business of which all the documents show you're now a Managing Director is called 'New Life'. We help people get a new start on life. Of course, they're too young to pay us, so we collect from the adults who adopt them. In short, we're sort of an adoption agency ... no, I guess not really an agency ... more like an adoption service ... and you, George, are part of this. Are you proud?"

George said, "Sure ... proud ... " and then waited.

Sen looked at George, smelling of fish, in his coolie outfit covered with vomit and shit. "Perhaps George, we might take another picture of you in this moment of pride. I'll give you a copy. You could use it to go with the article in the Harvard magazine." He reached into his briefcase, removed a small camera and quickly took three pictures.

"Sen, can you just cut to the chase and tell me what's going on?"

"My, these Washington attorneys, always right to the point. Very well, let me try to be equally direct. Every year there are about one hundred thousand reported drownings or abandonments of babies in China. That many being reported means the actual number is probably at least five times that. Think of it George, you're Managing Director of a company with an inventory of half a million human babies each year. People just keep producing babies. I guess it must be a natural instinct. And ... the demand is endless. Do you want to know what the price is?"

Sen didn't wait for an answer. "Of course you do. It's only your high executive position that keeps you from asking directly. We wholesale them for five grand each. They end up in Taiwan, America and who knows where. Just think of it, George. That little boat trip grossed one hundred and fifty thousand dollars. You ARE a keen businessman. Yes sir, George Chambers knows a good deal. No wonder you've done so well in the law, George."

The room was silent when Sen paused. George just continued to sit with his head in his hands. So Sen continued. "Of course, as a Director you want to know all about the supply and demand. I understand, George. This happens because China has a one-child rule. It's rigorously enforced. If a woman in China, who already has a child, gets pregnant she's put through a forced abortion. In rural areas they want boys, not girls.

Needless to say, all of the babies you just accompanied were abandoned girls."

"Unfortunately, the authorities in both countries are not progressive. In China, saving these unfortunate babies is considered kidnapping … with, of course, the death penalty. And it isn't much better in Taiwan. But, under your excellent management, your company, New Life, has anticipated these shortsighted people. You've paid off all the right high officials. Your only problem is that someone might tip them off that you keep a little black book of dates, amounts and most important, George, names. The problem is they're shortsighted people, and because of that, they kill."

George neither raised his head nor said anything. Sen waited a moment and then continued. "I know you're already impressed with your investment. But that's only the half of it, George … literally only half. You see, the very fishing boat that brought you here was in our employ going to Xiamen, too. It brought in the stuff you know about for our technology joint venture. So, as the truckers say, you had a return haul. What an outstanding manager you are. You figured out that fishing boats are the only thing allowed to go directly between China and Taiwan and you took advantage of that. I read the memo you wrote on the subject. It was first class, George. I can understand why you were proud enough of it to sign it."

George's head rolled back onto the couch. Sen asked, "Are you tired? I understand. A Director's duties can be exhausting, let alone a Managing Director who has personally signed every document. Let me show you to your own room. You'll be safe there. There are bars on the windows and the door is steel with a triple lock."

CHAPTER 11

When they got in the car, Janet handed Brad the brochure from the weekend retreat and said, "Look at the list of sessions. I'm gonna drive 'cause you should take the time to read this and decide which you want to attend."

He said, "How am I gonna decide? I don't know anything about this stuff. There are dozens of these sessions."

As she drove away from the house, waving to the children and their baby-sitter, she said, "You'll have time for lots of them. We'll be there tonight, Saturday and Sunday."

He smiled. "And I have you to thank for that. Otherwise we'd spend this weekend doing something dull ... like you know, maybe a dinner and a show or with the kids."

"No we wouldn't. I'd spend it with the kids and you'd spend it at the firm or with Dinky at the printer, or with George Dickhead on that stupid cellular phone, or some other such thing."

Well, George Dickhead is still in the hospital. Dinky finished the prospectus and Miles doesn't work people to death. How'd you find this place?"

She said, "I saw an article about it. It's a once a year thing and it's way up in the Maryland mountains near Hagerstown, so it'll take us at least two hours. It's only three now, so we're ahead of the rush hour. We're driving in daylight. So read and pick. Don't get there and go into your confused defense."

"My confused isn't a defense. Sometimes I'm just confused."

She said, "Right, but your confusion always seem to be when you don't want to do something."

"I don't want to do this, but I promised and I'll live up to that promise."

She said, "I know you will, darling. You're so damn honorable, it's disgusting."

He said, "Hey, look at this. There's a Career Planning session. I'm gonna do that. What's the Course in Miracles?"

"I'm not sure, but if anyone can use one, it's you. Maybe we should go to Lourdes, too ... sounds like it was made for you. Go for it."

"Janet, some of this stuff sounds pretty far out. Listen to this, 'The Power of the Indian Totem Pole', or how about 'Do a Real American Indian Sweat Lodge'? But, what are you gonna do while I'm in sessions?"

"I'm gonna be right there with you, baby."

"All of them?"

"Every last one. I'm gonna see this through with you. Besides, I've got to guard you."

"Guard me from what?"

She said, "From all those little Indian maidens who'd like to experience the power of your Totem Pole or help you to sweat by doing it with you."

"Well, they wouldn't get a chance anyway, 'cause I'm not gonna sweat. I think I'll go to 'Divine Spirit at Work' and 'See the Holy Loving Child at Work'."

"They sound just like the subjects George's so expert at. Are you sure he's still in China?"

He said, "Right, I'm sure they got George as a teacher, and if he's teaching, I sure want to attend. Hey, how about a 'Trust Walk'? You always say I don't have enough trust, so that's why I'm afraid to talk to people. Here's an interesting one on 'Improving Business Relationships Using Spiritual Principles'."

"Look for ones about self examination. You know ... looking inside yourself ... looking at your beliefs ... all that stuff."

Because of Friday traffic, it took them almost three hours to get there. The cool, pine covered rural site was a rustic former church camp. It had about fifty cabins and three big buildings, all made of logs. After registering, they put their stuff in their assigned cabin. Dinner was being served in a central dining room, with a number of long wooden tables. They picked up their paper plates, passed down the simple buffet and sat next to an Oriental couple.

The man said, "I'm Deng Chen. This is my wife, Luang."

Brad stared so hard and so long at the man that Janet kicked him under the table. Brad flinched and whispered, too loudly, "I know that name ... Deng Chen ... I know it."

Janet smiled at the couple and shrugged her shoulders as though she hardly knew Brad. Suddenly, Brad said, "Are you THE Deng Chen … the Tienamen Square Deng Chen?"

"That's me, the Deng Chen who was granted asylum here and who now teaches Feng Shui. In China, I'd still be in prison, if I was alive at all. Did you read about it in the papers?"

Brad said, "Read about it? Hell, Deng, I lived it. I was in law school then, taking Constitutional Law. We used you as an example of Civil Rights. It's always easier to use some other country, rather than our own."

Chen said, "I was in law school, too. My family has always been teachers of Feng Shui. I practiced it too. So, when I came to the states, I started teaching it. It doesn't pay as well as law, but it's a lot more peaceful."

Janet asked, "What is it?"

Luang said, "It is to arrange your surroundings to improve your Chi or life force, so that you will be able to access the well spring of abundance, harmony and wholeness that is rightfully yours."

Janet said, "I'd like to go to that. Brad, do you think you can tend to your own medicine pole and sweat alone, I mean really alone, if I go to one separate session?"

Brad said, "Sure." But then immediately changed the subject. "Deng, I have a partner in China right now, representing a client in a joint venture."

"Was the joint venture a competitive bid?"

"No, it's an exclusive."

"You don't seem like that kind of guy."

"What kind of guy?"

"The kind who does payoffs. That's one reason why we were demonstrating in Tienamen Square. The government of China is mostly corrupt. They're trying to change, but it's tough, 'cause it's become institutionalized. The Army, some police units and law enforcement people all have the right to muscle into anybody's business and own it. As a result, they're totally corrupt. They use their power to do mob type takeovers of business. If you did an exclusive in China, they're in the deal."

Brad said, "The deal's already signed. I have the papers. It's direct … a big Chinese University and our client. There's nobody else in it."

Deng said, "Believe me the police or the Army are in the deal, and probably both of them if it's in a big city."

"How can I find out?"

"That's very hard to do, but maybe you're better off not knowing. You can be almost certain there's someone giving part of your client's payments to the bad guys."

There was a moment of awkward silence, then Luang said, "So, Janet are you coming to our Feng Shui workshop at nine tomorrow morning?"

Brad thought, *Thanks, Luang, for asking her. I don't want to be in these sessions with Janet ... probably for the same reason she wants to be there ... to monitor me. She'll give me hell if I don't spill my guts, participate and blabber my innermost secrets.*

But Brad said, "The Course in Miracles workshop's at the same time. There shouldn't be many Indian maidens in there, so why don't you go with Luang and Deng? I'll be fine."

Luang said, "That's okay, were giving Feng Shui twice, the second is the same time the next morning."

Janet said, "Sweetie, I don't want to miss the opportunity of seeing you in action."

Brad said, "Swell."

They were surprised to find about ten people assembled in the Course in Miracles meeting room. The leader said, "Welcome, my name's Carl. There are three Course groups this weekend. I'm facilitating this one on using the Course in work settings. We're just ready to start now. Can you tell us your names?"

Janet and Brad introduced themselves.

Then Carl said, "The book we're using is 'Career Miracles'. Brad, we use an accounting rule here, 'LIFO'. It means last in, first out. Since you were last in the door, you're first out the gate. Tell us a particular challenge you have in your job."

"Well, actually I didn't come prepared to talk."

Janet, who was sitting next to him on a couch, gave his leg a quick pinch.

"That's okay. Just wing it. The Course isn't about miracles in the common sense. The miracle happens inside us. We change our negative minds. So you don't have to be prepared. Just share your thoughts about your job challenge, whatever it is."

"But I didn't bring the book."

Janet glared at him.

"We have extra copies for those who didn't bring one." He handed Brad a copy.

"I'm new to this. I don't know anything about the Course."

"That's alright, Brad. We're all students on the path." The room fell silent and twenty pairs of eyes were on Brad. Everybody waited.

Brad thought, *I can tell him I won't participate. But doing that doesn't feel really good, and besides, Janet will kill me. Maybe I could ask to talk after others are done, but then I'll probably chicken out and Janet will kill me. So, what the hell ... damn that pinching hurts ...*

He started, "My name's Brad. I must confess, I haven't ever done this before, so be patient with me."

The ladies smiled and Brad continued, "I have some problems with my boss." He stopped for a minute and saw Janet's arm begin to wiggle closer to his leg.

Janet glared at him. He quickly continued, "The truth is I have big problems with my boss ... actually, really big problems. I don't need to go into where I work or what I do ... do I?"

Carl said, "You don't need to do or say anything you don't want to, but we want you to be motivated to contribute, Brad. That's the way you get benefit from it."

Brad looked at Janet's arm buried between them and said, "Oh, I'm motivated."

Janet smiled, looking at him lovingly.

Carl continued, "You should know that in the Course, we always look for the ways in which we contribute to our own problems. What do you do, Brad, that causes this to be a problem?"

The room was silent again while everybody waited. Even Brad, who was used to long periods of silence, felt uncomfortable. Nobody spoke. A few people shifted in their chairs. The silence was so long and so uncomfortable that most people avoided looking at Brad.

Finally, Brad said, "It depends on what you mean by the definition of that word, 'contribute.'" That was as far as he got before he felt the burning pain up and down his leg. This time Janet really pinched him ... a hard pinch. He glanced over. She was sitting next to him with her best, pasted on smile. She had a firm grip. Her hand was buried between them. She had pinched his leg and didn't let go.

He tried to move his leg away, but she just held on. He thought, *I could easily raise my foot a few inches and then come down hard on her foot. Can I do it and not be seen? Maybe if I stomp her foot hard enough, she'll let go. But if anyone in the group sees me do it, they might not understand, particularly if she screams.*

Brad started to raise his foot, but then thought better of it and said, "The problem is, he has all the clients and I do all their work."

He felt Janet's pinch stop and Carl said, "I don't understand what you're saying you do to contribute to that, Brad, or even why it's a problem."

Brad was trying to figure a way out of giving a direct answer, when he saw Janet's arm begin to move. He quickly blurted out, "My boss ... "

He felt the pinch start, and quickly changed, "No, I'm sorry. I misspoke ... it's not my boss. It's me. I can't get clients." He felt the pinch change to Janet's soothing stroking of his inflamed leg.

Everybody waited. Carl said, "Yes, go ahead please."

Brad thought, *These people are so damn patient. Why don't they just give up and go on to some other victim? I'm caught between these saints and a sadist pincher. Why'd I ever agree to come here in the first place?"*

Brad felt himself sort of shrinking into a smaller person when he said, "I'm too shy, so I hide from clients as much as possible. My boss is so dominant he won't let anyone near clients, so he fills my need to hide."

Carl said, "Well, if you've got your needs met, why are you unhappy?"

"'Cause in what I do, if you can't get clients, you eventually get eased out, or at least you don't make much money."

Carl asked, "What keeps you from getting clients?"

"I guess it's a lousy self image. I think clients aren't going to like me, so I avoid them as much as possible."

"Why won't they like you?"

Janet began stroking his leg and he said, "Oh, it's a childhood thing."

Carl asked, "What kind of childhood thing?" and Janet's stroking stopped as though she was the poised pincher.

Everybody waited. After awhile, Brad said, "I always felt abandoned and rejected. I felt my own family didn't like me, so I feel I'm not very likeable."

Carl said, "But are you lovable?"

Janet blurted out, "You bet he is ... the best ... the most ... "

Carl put his finger to his lips to remind Janet that only Brad could answer.

Brad said, "I don't really know what that means."

Carl said, "I'll tell you what we Course people think it means, Brad. It means that first we have to think of ourselves as holy, loving children of God. Then we can think of others that way, too. Do you think of yourself that way?"

Brad felt them coming, but he couldn't stop them. He tried to stop them, but they just kept coming. They ran down his cheeks. They fell onto his shirt. Some rolled down his shirt onto his pants. But he just sat there and felt them. They increased. When Brad could look out of his blurry mist, he saw Carl crying, too. As he glanced around the room, Janet and almost everyone else had tears.

He felt Janet holding his hand, but that didn't stop his tears. He just sat there, without moving. *I'm all wet … all stupid wet … in front of all these people … what do I do now? … How embarrassing … I can't stop.*

Carl waited and then said, "Thank you Brad. Who else would like to share?"

No one said anything, so Carl said, "For those who are in our weekly group in Virginia, we'll meet again next Wednesday, as scheduled. See you then. Have a great weekend."

Brad stood up. Carl, and a number of others, hugged him. The only people Brad had hugged in the last ten years were his mother, Janet and his children. It was awkward, but he felt himself hugging them in return. *How extraordinary,* he thought.

There was a little alcove outside the meeting room with snacks and beverages. Janet and Brad stood there alone. Neither one said anything.

He hugged her again and said, "Can we talk about it later? I just can't now."

"Sure, sweetie. Are you up to going to the next one?"

"I guess so. My leg is pleading with me to go."

"How is it?"

"My leg hurts like hell, but my heart feels … sort of … well, you know … sort of … better."

"Does 'better' mean a broken heart that's starting to mend, darling?"

Brad shook his head yes and they walked away in silence.

They walked the path shown on the map and found the woods for the Trust Walk. It was near the main lodge. There were only six people gathered.

The leader, a late 30's jock, rose to greet them. "Hi, I'm Jake. Are you here for the Trust Walk? Okay, good. We've got a total of eight people now, including you. That's the minimum number. So, we can go ahead. We're only gonna do one part of the walk this morning. Then we come back twice more this weekend for the rest. But Janet, I'm concerned 'cause you and Elaine may not be able to catch these men when they fall."

Janet's eyes widened. "I don't think I can do that. Some of those guys are pretty big. Do they … like … fall out of a tree into my arms? I thought this was a trust walk, not a crush walk."

Jake laughed. "I don't mean catch them by yourself. We line up opposite each other and join hands in a firm grip. It provides a sort of bed of arms for the person to fall into, backwards."

Brad said, "Backwards? You mean without looking? If they're not ready, I'll fall to the ground. I could get injured. How far do I fall to their arms?"

"A couple of feet."

"That's a lot of trust."

"Yep, that's the idea. Can you do it?"

Brad looked at Janet. They both shrugged. Janet said, "Let's try it."

Brad said, "Can I go last after I see how it works?"

"Sure."

One of the men stood backwards on a wall about five feet high. The eight others lined up facing each other, right under him. The rest of the people faced each other, locked their arms tightly and waited.

Jake said, "Go." The man fell backwards and lay cradled in their arms. As he lay there, they all looked at each other. Brad felt it as a real moment of trust. But he was also feeling increasingly anxious as each person did the backward fall. His anxiety was highest when he stood himself, backwards on the wall.

Jake said, "Go."

Brad couldn't move. He willed himself to move. He started to move. He forced himself to move. But, he didn't move.

Jake said, "Go" twice more. But Brad couldn't do it then either.

Finally, Jake said. "That's all Brad, at least for today. If you can't do it today on three tries, you won't do it on thirty. Don't feel bad. There's usually at least one person who can't do it. We can try again tomorrow, if you like. Okay, everybody, time for lunch."

As Brad and Janet were looking for a seat in the dining room for lunch, they saw Deng and Luang sitting at one of the few small tables that seat four. Deng stood when they came near and said, "We saved these seats. I have some interesting news for you about China. Won't you join us?"

After they sat, Deng said, "How was the morning?"

Janet looked at Brad. "Do you want to tell him, or should I?"

Brad said, "Tell you what, Deng, why don't you tell us your news first. I don't know if I've even figured out all the things that happened to me this morning."

"This morning after we talked, I got in touch with my family in China."

"In China? You called them?"

"I do it on the Internet. My father's at home now and is on the net most of the time. When I was arrested, my father lost his job teaching at the University. So, the net's his thing."

"Can he do that in China?"

"Sure, it's a police state. But they've loosened up a lot 'cause the Communist guys in charge have got it all pretty much under control. Dad knows they can arrest him any time they want, with or without reason.

Trials are secret, so the press can't even attend. I'm sure they monitor his email traffic, but we both just use someone else's email to send anything important."

"What a way to live."

Deng said, "Yeah, it's like being a fugitive in your own country."

Brad started to ask him, how he knew about the fugitive analogy, but then thought better of it.

"Anyway, my Dad and I have a code for stuff going to or from his email. The text looks good to the police. But it really means something else. He monitors the net all the time for inside reports on what the government's doing. They try to keep everything secret, but word gets around. I asked him if he knew of any sizeable deals where someone with the government didn't get a cut. Do you want to know his answer?"

"Sure."

Deng said, "Dad said such a thing is theoretically, but not practically, possible in China. He gave me an example. He knows of a big local deal that hasn't even been announced yet. It's a joint venture with our local University. The government guys got paid off to make sure it only went to the one American company, the one that paid off. When another company showed up, their representative was mugged and his passport was stolen. All of this was to put him out of circulation long enough to wrap up the exclusive. But the interesting thing is the muggers were policemen. They sold his passport to someone Dad knows who deals in that stuff on the side. But that's only one way Dad found out about it. Do you want to know the others?"

Brad looked at Janet, but only asked, in a weak voice, "Where does your Dad live?"

"It's a city of only about a half million. You've never heard of it."

"Try me."

It's a seaport about half way between Hong Kong and Shanghai, but it has a famous University where Dad used to teach."

As he listened, Brad went into a deepening depression. He closed his fingers around Janet's hand when she put it in his.

"What did he teach?"

"Political Science, that's why they fired him. They thought he gave me all my liberal ideas. They're right. He did. But the school's famous for … "

Brad broke in, "The Physical Chemistry of Solid Surfaces … it's Xiamen, isn't it."

Deng's eyes widened. He thought for a minute, then said, "Is it your deal? ... your client?"

Brad said, "I assure you I know nothing of this payoff stuff. My partner's over there now and he manages the relationship. I've never been to China or even talked to anyone there."

"I don't mean to be suspicious, Brad, but how could all this go on and you not know about it?

Janet said, "Deng, do you know Carl, who facilitated this morning's Course in Miracles career group?"

"Sure, he's been coming up here for years."

"Then, if you have any doubts about what Brad is saying, ask Carl what happened this morning."

Deng said, "I hope you understand I have to do that to protect my father."

Brad and Janet were so shocked they didn't go to any other sessions. They went straight back to their cabin and spent the afternoon there. They walked in the woods a little, and did a lot of talking.

Late that afternoon Deng came to their cabin and said, "I talked to Carl. He told me. I understand why you wouldn't be involved. Have you thought that you may be being set up to be the fall guy, if one's necessary?"

Suddenly, Janet jumped up. "That's why ... I understand now. Remember Brad ... the guy the police mugged in Xiamen ... called to get you not to talk to George's clients? I wondered what the hell that was all about. It didn't compute. You're wonderful darling, but nobody has to worry about you stealing their clients. You can't even bring yourself to talk to their clients, let alone steal them. Now I understand what he really wanted ... to keep Brad away from Tensitron."

"But I talk to Tensitron people all the time."

"Sure, but let's face it darling, only about routine matters. George wants to keep it that way while he's gone, so nobody at Tensitron pieces things together."

Deng said, "Maybe the company, Tensitron, is in on the payoff with your partner, George."

Brad said, "It could be, and I have to be careful. But, I don't think so. This is much more George's pattern. He gets lots of money from the client and produces results. In fact, it's a lot like his pattern.

Janet said, "I remember you were really suspicious a number of times before. Were those the same?"

Brad thought for a minute. "No, it wasn't the same environment. But they were the same pattern. They were all litigation matters here in the States. They were really important to the clients … sort of 'bet the farm' litigation. If the clients lost, they might be out of business. In each case, just before the judge was going to issue a decision, George billed the client a big premium incentive fee … like a couple of hundred thousand dollars."

Janet asked, "Didn't anybody at the firm question it? I mean a client paying a big premium fee before a decision. When clients pay premiums, don't they do it after they get a good decision?"

Brad laughed. "No, but in the firm's defense, firms don't tend to question big incoming fees. I asked George what the premiums were for. He just brushed me off. The litigation partner who actually tried the cases asked him, too. We both felt our client's cases were not good and we were pretty sure our clients were going to lose. A big percentage of those incentive fees were paid out to George as bonuses. Then … poof … the judges issued decisions in our client's favor."

"Later, George lorded it over we 'Doubting Thomases'. What could we say? He was right about the decision and we were wrong. There were a number of these and they were always about a Court's decision. That's how he got his reputation. He did the same thing in his call from Xiamen the other day. That was another big payment. Tensitron covered it. But they would take George's word that it was necessary in China. The money went to his account in Xiamen. He said it was to pay local specialists. This time it was only fifty thousand dollars."

Deng said, "What a great piece of international data, bribes in China are only a quarter of bribe amounts in the States. There's a solid figure for the World Almanac. The bribe dollar must go a lot further in China … good exchange rate, lower cost of living for hired guns and all that."

Brad said, "I guess there's some humor in anything. But, this one's a real problem. If George is doing what we think, it could bring down the firm, Tensitron and me. This is so important I need to ask you a question, Deng."

"Sure, anything."

Brad said, "You may not like this one, but here it is. You checked up on me this morning, now I would like to do a checking on you. Can you ask your father for the name on the American passport that was stolen in Xiamen?"

"Sure. It's about three in morning in China now. I should have it by breakfast tomorrow, our time. But, Brad, even when you're certain there's bribery going on, you can't do anything about it."

"If we had the facts, we could blow the whistle."

Deng asked, "What happens to whistle blowers in the States, even when they're right?"

Janet said, "Something close to crucifixion, and if they're wrong, crucifixion itself. Either way their life is hell."

Deng said, "The difference in China is that they wouldn't be alive. The life expectancy of a whistle blower in China is minutes. The entire government closes around them and the police kill them. So, your ability to prove anything in China is minimal."

Janet asked, "Aren't there any honest people in government in China?"

"Sure, but they're in the minority and they keep their mouths shut. A good way to understand how it works in China is to compare it to what happens in the U.S. The U.S. government says there's a forty-hour work-week. Just like China says there's no corruption. There are some government employees who do put in a workweek of forty hours or even more. But they have long since given up trying to do anything about the majority who only put in about four hours a week.

You live in Washington. You probably know dozens of government workers. Think about what would happen to anyone in the forty-hour minority worker's group who tried to blow the whistle on anyone in the four-hour majority worker's group. You don't even have to imagine it, the newspapers have those sad stories on a regular basis."

Janet said, "I get the picture and I've seen the stories. The whistle blowers are treated terribly."

Brad wasn't really surprised the next morning when Deng said, "The passport belongs to a David Glass of Chicago."

The four of them talked about the problem for another two hours. They agreed to get together again in the future in Washington, where they all lived.

Deng said, "My Dad is devoting his life to cleaning up the Chinese government. You can count on his help, if you want to check out what's happening in China. But, don't get your hopes up. Most of it takes place behind a real thick bamboo curtain."

The next morning a dejected Brad and Janet packed and went home right after Deng and Luang's Feng Shui class.

CHAPTER 12

B rad was distraught when he went into the office on Monday morning. Because of Deng's scary information, Brad had gone onto the Internet on Sunday. What he found, the "Foreign Corrupt Practices Act," was right on point. Brad could be in trouble, even though he didn't have any direct knowledge of what was going on. He now could be in the position where he should have made further inquiries. What he strongly suspected George was doing, was a crime. The penalty was a one hundred thousand dollar fine and five years in prison. It was even worse for the Firm's "partnership," which was really a corporation. That was a fine of two million dollars.

He thought, *God, I'm having lunch with Miles today. What do I say to him? If I tell him about what Deng said, he may think I'm a whistle-blowing sneak … to rat on my boss like that. If I don't tell him, I could be in bigger trouble. Goddamn George. Maybe Art's right. This is what happens when you're totally dependent on someone. I don't even know what the "critical matter" is that Miles wanted to talk to me about. What the hell did Sheila mean by all those warnings?*

Brad got a stream of incoming calls all morning, but had trouble concentrating. One of those calls was from Dinky. "Brad, we put Tensitron's prospectus to bed, but are we gonna have to amend it for what's going on in China? What the hell is going on in China?"

"Dinky, I don't really know."

"What do you mean, you don't know? Aren't you the responsible partner?"

"No, George is."

"No, he isn't. At least not according to the Firm's records. You are."

Brad felt his heart stop and sweat began to ooze out of his pores. "That can't be right, Dinky. Let me check it and call you back."

"Sure, but get back to me, will you? I've got to decide about this prospectus."

Brad decided he better not call with a question about who the Tensitron responsible partner was ... just in case someone made a record of those calls. So he walked to the Chief Financial Officer's office where those records were kept.

Keeping his voice in control, but with his heart in his pants, he asked the secretary, "Could I please see the list of responsible partners?"

"Sure, Mr. Talbert. It'll take me a few minutes to pull it up and print it out. Do you want me to send it to you?"

"No, that's okay, thanks. I'll just wait. I have some papers with me I need to review." Brad was thankful he seldom went anywhere without a file to read, in case he had a spare moment. Besides, it kept him from having to think about things.

When he reviewed the list, he saw it. There he was ... responsible for Tensitron. He pointed to the item and asked, "When was this effective?"

She punched a couple of computer buttons and read the date from the screen. Brad computed the date and began to realize his danger. He thought, *George switched it during the week after he arrived in China. In the normal course of things, I wouldn't find out 'till a month later. By then it would be too late. Am I being too suspicious? Maybe it's just an error. What if I tell Miles now? He may think I'm paranoid. Maybe I am.*

Then he heard the paging system. "Mr. Talbert, Mr. Brad Talbert. Please pick up."

When he picked up the phone on the secretary's desk, the operator said, "Mr. Dean's secretary, Sheila is on hold for you. I'll connect you now."

"Mr. Talbert, this is Sheila. Mr. Dean has been delayed with a client and has to cancel your lunch for today. When would it be convenient to reschedule?"

Brad felt a deep surge of relief, but stayed calm as he said, "I'm not in my office, Sheila. May I get back to you?"

"Sure ... Mr. Dean had asked if you were free for dinner this evening, but—"

Brad felt a great sense of relief. "You bet Sheila. This evening would be great. What time?"

Sheila continued. "But when I couldn't reach you I called Mrs. Talbert about your schedule. She said that unless it was life and death not to schedule you for anything this evening because you would accept."

"Because I would accept?"

"Right ... she said you would accept in a heartbeat. She asked me to tell Mr. Dean that she finally got you to start a weekly interpersonal self-help group and the first meeting's tonight. She asked Mr. Dean, if possible, not to schedule a conflict."

Brad said, "But, I'd be happy to have dinner with Miles tonight. Don't I have anything to say about it?"

"I don't think so, Mr. Talbert. They already decided. Mrs. Talbert told Mr. Dean this is your first independent follow up about you getting your own clients. She told Mr. Dean that if he felt his meeting was more important she would cancel your group."

"Let me guess, Sheila. You asked Mr. Dean and he said to schedule our meeting some other time, Right?"

"Right."

"Sheila, did you ever have the feeling that your life isn't your own?"

"I have that feeling all the time, Mr. Talbert."

"How about the feeling that you haven't got any secrets from anyone?"

"That too ... "

"I suppose Mrs. Talbert also gave you the directions for me to get to my meeting tonight."

"How did you know? I put them on your email."

"Did she also tell you where I was permitted to go for dinner?"

Sheila snickered. "I could ask her if you like."

"No, that's okay, thanks, maybe I'll just go get some cheese with the other mice."

"Oh, Mr. Talbert, you're not a mouse. Everyone here thinks you're wonderful. We want you to succeed. We're all worried about you. I'm sorry Mr. Talbert. I know I shouldn't say that. But I don't care. It's true. We're worried about you."

"Sheila, what else do you know that I don't?"

"Lots ... but I've been Mr. Dean's secretary for seven years and I don't blab about problems."

Brad said, "Well, at least I've been upgraded to being a problem with clients, instead of being hopeless with them."

Sheila said, "I had a long talk when I called Mrs. Talbert, ... about your group tonight. We're both rooting for you. It sounds wonderful."

Brad said, "Yeah ... wonderful. I can't wait. Thanks, Sheila."

"Anything for my favorite lawyer ... except for Mr. Dean, of course, ... bye." She hung up.

That night Brad went directly from the office to his new meeting. He only stopped at a fast food drive-thru on the way and ate his soggy hamburger in the car while driving. He was still thinking about the office when he pulled up in front of a modest two-story office building on a side street in suburban Virginia.

When he walked into the meeting room there were already three men and two women talking and drinking coffee. Another man and another woman came in after him. About five minutes later, one of the men said, "Okay, gang, it's seven p.m., on the button. Let's get going."

Everyone sat in a semicircle and the same man said, "Since we have a new member tonight, I'll quickly recite the way this group works. Then I'd like each of us to briefly recite our experiences and results with the group.

First, anyone can speak whenever they like, as long as no one else is speaking. We don't interrupt, nor criticize. You all get enough of that at the office. This should give comfort to everyone so they can speak openly, otherwise there's no point in being here. What you hear here stays here. You all share a common problem, a lack of client relationships. There are no two people here in the same business or profession … so, no competition. Any questions?"

He paused a minute and said, "Okay, I'll go first. My name's Bill LePort. I started this group eight years ago, because I had these same client problems in building my own therapy practice. Even with a Ph.D. from a fancy school, or maybe because of it, I couldn't develop new clients. I advertised and started four of these groups, each on a different night. In those eight years there have been over two hundred people through these groups."

"The average time people stay in the group has been about a year and the results have been quite good. That is, except for those who drop out without reporting results. Those we don't know. We use first names only, no necessary indication of company affiliation … and no titles. We've got all kinds of degrees here. It doesn't make any difference. The problem's the same for every one of us … a crappy self-image … that's a technical term from a psychologist's dictionary. Okay, lets go around the room clockwise with brief introductions. We'll start with you, Jim."

"My name's Jim. I'm a CPA … made partner last year … joined this group about three months later … my firm's been beating on me since, about getting clients … it's a real struggle. I can't seem to be natural when I'm trying to get clients. There's something about being in a selling mode that makes me freeze up. I've made some improvement, but it's too early to tell how good it's gonna be for me."

Bill nodded to the lady sitting beside Jim and said, "Go ahead, Nancy."

"My name's Nancy, I'm a computer software engineer, but I'm expected to do follow up on sales when I'm doing an installation. I haven't done it and it's kept me from getting promoted. I kept telling my company I didn't get two degrees in computer science just to be in sales. I tried to change jobs but I found out they all expected that. So about six months ago I decided to join Bill's group. I'm far from a sales queen yet, but now I understand better how to relate to people."

"Next."

"My name's Hank. I'm a banker … a commercial lender … I still have trouble believing that the personality that goes with the money is real important and I always seem to lose out on the good loans. I can't get over the idea that I have the money and they want it, so they have to kiss my butt, not the other way around. My boss has as much as told me my days are numbered. Part of the deal I made with him about a month ago, was that he would let me stay with the Bank for another six months if I joined Bill's group and attended every week."

"Next."

"My name's Frank. I'm an editor at a big publishing house. I worked hard to get my Ph.D. in Creative Writing. I'm a great editor, but I'm also supposed to schmooze good authors and get selling titles. I always thought any gladhander out of high school can do that. It's a waste of my talent. I just didn't think that was fair."

"I've been in Bill's group over a year, now. I still don't think it's right. But now I have a better understanding of why firms have to do it and why I resist it. Maybe it's a chicken and egg deal. As I've gotten better at selling, I understand my own reluctance more. Frankly, some of it's kind of sick."

"Next."

"My name's mud, or at least my company was ready to change it from Richard to mud, if I didn't reduce the complaints. I'm the regional floor plan guy for one of the big car companies. I monitor our dealer's car inventory, part of which we finance. I always thought someone needed to stay on top of those sleazebag dealers or they'll steal you blind. For some strange reason, they got the idea I don't like them, or that I was too hard-nosed. Who knows? Anyway, they got together and told my company it's either them or me."

"I've been in Bill's group for about two years now. Most of those 'sleazebag' dealers are now pretty good friends. For the most part, we trust each other. There are still a few sleazebags, but I don't let them ruin my relationships with the others. In short, I think I've learned how to boost my own self esteem enough so I'm not on the defensive, when there's no need to be."

He nodded to the next person.

"My name's Susan. I'm with government … well, hell, I'll tell you. I'm with the State Department. I answer telephone questions about passports. People pay to talk to me. They charge it to their credit card and then they complain to management. Why don't they just look it up themselves, if they know so much? I think they just want to cancel the five-dollar charge. Anyway, I seem to get all the turkeys. You know, the ones with a negative attitude. My Department monitors the calls. My boss listened to them and said I don't give good phone and I better fix it. I just joined Bill's group two weeks ago. I haven't seen any change yet."

The woman next to her waited a minute then said, "My name's Elaine. I'm a dentist. I had my own practice for awhile, but I work for another dentist now. My practice crashed … not enough patients. It's so hard to establish a new practice. I just couldn't seem to keep patients. I didn't know why. I was near the top of my class and I'm very efficient."

"I joined Bill's group about three years ago … dropped out after six months … didn't find any better group … rejoined about a year ago … restarted my own part time practice two months ago … so far, so good.

Bill LePort said, "Okay, Brad, you've heard everyone else. It's your turn."

Brad was listening, but dreading this moment. He asked, "Can I pass for now?"

Bill said, "Nope, you can't pass, unless it's gas, and only that 'cause we can't stop you. Sorry, Brad, but everyone here is a participant. There are no observers … not even me. So, you're up. Go for it. We'll support you."

Brad gave a big sigh. "Okay … My name's Brad. I'm part of America's most beloved profession, lawyers. I made partner a few years ago, but I can't seem to get any clients. My boss is a rainmaker and he keeps me busy, but I pay a big price for that. I just seem to freeze up when I'm with a client … I don't know what's wrong … no, that's not really true … I think I do know what's wrong. I was abandoned when I was a child and I have this fear of authority figures … you know … like they're gonna abandon me, too … unless I do the right thing … But I don't really know what the right thing is. I think that's it. I don't know what to do, so I get real nervous and screw it up. The clients think I don't like them."

He paused and waited. Bill said, "Do you?"

"Sure I do. I just get choked up when I try to express it."

"Why?"

"I don't know why. Maybe it's because I'm afraid of being rejected."

"When you were rejected, what hurt the most?"

"My parents when I was a child."

Bill LePort asked, "Who in here thinks they have a similar problem?"

Everybody in the room raised their hands, including Bill, who said, "Will some people tell us about what you've done before this to fix it?"

Hank said, "My former bank paid for a therapist. I went once a week for almost a year. We covered my whole life, ever since I was a little kid. The result was I didn't get any more business, but I felt better about being fired. The cost for the therapist was so high that my bank's health insurance premiums increased for everyone. I was forced out and had to look for a new job. That's how I ended up at my present bank where I still have the same problem."

Elaine said, "Another dentist I know, is a nutrition nut. He was sure my shyness was due to poor kidneys. I still have a closet full of health supplements for the kidney. Then, when those didn't work, he was sure it was a jammed up colon. I had my colon irrigated so many times, it became a habit."

Jim laughed harder than anyone. "CPAs are immune to that kinky stuff. If it isn't numerical, we won't be involved. I went to a weekly meeting called the Advanced Calculus of Esoteric Healing."

Brad asked, "What's that?"

Jim said, "I didn't know when I signed up. I went every week and I still didn't know when I quit six months later."

Frank said, "I tried to sign up in one of those EST descendents. I don't remember the name, but they have these consciousness-raising weekends, all over the country. You know, with leaders or trainers, or whatever they call them, where everybody pours out their innermost secrets. Anyway, I went to their introduction night. It was all about integrity, keeping promises and trusting people. It sounded good to me. I told them I wanted to sign up.

They said, "Sign here." It was a document that looked like a concentration camp internment agreement. I was agreeing not to use their methods, ideas, concepts, thoughts … I mean like everything.

I told them, "Look, I'm a professional editor and work on twenty or more books a year, plus what I write myself. Your agreement would put me out of business. You'd be able to sue me for anything.

They said, "Trust us. We don't sue."

I said, "Trust me. I don't either. I want to attend. How about a waiver from the vaguest part of the toughest language? Just make it specific and I'll sign it."

They said, "You'll have to talk to our legal department, but they won't call you." So, I called them.

They said, "We've never issued a waiver and we never will."

I said, "It says right in your agreement to apply for a waiver. What does that say about your own integrity?"

They said, "We don't think you're our type."

I said, "I agree."

Frank said, "My point about all this is that it's easy to talk the talk, but damn few walk the walk."

Bill said, "Thanks, Frank. Anybody else?"

Brad did something totally uncharacteristic. He volunteered to speak. "Last weekend I went to that annual 'Total Person' weekend up in the mountains. They had a session on applying the Course in Miracles to business. I was impressed even though I hate religious things."

Bill asked, "What impressed you most about it?"

"I guess, it just felt good."

Bill said, "Could that be 'cause it was spiritual, not religious? Brad, any one of these things that works is spiritual, at its core. It takes that to pull people out of lifelong patterns. They're usually hard wired in, 'cause they were set in childhood. That's why a lot of motivational talks sound great when you're listening, but that good feeling leaves quickly. They're like a locker room pep talk. They don't have substance, so they only last for the next quarter of the game."

Brad got home about ten that night. As he walked in the door he said to Janet, "That was great. I don't know why I didn't go sooner."

"It's probably my fault, darling. I should've found it sooner. You certainly were pressuring me about it."

"Very funny. Anyway, it was great."

Janet asked, "Did you bring your cellular phone into the meeting with you?"

"No. They don't allow cellular phones into the meeting."

"I thought so. Your favorite person in China called and left a message on our answering machine."

"What did he say?"

"He said that you better be able to prove you were unconscious in a hospital, if you're not carrying your cellular phone. You got another call, too."

"Who?"

"Miles Dean. He wants to know if you're free for lunch tomorrow."

Brad said, "Shit."

"Shit ... for Miles?"

Brad explained about George's setting him up by quietly substituting responsible partners. "I don't know what to say to Miles. It seems like heads I lose, tails I lose."

CHAPTER 13

When George woke up, the first thing he saw was the brilliant sun streaming through the bedroom windows. Had it all been a bad dream? Where was he? Then his eyes focused on the bars across the windows and he remembered. Last night after they forced him into this bedroom, he had waited. As soon as he heard the bedroom door lock, he peeled off the stinking coolie outfit, dropped into the bed and slept immediately. This must be the next morning. He remembered illegally taking thirty babies out of China … the fishing boat … the shot in his groin. He reached down and felt around his testicles. He was relieved to find the right equipment seemed to be in the proper places, even if it burned from the pistol being fired so close.

Then he heard noises outside in front of the house. He got up and went to the window. The van had returned and the driver was handing Sen a suitcase. George thought it looked like his suitcase. Sen was talking to the driver. Suddenly, as though he had a special sense, Sen turned and looked at George. Then Sen smiled, waved and held up the suitcase, pointing to it and then to George. He put the suitcase down on the driveway and signaled to George with both hands to pull the window up.

After the window was open Sen said, "Good morning, counselor. I hope you slept well."

George put his head to the bars and said, "How about letting me out of here?"

"Your bedroom door's open. You've been free to go since early this morning. I just thought you might not want to wander around this island in your birthday suit, particularly with powder burns on your balls. You wouldn't even have a pocket for your fake Russian passport. I was concerned you might stick out in a crowd, since you're the only white man on this island and you do have a lot of skin. You really should go on a diet, George."

"Now that you've gotten me here, what are you gonna do with me?"

"Why, George, we're going to take you back. You certainly don't want to stay in Taiwan illegally. They frown on that."

"When?"

"As soon as we clear up a few matters. The driver will bring up your suitcase. I hope you find everything you need to dress the part of the Washington lawyer, vacationing in Taiwan. We took the liberty of removing the coolie outfit from your room last night, George. You shouldn't wear those coolie clothes. They don't fit you well, at all. You can go native some other time."

There was a knock on the door and it opened. The driver dropped the suitcase on the floor and closed the door.

Sen stood in the driveway and shouted up. "How about some breakfast, George? In about thirty minutes, okay?"

George just looked at him.

Sen said, "I'll be in the dining room waiting … bacon and eggs okay?" He walked into the house without waiting for an answer.

George poked around in his suitcase. Everything he needed seemed to be there. So he showered and dressed.

When he came downstairs, George saw Sen sitting at the dining room table having tea and reading the morning paper. Sen looked up and rang a little bell on the table. A man appeared and Sen gave some commands in Chinese. The man bowed his way out of the room, reappearing a few minutes later with breakfast for both of them.

"Well, George, you look rested. I hope you're ready to return to China today."

"Come on, Sen, what the hell is going on?"

"Going on? Nothing's going on, George. But what's going to happen is that you're gonna get that password and get that fifty grand for me and then you'll be able to check back into the Lujiang Hotel. It's a comfortable hotel, isn't it?"

George said, "Yeah, it's fine. What then?"

"Then? Then it's business as usual. After all we're partners."

"It didn't seem that way last night."

"Oh that … that was just a … sort of indoctrination into your new baby business. But shouldn't we be talking about our main business ... the technology joint venture with Xiamen University?"

"What's there to talk about?"

"Now, now George, don't pout. It doesn't become someone of your stature. Besides, what would they say at Harvard?"

They were interrupted by the van stopping in front of the house. Sen said, "That would be Chang, just over from the mainland."

As Chang walked in, Sen said, "How nice you could join us for breakfast. We have so much to talk about. Chinese or Western breakfast, Chang?"

As soon as they were settled, Sen said, "The first thing we have to do is to figure out what's going on at the University Lab. How about it Chang?"

Chang said, "We've got some political problems in the lab, and some outside, too."

Sen said, "This is what we're paying Chang for, George. He keeps an eye on any problems that develop. Give us the inside problems first, Chang."

"Well, Dr. Fu, the principal scientist, has to be handled carefully. He's too straight. It's disgusting. He hasn't got any idea what's happening. In fact, the idea that anything, other than what's supposed to, could happen, isn't something he would even think about. If he knew how this deal really came about, he wouldn't believe it."

Sen said, "So?"

"It's important that he never know, 'cause he'd blow the whistle in a minute."

Sen said, "So, how much will it take to buy him off? He can't make much money."

"He doesn't make much. But he's in his sixties. He's come through the Cultural Revolution, Tienamen Square and six changes of government and still believes in Communism. There's no way you're gonna get to him with money. If you try, we'll be in big trouble."

"So what does he like ... girls, boys or something in between?"

"He likes chemistry."

Sen said, "So, get him his own lab."

"He already has one. It's called the University Lab. He runs it."

"Can we get rid of him?"

Chang said, "Not if you want a deal ... the key Tensitron scientists are mostly sharp Chinese Ph.D. chemists who fled the country during the Cultural Revolution. That's how Tensitron found out about Fu's nano-technology breakthrough They don't respect Fu's politics, but they do respect his science, and for good reason. He's the best scientist in the place … world famous reputation and all that. On top of that, they like him. He's a nice guy."

George said, "I thought nice guys came in last. What's the other problem?"

Chang said, "It's tied into this one … those Tensitron Chinese chemists … "

"Yeah?"

"They won't come onto the soil of Mainland China."

"Why?"

"Because as much as they like Dr. Fu … they don't like the Communist government in China … about the same amount. In fact, they love Fu and hate the government. In addition to hating them, they don't trust the Communists either."

Sen said, "What's the big deal? Nobody with any sense trusts anyone in any government."

Chang said, "You forget, these guys are still technically fugitives from China. They escaped in the sixties, during the Cultural Revolution. Fu stayed. They fled. It's that simple."

Sen said, "We'll get the government to give them amnesty."

"The government could give them golden parchment scrolls of amnesty, elect them to the National Congress and send litter chairs, hauled by beautiful maidens with undying promises of love, to carry them back from the U.S., and they still wouldn't come to China."

George said, "I'll be damned."

Sen said, "You probably already are, but back on this subject, let's see if we can talk them into it."

Chang said, "You're wasting your time."

Sen ignored him. "George, who do you have in the States, who can sweet talk these guys?"

"I've got just the guy. He's so straight … he's like Dr. Fu. He doesn't know the score. Where's the phone?"

Brad and Janet had just climbed into bed, when the cellular phone started ringing. No one except George had the number, so they both knew who it was.

They looked at each other. Brad reached for the phone. Janet put her hand on his. "Tell him to go fuck himself."

"You tell him. I've still got to meet with Miles tomorrow and I want to get to Miles before George does."

Janet said, "What would he do if I did?"

"Nothing. He'd probably hang up, figuring he got a wrong number."
Brad reached for the phone and said, "Brad Talbert."

He listened for a long time. Then he said, "George, I've got an important lunch date with Miles tomorrow and we've already postponed it twice."

Then he listened again and said, "All I know about the Tensitron prospectus is what Dinky told me today. It's ready at the printer, but hasn't been circulated yet. ... Tonight ... you want me to go to San Diego tonight? It's ten at night here. I don't even think there are any more flights."

He wanted to say, "You asshole. You don't have any respect for anyone else. Why don't you understudy Miles for awhile and see how it's done?"

Brad listened again, then said, "Okay, George. I'll take a red eye tonight, if there is one. I should be able to drive to Tensitron in less than an hour. The rush hour traffic's the other way. That would put me there about ... let's see ... if the plane leaves at one a.m. I should get in about four a.m. tomorrow, local time. The flight takes about six hours and I gain three. Then I need an hour for the plane to be late, get a car and get out of the airport. I should be at Tensitron about six tomorrow morning."

Brad waited again while George spoke. Then he said, "Yes, I understand the issue. I'll do my best."

He waited again. Then said, "George that's all anyone can do ... is their best. I can't promise I'll be able to convince them. But, I will do my best and yes, I'll turn on all my best charm. How do you know they'll even be there?"

He listened. "But even if you call Jack Mann, he can't produce them if they're somewhere else."

Brad listened again. "I guess you're right. Lab scientists do tend to be in their lab. Okay, I'll wait for your call back after you talk to Jack."

George called back about five minutes later. "Jack said, 'Try to convince them, but don't push too hard or piss them off. He likes them and he needs them.'"

Brad said, "That's a tight tightrope to walk, George. You want me to convince them, but not to be too forceful."

He thought ... *typical George ... doesn't give a shit ... impossible task ... I'm not even good at convincing people to begin with ... now he lays this at my doorstep.*

The first beads of sweat began to break out on Brad's body. He could feel them ... on his head, in his crotch, on his armpit. It was that cool feeling, coming from uncontrolled evaporation of uncontrolled sweat. He waited until George was finished.

Brad listened again. "Okay, I'll call you from San Diego after I talk to them and let you know. ... Yes, I understand it affects the prospectus. ... Right George ... Yes, I understand. ... right ... Okay, I'll be sure and get back to you. Bye."

After he hung up, Janet said, "I gather I'm going to be sleeping alone tonight?"

Brad said, "Maybe you could come with me and we could curl up together in the back of the plane. They have these two for one tickets now ... besides, I've got lots of frequent flyer miles."

"Do they charge more miles against your account if we screw on the way?"

"That's a very complicated legal question. It depends on the state over which we screw. There's a form we fill out. We have to certify when we each had an orgasm. If we do it over Iowa, they deduct a lot more miles than they do over Colorado. But there's a use tax in Colorado. Actually, that whole matter is a practice specialty called Aircraft Fornication Law. We have a couple of partners who specialize in it. I could call them."

"No, that's alright. I'll stay home and whip out my vibrator, but it's on its last legs ... no pun intended. When can I expect to see you?"

"Brad thought for a minute. "George wants me to convince these Chinese scientists to go into Communist China. They don't want to do it. I'm supposed to be forceful, yet diplomatic. It'll take something between five minutes and five years. He doesn't want me to come back without their promise."

Janet said, "Maybe you could swap some frequent flyer miles to get me a new vibrator."

"I'll look in the gift catalog on the plane ... any particular kind?"

Janet hugged him. "One that looks like you, darling."

When Brad arrived at Tensitron, he was exhausted from thinking about how to do this. But he was pleased to find the three scientists waiting ... well, not exactly waiting ... but at least working in their lab. They were expecting him, but clearly not happy about the reason he was there.

He gave them his card. "My name's Brad Talbert. I'm a lawyer with the Firm representing Tensitron."

They were so short, Brad had to bend low to shake hands. All of them were in their fifties and wearing lab coats. One of them introduced the others.

He said, "We know who you are, Mr. Talbert. Jack told us. My name's Arnie Fong. My colleagues are Jing Guangwen and Liu Pang."

There was an awkward silence, then Brad said, "Can we go some-where to talk?"

Arnie said, "We've arranged to use a conference room. Please follow us."

When they were settled, Brad asked, "Do you know why I'm here?"

They were silent for a few minutes, then Arnie said, "Yes, we do, Mr. Talbert. You want us to go into Mainland China, a place where none of us have been for thirty years."

"Please call me Brad."

Arnie said, "Alright, Brad. Jack Mann called me last night. The three of us met within an hour of that call. We decided to try to help you un-derstand why we won't go back. We owe Jack a lot. We like him, too. He gave us jobs when they were hard to get. He's a fine human being. We would do anything we could to help him, but you may not understand how difficult this is for us."

Jing said, "I don't see why we have to go there. We can cooperate with Dr. Fu from here. We'll exchange data and specimens. Air express is fast these days, and- "

Liu interrupted. "That's wishful thinking, Jing. My preliminary analy-sis is that we won't be able to ship the specimens so far. They're not stable enough. I don't see how we can do it with them in China and us in the States."

Arnie said, "I agree with that. A lot of specimens can't ship fast enough to survive.

Brad thought, *These guys are so sincere. I don't want to convince them of anything.*

"I tried to think of an example to help you understand." Arnie said, "Asking us to go there is like asking an American Negro to go back to the South where his family was hung. Try asking a Jew to go back to Jordan or a Cuban to return to Cuba. He hears the reports about change, but he doesn't trust his rednecks. We particularly don't trust our Chinese red-necks either. They run the government."

Brad said, "I don't understand. They'll give you whatever assurances you want, in writing. And our State Department will guarantee them."

Liu said, "A State Department guarantee isn't worth anything. If push came to shove they couldn't and wouldn't honor it. What are they gonna do, sue … or go to war with China, over three scientists?"

Jing said, "I don't think it's possible for you, as an American, to un-derstand. You have all the problems of big government here. But you have some protections for the public, even if they're minimal. There are a few courts and judges who will protect human rights in the States. It may only be available to those who have the money to fight for it. But it's still there."

Arnie said, "What Jing's saying is, in China, there are none of those protections. The courts and the judges are just extensions of the government and they do what they're told. The closest you can imagine is to think of some U.S. cities with big corrupt political machines. Imagine all of the rest of the U.S. is like, say, Chicago or New Orleans or Providence. Judges do what the political machine tells them. That's China, only worse, 'cause there's no review process. There's not even the pretense of fairness you see in the States. Would you trust your freedom to that?"

Brad said, "I can't believe it's that bad."

Jing said, "It's worse. During the Cultural Revolution, when Mao had his fight with Shaoqi, his number two, he created the Red Guard to crush Shaoqi's followers. They crushed everything and everyone else. Whether or not it had to do with Mao. They destroyed everything that was fine and beautiful and educated … everything. And the courts did nothing."

Liu said, "I was just twenty years old. They closed my college, beat my father who taught there, ransacked our house and deported me to a state farm in Ruili, a far corner of China. There was no reason for all of that. No judge opposed them, 'cause if any did, they would have been sent to a farm, too. The Red Guard murdered ten million people. The courts did nothing. They burned temples, museums, homes and the courts did nothing. Now, what is it you wanted me to believe?"

Brad said, "But that was all over thirty years ago. Things have changed in China."

Arnie said, "Things have changed. But that hasn't changed. Government controls and does what it wants. We escaped and we're still fugitives."

Liu said, "I don't think any of this has changed in China. Look at Tienamen Square. That was less than ten years ago. They did it all over again. Just talk to anyone who went through it. There are plenty of refugees here in the states from Tienamen."

Arnie said, "Brad, we appreciate your coming. But I don't think we're going to change our minds. You've got to find another way to work this out. Maybe Dr. Fu would come here."

Brad said, "We already tried that. The Chinese government wants the work done at their lab in Xiamen. They say they developed the technology and they want to control it."

Liu said, "That's reasonable. But it looks like we've got a stalemate."

Brad stayed with the Tensitron scientists through lunch, trying to convince them. But nothing worked.

He called George right after lunch. "I tried everything, except kidnapping them. They aren't going to do it."

George said, "Has Jack Mann told them they have to do it? He's the damn President."

"They already told me they'd quit before they'd go back. But I've got an idea."

"Try anything Brad. You know how I depend on you."

Brad hated it when George threw up those phony compliments. They were so insincere. But he said, "The most recent convincing thing for them is what happened at Tienamen Square. I met a Chinese couple in Washington who were student leaders in Tienamen Square."

"What's Tienamen Square?"

"Tienamen Square ... T-i-e-n-a-m-e-n Square. It was about ten years ago."

"Where?"

"In Beijing, China."

Brad thought, *I hope he's only kidding. Could it be possible that he really doesn't know what it is?*

Brad continued, "Anyway, this guy's real metaphysical. Maybe he could get them to change their minds."

"Good idea ... try to do it as fast as possible. I'm lucky to have you for a partner."

Brad thought, *I feel like throwing up. Doesn't George realize how he comes across? Why can't others see what a phony he is? Maybe I do 'cause I know him so well. No wonder, I think it's better for me to just keep my mouth shut rather than to be a transparent phony like him.*

CHAPTER 14

When Brad called the office from San Diego, his secretary gave him his messages and then said, "Mr. Dean asked me to transfer you to him when you called in. Hold on."

Miles came on the line immediately. "Brad, I'm glad you called ... enjoying the weather out there? ... I understand you took an overnight flight, you were so eager to go on your extended vacation in San Diego. Have you convinced those Chinese fugitives to go back? I'm anxious to hear if you did it, but that'll wait. You've had a whole night without sleep and a day of being powerful and persuasive. That's long enough without any challenges. I'd like you to join me in making an important call tomorrow on a company in Los Angeles. They're a minor client now, but could be a significant one. Are you up to it?"

"Sure, Miles, but as you know I'm hardly the firm's best salesman. I'm here on the West Coast, but are you certain it's me you want to join you?"

"They're doing a joint venture in China. Didn't you do all the work on the JV agreement for Tensitron?"

"I drafted it, but I didn't negotiate it."

"Well, did you do the research, leading up to it? I know George. I'm sure he didn't do it."

"You're right, I did it."

"Okay, ask your secretary to give the file to Sheila. I'll bring it with me and I'll meet you in our Los Angeles office about three, tomorrow afternoon. I'm too old to do your overnight flight thing ... and Brad ... "

"Yes?"

"The rainmaking part of this will be okay ... honest. You've got the right stuff. You're one of the best lawyers in the firm."

Brad hung up the phone and almost cried. He sat in the empty Tensitron office, motionless for almost ten minutes. He thought, *What is it about Miles' style? What is it? I wish I could bottle it and then sprinkle a little on me every time I get depressed.*

He looked at his watch … a whole twenty-four hours 'til he had to be in Los Angeles. On an impulse, he picked up the phone and called Jim Ward.

Jim answered on the second ring. "Jim, this is Brad Talbert. I'm here in San Diego at a client's and I don't have to be in LA 'til tomorrow afternoon. I'd love to get together, if you have time."

"Brad, it's great to hear from you. I'm flattered. Are you staying in San Diego this evening? … How about dinner? … Wherever you like. … Sure, your hotel's great. I'll look forward to seeing you … and Brad, remember San Diego's casual … no Washington coat and tie stuff … that way they won't suspect we're lawyers … This is a real treat for me … I'm delighted you called … look forward to seeing you."

As they were finishing dinner Jim said, "I notice you stay up here in Sorrento Valley, so I assume your client is a technology company. I have a number of those companies and executives as clients. Those guys are under a lot of pressure."

"Do you think it's more than other executives?"

Jim said, "I do. And it's mostly 'cause their technology moves so fast, they can't focus only on the standard things like production, sales and personnel. They always have to be fixated on the next stage in their technology. It's a special breed all right. And technology doesn't have boundaries. They're vulnerable to developments all over the world."

"I hadn't thought of it that way. But that's true. My client is a technology company and the President has all the problems you described. Right now he may lose an important JV in China 'cause some of his scientists won't go there. In fact, that's why I'm here."

Jim's desert fork stopped in midair, leaving his jaw hanging open. He slowly put the fork back on the plate. "Brad, this is none of my business, but is your client Tensitron?"

Now it was Brad's turn to be stunned. "Do you have a conflict? If so, neither one of us should say anything more."

"No, not a conflict in the sense you mean it. Brad, I basically represent Jack Mann personally."

"Well, I don't see any problems there. He's not even potentially adverse, or opposed, to his Company in anything I'm aware of."

Jim said, "You're right about that. Now I know who you are."

"You knew before."

"No, before I knew how you suffered. Now I know what you stand for."

Brad was really puzzled. "What does that mean?"

"You work for a guy named George something, right?"

"Right."

"He's a miracle worker in getting favorable court decisions and deals, right?"

"Well, I guess you could say that."

"Do you know how he does it?"

"Jim, maybe we shouldn't continue this conversation."

"You're right, Brad, we shouldn't. ... Brad?"

"I'm going to move that sealed envelope I witnessed to a fireproof bank vault. You may need it."

" ... And Brad ... "

"Yes?"

"Be careful."

They got up and said goodnight in the hotel lobby. Brad felt severely strained in the relationship. Jim was as warm and cordial as ever.

The next morning as Brad was creeping along the freeway in his rental car in the Los Angeles traffic, he returned his calls on his cell phone.

The first call was to Deng Cheng in Washington. Brad quickly explained the problem with the three Chinese scientists at Tensitron. "I'm on my way to meet an important partner in Los Angeles. He's going to ask me about what's happening in China and I'd like to be able to tell him you're gonna solve the problem. My client will be glad to pay you for your time, win, lose or draw."

He listened and then said, "Yes ... I suppose it can wait 'till I get back to Washington tomorrow. But it's really urgent. Do you think you can help?"

Brad listened again, then said, "I understand you're not optimistic about it, but ... Okay, let's talk about it when I get back. Are you free for dinner tomorrow night? ... Where? How about a Chinese restaurant? You pick it. ... Where? ... Okay, see you there about eight."

Three and a half hours later, Brad had completed the two hour drive to the firm's Century City office.

An hour later, Miles came into the Century City office, took one look at Brad and thought ... *that look, it's so sad, for such a solid guy ... worry, uncertainty, lack of confidence ... I feel so sorry for him.* He said, "Great to see you, Brad. Thanks for joining me. Sorry to be late ... it took me an hour to get here from the airport and it's only about twenty miles."

"It was a parking lot driving up here from San Diego, too. I could have walked faster."

"True, but then you wouldn't have been rested to meet the client for dinner."

Brad said, "I've got to tell you, Miles, I'm pretty nervous about calling on a new client. George has never taken me with him on a new client call. I'm a technician, not a salesman."

"Now Brad, remember 'From our perception flows our reality'. And that's not a very good perception you have of yourself."

Brad didn't respond.

Miles said, "God knows I've had my share of practice problems too, Brad. This isn't my first firm. In fact, as a young partner, I had more than my own share of problems ... bad firm management ... I had to change firms three times ... clients who didn't pay ... more senior partners who wanted to work me to death ... but there was always someone there to mentor me."

Brad was silent. Miles asked. "Do you have someone to mentor you, Brad?"

"Janet."

Miles said, "That wasn't quite what I had in mind." He thought, *I like this boy ... he's amiable and smart ... I'd be proud to have him as my own son ... he doesn't deserve George ... but, maybe I'm wrong ... maybe he's in it with George ... and fooling all of us ... me too.*

Brad didn't say anything. Miles reached into his briefcase and took out a file. "Here's your China joint venture file. Would you please go over the key points with me before our client dinner meeting?"

Brad started to talk, but Miles couldn't focus. His mind kept wandering off Brad's comments as he thought *how much empathy I have for this superb young man ... he's headed for the abyss. What a disaster his life will be, if he continues on this course. What a shame to lose all that talent and for him to have all that pain. I wish I could give him an infusion of self-confidence.*

Then Miles heard Brad's comments through his thoughts. " ... So, the agreement provides for mandatory arbitration by the World Intellectual Property Organization, if there's a dispute. My experience is these international JV's just aren't practical to litigate. Tensitron was going to put litigation language in the agreement. I sent them a strong letter warning them that the Firm had advised them against it. George was pissed, but Jack Mann said he appreciated it. Then George changed his tune."

Miles asked, "Did you have a chance to look at those few pages I had faxed to your hotel last night about this deal? How long will it take you to draft the agreement for this client?"

Brad said, "Well, that depends on ... Miles' mind wandered as he watched Brad, without really listening. He thought ... *God, he's so long winded. Just give me a range of time Brad. Don't tell me how time is measured. He's so mature in his integrity, but so immature in his understanding of human nature. He's so damn sincere. I don't think he even knows how to be misleading. Maybe he shouldn't be a lawyer. No, I was like that at his age, too. I was lucky. I just didn't have a George in my life.*

Miles said, "At dinner tonight, let me try to answer most of the questions. When it's a technical matter I don't understand, like these agreements, I'll ask you. But don't feel put off if I cut you off. You do tend to be somewhat long winded on technical answers, Brad."

"Janet tells me that, too."

"Just try to be less of a lawyer and more of a regular guy."

"But clients pay us to be lawyers."

"Brad, they pay us for some of both. Are you so conservative that you have both your suits and your pajamas made with vests?"

"No. Should I?"

The next morning as their plane took off from Los Angeles, Brad was still undecided about how much to tell Miles about China. But here they were, for a six hour flight ... just the two of them together ... "

Miles said, "Brad, I can't tell you how well that went last night. Whether or not the client gives us the matter, you did a superb job and I want to congratulate you."

Brad made the decision. "Thank you. ... Miles?"

"Yes?"

"There's something else I'd like to talk to you about."

"Sure."

"It's about China, Miles."

"Yes?"

"There's something wrong there."

"Tell me about it, Brad."

Brad talked through breakfast and lunch. Miles asked a lot of questions, but mostly listened. He interrupted only twice. Once to go to the bathroom and once to call the office.

He even made the office call brief, "Hi Sheila ... everything under control, as usual? ... Any other messages? ... Okay, fine. Would you ask

Dinky to finish up his file and tell Tim Long that our mutual friend is fine. We get into Dulles at six this evening … Flight 732, nonstop from LA … Right, I am too … very much so. Thanks Sheila."

After Miles replaced the phone, into the recess built into the rear of the seat in front of him, he sat reflectively for a minute looking out the airplane window.

Then he turned and said, "I hope you don't mind, Brad, but I've had to schedule a meeting at the office tonight. You can join us. I think you'd be a major contributor."

"Who's the client?"

"The firm, it's sort of a firm strategy planning session. You'll find it challenging. Our time together on this trip enables me to tell you what it's about."

Brad said, "I've never been in a firm strategy meeting except for the rubber stamp general partnership meetings."

In a sense Brad, this one's about you. It's what I've been trying to get together with you about for the last week. The Firm's doing fine, but we're like all firms; under constant pressure to deliver results at less cost to the client. That means we're always looking for ways to cut costs. Our biggest cost is salaries and the biggest part of that are attorney's salaries. Any attorney who doesn't generate billable hours is vulnerable."

Brad said, "I bill out lots of hours."

"That's true, Brad. In fact, you bill out more than most, and they're good hours, too. Your clients don't complain 'cause they sense you're more than worth your billing rate. But you don't originate those hours."

Miles wanted to ask for a drink. He thought how difficult this conversation was going to be and pushed the flight attendant button. "A white wine please."

Then he continued. "Do you realize, Brad, that you're doing sixth or seventh year associate work but getting paid about fifty percent more than that as a sixth year partner?"

Brad said, "I hadn't thought about it that way, but I think I bring more experience to it than a sixth year associate. Isn't that worth something?"

"You do bring more experience, Brad … about ten years more experience. But your experience for the last of those ten years has been doing the same thing over and over again."

Brad said, "The challenges are all different."

Miles said, "I don't share your view. The clients are different, but the challenges are pretty much the same."

"China's different."

Miles said, "Yes, China's different, and it's that very difference that's causing this conversation. But I don't think the difference I'm thinking about is the same one you're referring to. Tell me what you mean by different."

Brad said, "I mean; It's international. It's a joint venture with a government entity. That government is both Communist and a former enemy. And it involves intellectual property."

Miles said, "That's what I thought you meant by different. Everything you said is true, from your perspective. Now, I'll tell you what I mean. This is painful for me to say, Brad, but this thing in China has magnified your problems at the Firm."

Brad interrupted. "Problems … problems? I didn't know I had 'problems'. I thought I had one problem … the inability to get clients."

"You've got other problems because you can't get clients."

"I don't understand."

"I know you don't. If you did understand, I don't think you'd have the problem. As a result of your dependence on George, you're viewed as his hireling, there to do his bidding … all of it."

Brad said, "What does 'all of it' mean?"

"It means there is a concern that you're a co-participant in whatever he's doing."

"Does 'whatever he's doing' mean what I think it means?"

"Brad, it means people don't feel free to be open with you about George 'cause you aren't independent of him."

"Hell, Miles, he's my boss, not my Master. Abe Lincoln took care of that problem."

"Lincoln freed the black slaves, not the white ones. You're beholden to George for your job. As good as you are, few other partners will take you on and then only on a temporary basis. You're just too damn expensive. That makes you owe George, big time. An associate can do your work for half the cost. George doesn't have that luxury of replacing you with an associate 'cause no associate will work for him … at least not for very long."

"That's pretty subtle, Miles. I understand what you're saying, but is the punch line that I'm gonna be fired?"

"Probably, if you don't take care of yourself. Not right now ... not today ... cause we're so busy now, but when things slump off again ... then you're in trouble."

"How much trouble?"

"Big trouble. You probably should be dusting off your resume now."

"Who's gonna hire me?"

"I don't think anyone will ... at least not at your current compensation. You'll probably have to take a cut."

"How much?"

"I don't really know, but I'd guess about thirty to fifty percent."

Brad sat up, bolt upright in his seat, "Fifty percent ... half ... a fifty percent cut in salary? Miles, you've got to be kidding."

Miles thought, *I hate this. Why me? At least I got his attention. Damn it Brad, wake up and smell the coffee. I don't want to go through this again with you and I'm not gonna. I like you, but it's just too damn painful.*

"Brad, we've talked about this a number of times. I'm speaking to you now as a friend. Take care of the problem before it takes care of you."

There wasn't much more to say about that subject, so they continued talking about China. They were still talking about it two hours later as they walked out of the airport terminal and entered the car waiting for them at the curb. Miles picked up the car phone, dialed and waited. "Sheila? Thanks for staying late. How's everything going?"

He listened, then said, "Okay, we should be there in less than an hour. Thanks for waiting. Why don't you go home to your faithful husband and unfaithful dog. Does he still go with whoever gives him a treat? ... No, I meant your dog. Does your husband do that too? Bring him to one of those dog psychologists. They'll give him some self esteem."

When they walked into the office, Brad saw Tim Long and three other partners who were on the Executive Committee, sitting around the table in the big front conference room. The huge marble table seated a couple of dozen people and gave them a panoramic view of the Washington skyline.

Tim said, "Come in, gentlemen ... that's a long trip from the West Coast. There's coffee on the side buffet. Welcome, we've been waiting for you. In fact, now that you're here, this meeting can start."

Brad thought, *I wish I could do that. He always knows how to make people feel good.*

Everyone, including Brad, sat. He said, "I'll bet I'm the only one in this room who doesn't know why I'm here."

Tim said, "Brad, your ability to be that open is why we've asked you to join us in this experiment. But the group you represent isn't in an enviable position."

Brad said, "The group I represent?"

"I meant 'represent' only in a metaphorical sense, Brad. When I became the Managing Partner my language skills declined. If I were to state it better, it would be the group of which you are most representative."

Brad said, "Do I dare ask what group that is?"

Miles said, "It's the non-originating partner group we talked about on the plane, Brad."

Brad thought, *oh, God, why me?*

Tim said, "We'd like to get your pledge of the secrecy of this meeting and its contents and then your reaction to our planning for your group."

Brad said, "Sure, I'll give you my pledge of secrecy and my reaction, but I don't feel those partners are my group."

Miles said, "It may be before this meeting is over. Here's the problem, Brad, and it's your problem too. You're a partner in this firm. We have about a dozen other partners in this group. None of you are carrying your own weight. In simple terms, we're paying you more than you're worth."

Brad asked, "Isn't worth a relative thing? I mean, aren't we worth the compensation the Firm's arrived at after years of seeing us in action. I've been here for twelve years, ever since I got out of law school. The Firm's certainly had an opportunity to evaluate me."

Tim said, "That's true, Brad, but we evaluated you in a different market. That market was one that demanded getting the work out. I mean, getting it done was the big challenge. Now, it's much more to get the work in, and you're not getting it in. In short, for a young guy you're living in another time, fifteen years ago. It's like you had Alzheimer's and you only remember ancient events."

Brad was feeling increasingly uncomfortable. *God, it was tough to be laid bare, like this, in front of his partners.* He thought about telling them he was suddenly taken with a rare form of Malaria ... or maybe now, that asshole George would call, for the first time when he was welcome or better yet one of the kids would have an emergency. But none of that happened.

Miles said, "Look Brad, we're not here to beat on you. We want your feedback; first, we'd like you to make some suggestions about what the firm can do to help you, and your group, become rainmakers. Then we'd like to bounce our ideas off you. And we'd appreciate your honest reaction."

Since Brad saw no way out, he smiled and said, "Sure."

Tim said, "Here's what we have in mind. First, we need to appoint a coordinator for this group. Then that person could arrange meeting dates, schedules, goals and all that stuff."

Brad said, "Whose gonna be crazy enough to volunteer for that kind of non-billing, thankless job?"

Tim ignored Brad's question. "Then, we're thinking about getting a trainer to meet with your group."

"It isn't my group."

Tim continued. "Okay, a trainer to meet with the group, which for purposes of this meeting we'll call Brad's Group."

Brad said, "Sometimes I'm dense and then it takes me awhile, but I think I finally got it. You want me to organize this group. Since I've got the same problems they do, they're less likely to take offense if someone like me suggests putting it together."

Miles said, "Why Brad, that's a brilliant suggestion. I wish I had thought of that. Don't you, Tim? How about the rest of you gentlemen ... don't you wish you'd thought of Brad's great idea?"

Everybody jumped up and came over to congratulate Brad.

"Great idea, Brad."

"Thanks for volunteering, Brad."

"We're lucky to have you in the partnership, Brad."

"That idea shows how smart you are, Brad."

Brad said, "So, now that I've 'volunteered', what do you want me to do? Wait, let me guess. It's entirely up to me, but you'd love to hear my plans. Right?"

Tim said, "Brad you're right on. We know how smart you are. Tell us what you have in mind."

Brad said, "Well, since it was only five minutes ago that I was railroaded ... whoops, I mean volunteered for this job, I haven't had much chance to develop plans. But you gentlemen have been thinking about this for some time. I don't suppose you, perhaps, have any ideas for the group?"

Tim said, "Sorry Brad, but we think plans are better left with the group leader."

Brad said, "Swell. How about if I ask the question a little differently.

Suppose I mention some ideas, would you be willing to give me your feedback?"

Tim said, "Why, Brad, we want to support you in every way we can. Go ahead and share your thoughts. Don't you all agree?"

Everybody immediately shook their heads in agreement and then the room was silent.

Brad said, "Okay, how about a trainer?"

Everybody shook their heads in agreement.

"Should we meet regularly to talk about our problems?"

All the heads went up and down again in agreement.

"How about a ten percent raise for everybody who participates in the group?"

All the heads shook no.

How about a promise that we'll be given three years to show results?"

All the heads shook no.

"Two years?"

All the heads shook no.

"One year?"

All the heads shook yes.

"My thought would be to give everyone six months to begin this process and come up with goals."

Brad waited and looked around the room. All the heads shook no.

"Three months?"

"One month?"

The heads started bobbing up and down in unison.

Brad asked, "There couldn't possibly have been any prior collusion here?"

All the heads shook no and Tim said, "Brad, we're your partners. How could you possibly think that?"

Brad said, "Sorry, I guess it's just my suspicious nature."

Tim said, "Brad, on behalf of the Executive Committee let me thank you for volunteering and coming up with those great ideas. I wish we could've thought of them. Don't you, gentlemen?"

Everybody got up again and came over to where Brad was seated. They all gave him another round of congratulations.

Tim said, "Well, there being no further business. I declare the meeting adjourned and instruct the Secretary to record the appointment of our partner, Brad Talbert, as the Chairman of the new Partner Development Committee. And, Mr. Secretary, please be sure to include Brad's wonderful ideas for the Committee in the minutes. Of course, Brad, we'll leave it up to you who should be on the Committee."

Brad asked, "Is there any other way you'd like to torture ... sorry, I misspoke ... like to help me?"

Everybody was moving toward the door as Tim said, "Can't think of a thing more, Brad. Keep in touch."

Brad sat in the big conference room alone, looked at his watch and mused, *less than an hour from entrance to slaughter. Am I lucky, or what?*

CHAPTER 15

The Chinatown section of Washington is small and the restaurant where Brad was meeting Deng was even smaller. As his cab headed for Chinatown, Brad thought about how he had been sucked into two thankless tasks, motivating both the Chinese scientists and his non-billing partners. He could hardly motivate himself. Brad wondered why people didn't just do things the way society required. Then he remembered he was one of the problem people. His only consolation was that he probably didn't have much choice about either motivation assignment … so he might as well do them graciously.

Brad was almost a half-hour late. Deng sat at a table in the almost empty tiny restaurant. He was sipping tea and reading. He smiled and said, "Okay, Counselor, since I'm on the payroll, who gets the bill for this half hour you're late?"

Brad said, "Are you sure you didn't take Billing 101, before you dropped out of law school?"

"We didn't have that course in China, since back then we all had the same client." He held up a big book. "I brought this book. It may help you understand why your scientists won't go back into Mainland China. It'll show you Tienamen Square, one of the most photographed mass murders of civilians in modern history."

"Look, Deng, all that stuff is ancient history. Can't you just talk these guys into going to China? What's to be afraid of?"

"Haven't you ever been afraid of anything, Brad, no matter how irrational? Think hard."

"I don't have to think very hard. You know the answer. That's why I was at that mountain retreat where we met. I still have unconquered fears, but they don't affect my client."

"No, that's right they just affect you. If I remember right, the effect is that you don't have a client."

Brad said, "Ouch."

I didn't say that to hurt your feelings, Brad. I just wanted to be sure you understand the power of fear … and believe me, the Chinese government is something to fear. You just fear some long ago worry about abandonment. Your scientists are afraid of the knife and gun. So, who's crazier?"

"Don't hold back, Deng. Just say what you think. Are you always so subtle? Besides, they aren't my scientists. They work for Tensitron."

Deng said, "My point is that your fears are about things that can happen only in your head. You don't want to get close to a client, 'cause they have the power to leave you. You don't want to give that power to anyone again."

Brad said, "It's different when you're a kid. Things make a lifelong impression. Kids are helpless. They become victims."

"Ancient Chinese saying is, 'Man who lives life as child, lives in fear'."

"Come on Deng, that doesn't sound very Chinese to me."

Deng said, "You're right. It isn't. But people like to hear Chinese sayings. I don't know any. So, I make them up."

"What kind of noble Chinese tradition is that?"

"No kind, but it helps me make a point, until some smart ass like you catches me at it."

Brad said, "I don't think there's any similarity between my situation and those scientists."

"You're right. Those scientists aren't living out childhood fears. You are. They're in the States 'cause they had to escape death. You're escaping a childhood fantasy. The proof is that there are millions of others in China who didn't escape. They're either dead or living zombies. All you have to do is walk out of your dream."

The restaurant owner came over and spoke to Deng in Chinese, then left. Deng said, "He's a fugitive, too. I talked to him while I was waiting for you. Would you like a loose translation of what he just said about you?"

"Sure."

"He said, 'Is this the dumb son-of–a bitch who's trying to convince fugitives to go back? Man, that's one crazy gringo. I wouldn't go back there for all the noodles in China."

Deng said, "I also took the liberty of giving him our order. I hope you don't mind."

Brad said, "No, what the hell. Between my partners and Janet, I don't have to make decisions any more. You may as well join them in directing my life."

"Don't worry. The owner doesn't know who you or your clients are or where they're located."

"I figured you to be at least that discrete, Deng."

Deng said, "I'm not sure those guys can be convinced."

"Deng, overseas Chinese go back all the time."

"Not fugitives, they don't. I wouldn't go back on a bet."

"The Chinese government will give absolute assurances of safety."

"Brad, no one gets rid of their fears until they confront them. I have my own fears. I remember the tanks in Tienamen Square as though it was yesterday. I can still feel the rumble of their tracks making my body vibrate. The smell of the diesel fuel. I can smell and feel them right now, while we're talking. The cannons and machine guns are aimed at me. The tanks are coming at me, only inches away. One little turn and they'll crush me. I see myself watching while they crush others. Can you understand that level of fear?"

"Sure I can, Deng. I have my fears, too. You know that. To some extent they've controlled my life."

Deng said, "To some extent … are you kidding? They're the dominant factor in your life. There's an old Chinese saying 'Man can't encourage client billings by denying fears.'"

"Is that another one of your made up Ancient Chinese Sayings?"

"Yep, but it's true. You don't like to be close to clients. When that happens, you're terrified they'll abandon you. I'm still terrified about being taken by Chinese secret police and I'm not even in China. We're both nuts."

Brad said, "You don't know what it's like to be abandoned as a child. To be completely alone … no father … no mother … just alone. I don't know if I'll ever overcome it."

"You better overcome it or you're gonna be chopped won ton. We've all got our thing, Brad. When I came to this country my English teacher was some old hard-bitten volunteer who taught a bunch of immigrants. You know the tough, but heart of gold, type. We all used to tell him our sad stories. He'd say, 'You want sympathy? You'll find it in the dictionary between shit and syphilis.'"

"Sounds like the Dale Carnegie of English tutors."

"My point is nobody knows how we feel. You can't know how I felt being the object of a house to house search. I moved every night. I wasn't safe anywhere. In the month after the massacre thirty people were sentenced and executed, with a quick single shot to the head. Not letting fear overtake me saved my life. If I didn't have the courage to get a false passport and find the Underground Railroad to Hong Kong, I'd be dead too. And you want me to convince these scientists that the Chinese government is swell?"

Brad said, "Well maybe not swell, but at least reformed."

"Reformed, are you nuts?"

The waiter brought some food and said something to Deng in Chinese.

Deng said, "He says he agrees. You're a fool, but at least you're a fool whose got a hero, namely me, for a friend."

"Great … isn't there such a thing as a private conversation in China? Why don't we get the kitchen crew out here as well?"

"You don't want them here. They have knives."

Brad said, "Right, they're gonna come out here with their kitchen cleavers."

"I don't mean kitchen cleavers. I mean knives … hidden knives, big ones, switch blades, all that stuff."

"Why?"

Deng reached in his pocket, pulled out a big switchblade knife and said, "For the same reason I carry one."

Brad pulled back. "Put that thing away, Deng. I thought you were into Feng Shui … you know loving peace and all that stuff."

"I am, but this is what fear does. I carry it in case the Chinese secret police come after me."

"In Washington, DC, USA?"

Deng said, "It's a hell of a lot less crazy than you being afraid some client's gonna hurt you by abandoning you. At least my fears are based on adult reality."

"What reality? The Chinese secret police in Washington?"

"When we were making our stand in Tienamen Square the government secret police infiltrated us. Yesterday's 'friends' were tomorrow's betrayers. I watched my fellow students being fingered by the infiltrators. One minute my friends were alive, an instant later they were a body, lying next to scores of other bodies. That's real."

Brad said, "Okay, I get the message. Are you gonna help us with the scientists?"

Deng said, "Not a chance."

Brad could hear the waiter's nearby grunt of approval.

That night Brad called George in Xiamen and gave him the bad news.

Finally, in exasperation, he said, "Look, George, there's nothing more I can do. I can't figure out anyway to convince those scientists to go to Xiamen."

Brad listened for awhile, then said, "Yeah, I know it's too bad you're not here. No, Jack Mann says he can't and won't order them to do it and they say they'll quit first. I tried everything I can think of. Okay, I'll wait to hear back from you."

George was back in his old room at the Lujiang Hotel. He hung up and rang Sen's room. "We've got troubles. The scientists won't come to China."

Sen said, "Okay, I thought that might happen. I've been thinking about what to do. I think we can work it into our meeting this afternoon at the University. Leave it up to me. Why don't you and I meet Chang at the shipyard at noon."

"Not a chance. The first time you got me to that shipyard is the last time. You've got your fifty thousand now, so no more games."

"George, my friend, you don't understand. We're going to use the shipyard as our alternative for the scientists coming here."

George asked tentatively, "How?"

"We've got to work that out with Chang."

"You work that out with Chang. That's not my department. Besides, I'm going back to the States tomorrow. I've got to be back for our annual partner's meeting this weekend. They'd think it was strange if I wasn't there."

"George, I thought you were gonna be cooperative. This is part of your complete involvement. You know, what you call being an accessory. Remember our deal George? You get a cut on the stuff that comes in and on the babies going out."

"I don't want a cut on the babies."

"But, George, my friend, you're Managing Director of that company. Get dressed and meet me in the lobby in an hour. We're going to the shipyard."

When they arrived, George saw the large shipyard shed first. At the same moment, he felt the same powder burning sensation in his crotch. This is where 'it' had happened. Next to the shed was the same fishing boat tied up to the same dock. Sen opened the padlock on the shed. They all went in and Sen closed the door, snapping on the lights.

The inside could not have been more different from the rusted, run-down outside. Sparkling white racks lined one side of the shed for about a hundred feet. The other side had three glass enclosed modern offices. At the far end of the shed there appeared to be a gasoline driven generator and locked heavy steel doors to a room made entirely of steel.

Sen said, "You're the Ph.D. chemist, Chang. What do we need?"

Chang took a slow look around and said, "I'd put three lab benches over there where the racks are with big lights above them. Put the three vats in one of the spaces where the office cubicles are and put air-conditioning in the whole place."

Sen asked "How long will it take?"

Chang said, "If we move on it, about two weeks."

Sen said, "Do it. There you are George, we'll be ready for your scientists in two weeks."

George felt frustrated. "Sen, I told you. They won't come to China."

"They don't have to. We'll bring China to them."

"I don't understand."

"Tell George about your great idea, Chang."

Chang said, with a lot of pride, "This shipyard is only a short drive from the University. The nano specimens are tiny. I can slip an entire day's experiments in my pocket, including their packaging, and bring them here."

George said, "So, they're here … they're still in China and the scientists won't come here."

Sen said, "Tell him the rest, Chang."

Chang said, "Remember the house in Taiwan where you were a … a … a guest? Well, it's right next to the harbor. We can move the specimens across in the boat."

George asked, "What about the authorities?"

Sen smiled, "Nothing money can't take care of, George, in both countries. In fact the Taiwanese are overjoyed. They see it as a chance to beat the Chinese out of their technology. We've already lined up special unlimited visit visas for all of us, the scientists too. We can come and go to the island all we want."

"From China?"

"… Um, no, not really, but the only people who know, find it in their self interest to keep their mouths shut."

"Don't the scientists need to have a lab?"

Sen said, "Sure, we're gonna duplicate this lab in the house on Quemoy.

They can talk to Dr. Fu on the phone about the specimens. He'll think they're talking from the states."

Chang said, "Dr. Fu's never had to think about moving the specimens. He doesn't focus on how short their half-life is, so he doesn't think about moving them long distances."

Sen said, "I assume Tensitron's scientists will go along. How about it, George?"

George thought a minute. "I don't see why not. They hate Communist China. If this helps Taiwan, they'll be all for it."

Sen said, "Okay, when can you give Tensitron a call, to check it out?"

"As soon as I get back to the hotel."

Sen said, "Okay, Chang, if you don't hear from me tonight, get this shed conversion started tomorrow morning."

Chang nodded yes, but neither of them noticed Chang quickly turn a switch under his shirt, controlling a hidden tape recorder.

After Chang left the shipyard he took a cab to the airport instead of returning to the University. He made notes and diagrams while waiting in a conference room in Xiamen Airlines' private lounge for its incoming flight from Hong Kong.

About an hour later a well-dressed man entered the conference room and said, in Chinese, "I'm from the chemistry department."

Chang said, "I work there."

The other man bowed. "I am Lao. Do you have the information?"

Chang bowed and handed him his notes. "You will find this very complete. It shows the locations both here and in Quemoy and gives all the registration information about the boat. Do you have my money?"

Lao handed Chang an envelope. Both men sat at the conference table. Lao read the notes and Chang counted his money.

"It's here, all twenty thousand American." Chang said, as he smiled. He bowed low and said, "Shea shea."

Lao said, "Such a formal Mandarin bow and thank you. Those of us in the Taiwan Secret Service who know about this, figured we would shortly be bowing to you, as the richest man in Xiamen. We figured you're making your University salary, plus your Communist party watchdog bonus, plus at least ten thousand a month from Sen plus another twenty thousand a month from us. Who's buying the drinks?"

Chang didn't pause. He smiled, bowed again and said, "You are."

Lao laughed. "Why did you waste your talents on chemistry? You could have been rich by now."

"I know I'm making up for lost time. The drinks are free here in the club anyway. Otherwise you would be paying. Do you have questions?"

Lao said, "Only a couple of dozen."

"That's not a bad price, about a thousand dollars each."

Lao said, "First, how do they plan to keep Dr. Fu from knowing what's going on?"

"That's my job. He trusts me, or at least the Communist Party does."

"Then my next question is what is going on?"

Chang said, "We're gonna bring the specimens over by boat. We'll basically set up a lab on Quemoy that's a twin to the nano lab at Xiamen. Since I'm the courier, I'll steal a representative sample of each specimen batch and pass it along to your agent in Quemoy or Xiamen, as the opportunity presents itself."

"Gee, we even get free samples for our twenty thousand."

"You do even better than that. Your boss drives a hard bargain. He got me to agree to throw in my consulting services to help you set up your twin lab on Quemoy. Your twin lab will be a twin to our twin lab on Quemoy, which is a twin to lab at the shipyard in Xiamen, which is a twin to the University lab. In fact, I already have an ideal place picked out near the shipyard for your twin lab. I'll front it for you."

"Why do we even have to have a twin lab?"

Chang said, "The specimen half-life is very short. Twenty four hours at the most. The twin lab is to try to stabilize specimens."

"How long will we have to be paying you the twenty thousand each month?"

"As long as I can milk it out of you. In fact I have a little bonus sample for you now." He reached in his briefcase and took out a small vial.

As he was handing it to Lao, he said, "Listen, they're calling departure of your plane back to Hong Kong, so here's the going away present."

Lao said, "The plane isn't leaving for a half hour."

That's what you think. Xiamen Airlines departure time isn't when they leave the gate."

"What is it?"

"It's the time their wheels leave the runway."

"You're kidding."

"If you really think I'm kidding, I'll bet you this twenty thousand that I'm right ... double or nothing ... that plane will leave the gate in five minutes which is ten minutes before scheduled departure time."

Lao quickly gathered his stuff, saying, "I'm convinced. I'll see you at our next Xiamen meeting site in five days."

Chang said, "Right." He stood and bowed. After that he stood and waited until Lao was past the customs barrier. Then he quickly glanced at his watch, practically ran out of the airport, jumped in a cab and said, "Marco Polo Hotel."

An hour later he was sitting in a room on the tenth floor, across from an American.

The American said, "Thanks for coming Chang. My name's Quan."

Chang said, "You sure don't look like any Quan to me. Your eyes are round."

"For our purposes, my name's Quan."

Chang bowed and handed Quan a copy of his notes. "You will find this very complete. It shows the locations both here and in Quemoy and gives all the registration information about the boat. Do you have my money?"

Quan handed Chang an envelope. Both men sat at the conference table. Quan read the notes and Chang counted his money.

"It's here, all thirty thousand American." Chang said, as he smiled. He bowed low and said "Thank you."

Quan said, "Such a formal bow and thank you. Those of us in the Secret Service who know about this, figured we would shortly be bowing to you, as the richest man in Xiamen. We figured you're making your University salary, plus your Communist party watchdog bonus, plus at least ten thousand a month from Sen plus another thirty thousand a month from us. Who's buying the drinks?"

Chang didn't pause. He smiled, bowed again and said, "You are."

Quan laughed. "Why did you waste your talents on chemistry? You could've been rich by now."

"I know it, and I'm making up for lost time. Do you have questions?"

Quan said, "Yes, a number of them."

"Go ahead please."

Quan said, "First, how do they plan to keep Dr. Fu from knowing what's going on?"

"That's my job. He trusts me, or at least the Communist Party does."

"Then my next question is what's going on?"

Chang said, "I'm gonna sneak the specimens out. We'll basically set up a lab here in Xiamen at a shipyard close to the University. It'll be a twin to the nano lab at Xiamen University. I'll steal a representative sample of each specimen batch and pass it along to your agent in Xiamen as the opportunity presents itself."

"You mean we even get free samples for our thirty thousand?"

"You do even better than that. Your boss drives a hard bargain. He got me to agree to throw in my consulting services to help you set up your twin lab. I even have an ideal place picked out. I'll front it for you. Your twin lab will be a twin to our twin lab, which is a twin to Xiamen.

"How long will we have to be paying you the thirty thousand each month?"

"As long as I can milk it out of you. In fact I have a little bonus sample for you now. He reached in his briefcase and took out a small vial, he said, "Would you excuse me please. I have to get back to my job at the University."

As Chang was in the cab leaving the hotel, he thought about his next two meetings. Another thirty thousand from the Japanese 'special representative' at dinner tonight and a meeting sometime this afternoon with a Russian. Why are Russians always so mysterious and bossy? They don't have any class. "Just get into the cab waiting at the curb. He will know where to take you."

Chang was still thinking when the cab driver pulled into a garage, turned and said in a heavily Mongolian accented Chinese, "I'm from the chemistry department. Do you have the information?"

Three weeks later, there were four secret nano labs in operation- all within three blocks of the shipyard and of each other. The only differences were the languages spoken in each one and the three rents, each of which Chang had tripled, pocketing the difference. Every other day, Chang made the rounds of the "secret" labs, delivering specimens.

CHAPTER 16

George barely got aboard his Xiamen Airlines flight to Hong Kong the next morning. He thought he was early, but got on just as they were closing the plane's door. It left the gate fifteen minutes before scheduled departure, but was airborne right at scheduled departure time. Since George was in the first class section, he could see the pilot and copilot through the 727's open cockpit door. They smiled at each other as the plane lifted off. The pilot pointed to his watch, made the thumbs up sign to the copilot and made an announcement. He said something in Chinese and then repeated it in English. "Thank you for flying Xiamen Airlines. We're right on time again."

While George was waiting to change planes in Hong Kong he called Brad. "We're all set in Xiamen. They're putting together a first class lab on Quemoy for the scientists. Is the prospectus ready?"

"It's ready, George. Don't you want to see it before we release it?"

"No. That's why I made you the responsible partner."

Brad thought, *that's not the real reason, you duplicitous prick.* But he said, "Does that mean I get part of the origination credit too?"

George was silent for a minute, then said, "We can talk about that when I get back. What else is going on?"

"The Executive Committee appointed me Chairman of a new Firm Committee."

"You? What Committee?"

"The Partner Development Committee."

"What the hell is that?"

"It's to help partners who don't have big books of business."

"You're the right man for that, all right. But isn't it gonna be the lame and halted leading the blind?"

"We've already had our first meeting. Everybody's enthusiastic. I'm interviewing trainers all day today."

"What's a trainer?"

"Someone who's gonna lead us to the Promised Land."

"You don't need a trainer. You need a Rabbi."

"If he's good, maybe he'll be both."

"Is all that shit billable?"

"Nope. Tim said I could spend ten percent of my time on this, unbillable."

"Unbillable?" George said the word as one might say Leprosy.

Brad said, "I'm not sure who I'd bill it to, George. The firm's the beneficiary."

"Find someone. I always do. Anyway, my flight leaves Hong Kong for LA in a couple of hours. I get there in about fourteen hours. I'm going to go to Tensitron, which will add a day, and then fly out of San Diego for DC. I'll be in DC two days from now. That's Friday at the end of the day. Tell my secretary to team me up with some good players for the golf tournament at the partner's outing on Saturday. Last year my foursome was all wannabes. Bye."

Brad buzzed his secretary and asked her to take care of the golf foursome matter for George. She said, "Mr. Talbert, I don't know how to say this, but none of the other partners want to play with Mr. Chambers."

"Well, work on it, would you please. Just do the best you can. Is my first trainer interview here? Just send him in please."

Brad rose to greet one of the most stunning women he had ever seen. As she came into his office, he said, "Dr. Jordan, I'm Brad Talbert. Thanks for coming by." He thought, *Janet would kill me if I hired her.*

Dr. Jordan shook hands, sat down and said, "You're probably thinking your wife would kill you if you hired me."

Brad thought about the Equal Employment Opportunity Act and said, "Why no, she's all for equal rights. She'd applaud your getting the assignment." Then to himself he said, "Provided she never saw you." He continued. "I assume you had an opportunity to review the material we faxed? I wonder if you'd be good enough to explain your approach."

Dr. Jordan said, "I don't think it's conceptually different than lots of others. It's all in how it's done. What I do that's different is to help people focus on tangible goals."

"I understand, but how do you help them achieve those goals?"

"Well, that varies according to the situation."

Brad said, "It seems to me it may be easy to set a goal of a million dollar book of business. But, unless I had a way to achieve it, I'd just be more frustrated than I am now."

"And we'd certainly work on your individual needs."

"Have you done this sort of thing before?"

"Very similar ... I've helped lots of people set goals."

"In business settings?"

"Goals are goals, Mr. Talbert."

Later that afternoon, after Brad had interviewed his fifth candidate that day, he composed a summary memo of the results on his computer and transmitted it to his secretary for editing. Toward the end of the day his secretary buzzed him to ask an editing question and added. "I squared away Mr. Chamber's foursome at the partner's golf outing. Mr. Miles Dean and Mr. Dinky Silver called and asked for Mr. Chambers as a partner. So I put you in as the fourth. Is that okay?"

Brad said, "Oh sure. When will you have the memo edited?"

A few minutes later the memo flashed up on his screen and was ready. Brad printed it out and read it.

TO: THE EXECUTIVE COMMITTEE
FROM: BRAD TALBERT
SUBJ: The right training for the Partner Development Committee members

You asked me to summarize my findings in as few words as possible. Subtlety has been sacrificed for brevity.

THE PROBLEM:

The Firm has about twelve partners, myself included, who have not been able to develop their own 'originations', meaning establishing significant client relationships. The result is that they suffer emotionally and both they and the Firm suffer financially. If the practice of law continues to be competitive, these partners will, in the near term, need to seek other employment.

MY APPROACH:

I have enrolled myself in a weekly rainmaking group, which is open to all professions, attended a weekend multidiscipline retreat and have interviewed six well-recommended, but widely different, professionals who could serve as a trainer or facilitator for our problem partners.

WHAT'S AVAILABLE:

The four broad types of offerings are: 1) Motivational Talks, 2) Marketing Training, 3) Sales Training, and 4) Thought Training.

#1 (Motivational Talks) are great for people who know what they're doing. None of the twelve of us do. It's hard to motivate a terrified kid. #2 (Marketing Training) is great to get an overview of a market. We need an overview of ourselves, not the market. We are our own principal problem. #3 (Sales Training) is great for imparting techniques. But we'd never use the techniques because we're too blocked emotionally. #4 (Thought Training) is what we need. Our beliefs are unhealthy and wrong. We won't improve until we do belief modification.

TYPES OF BELIEF MODIFICATION:

The offerings are as varied as mankind's beliefs. However, they tend to fall into five basic types: 1) Emotional Catharsis, 2) Analyzing Reasons, 3) Magic, 4) Placing Blame, and 5) Rational Grounding. I will describe them in absolute terms for brevity: #1 (Emotional Catharsis) works best for people who benefit from letting it all 'hang out'. Most attorneys have the opposite profile. We hold it all in. We are a circumspect bunch. #2 (Analyzing Reasons) works best for non-analytical people who are thereby forced to address their motivations. A group of attorneys in this milieu could happily, but unproductively, spend many lifetimes in endless debate. We are the epitome of analytic personalities. #3 (Magic) depends on gurus, incantations and devices. It is diametrically opposed to the logic of the law. As such, it wouldn't tend to cause change for us. #4 (Placing Blame) is a painful search for the person or persons responsible for our negative thinking. Our legal training would cause us to enjoy the process, but it isn't productive. #5 (Rational Grounding) is covered below.

RATIONAL GROUNDING:

This title, "Rational Grounding" is my invention to make "it" palatable. But whoever guides "it" and whatever they do, "it" should have these five elements to succeed: 1) It must confront, because our legal training makes us excellent evaders. 2) It must nurture, because we require patience to drag these deep problems out of us. 3) It must focus on low self-esteem issues, because they are our common malady. 4) It must be ruthless for results, because we are experts in procrastination. 5) It must be spiritually based because if we could do it alone, it would not now be a problem. The first four elements are the "what to do." This fifth element is the "how to." This has nothing to do with religion. I am aware of the dangers when mixing the water of commerce with the oil of spirit. But unless there is attribution of, at least, a higher power, the twelve of us are doomed to live our lives in our current autistic client withdrawal.

MY RECOMMENDATION:

I have attached two resumes of people I believe capable of accomplishing this result. They both have these four qualities: 1) long experience with others, 2) strong spiritual foundation without pushing any creed, 3) professional, but with a strong personal goal which makes them 4) dedicated to ending our personal pain.

After reading it, Brad faxed it to his home with a cover memo. "TO: Janet, the Wonderful. Roses are red, violets are blue — This wouldn't be possible without you. How about just the two of us for dinner tonight at the place where they stick us in that lonely corner?"

About an hour later an email message appeared on his computer screen. "I read your memo, but I couldn't answer earlier because I've been crying for the last hour. I love you — you're terrific and so is your memo — can't wait for our date tonight."

George's prop plane from LA to San Diego made him airsick. He hated those little planes, particularly after a twelve hour Pacific flight. It was late afternoon in San Diego and he needed some sleep. He was so tired that he didn't notice the man who waited at the gate, followed him to his hotel and checked in after he did.

When George met Jack Mann for breakfast the next morning in the hotel dining room, that same man sat down at the next table, and started reading the morning paper.

Jack said, "Well George, you've done it again. We got the deal in Xiamen, thanks to you. How did you do it? I thought all those deals had to be competitive bid."

George flashed his best three hundred-dollar an hour smile. "Not for a company with Tensitron's technology, Jack. The Chinese government realized there weren't any real competitors, so they awarded it to us."

"What happens now?"

"You can just go forward on the joint venture. We've arranged for Tensitron's scientists to do their research on a little island right next to Xiamen, but owned by Taiwan. That way they won't have to enter China."

"Is that legal?"

"Legal? Sure it's legal. But we don't want to offend the Chinese so we don't talk about it, okay?"

Jack said, "I don't pretend to understand this stuff, but don't we have to put something in the prospectus?"

"No, it's not material."

Jack leaned forward and said, "George, every once in a while the Board complains about your bills. I remind them that Tensitron wouldn't be where it is today if it weren't for George Chambers. You've saved us in our two critical litigations and now you've made us in China. How can I ever thank you, my friend?"

George shifted uncomfortably in his chair. These kinds of conversations always made him feel uneasy. So, he bribed two judges and who knows how many Chinese. So what. That's the way the game's played. For Christ's sake, Jack, stop applauding and throw more money.

He said, "Jack, it's always a pleasure to work with someone like you." He thought, If you only knew. I always took care of myself Jack. Anything goes wrong, it's your head on the block, not mine.

Jack interrupted his thoughts. "When can our people go over there?"

"In about two weeks, I'll let you know. Right now I'm concerned about getting the prospectus finalized so you can get that money."

"When can we close on it?"

George said, I'm going to try for Monday."

"You mean, this Monday, four days from today. Is that possible?"

"Sure, everything's all done in China. We've got nothing else to disclose."

CHAPTER 17

Two days later, the Saturday morning of the Firm's Annual Partner's Golf Outing, was beautiful. The Club considered this one of their most important annual events, so everything was perfect. The greens, carts, tees and fairways all looked as though they were movie sets, painted in place. Early arriving partners were assembling at the coffee shop. There was a murmur of comfortable conversation from people who had been partners for years.

George was just arriving too, nodding hello to his partners, saying a few words to people he knew well. As he was unloading his golf bags from the trunk of his car onto a cart, another car pulled into the lot, but parked without unloading any bags. George looked up to see someone who looked familiar, but George didn't think he was with the firm. He must be with the Club.

As he walked to the clubhouse he saw Miles and Dinky waiting in line for coffee, joined them and said, "Well, a beautiful morning for a beautiful game. Are we doing this for money?"

Miles and Dinky looked at each other. Miles said, "Not this year, George, I may have an emergency so we can't finish in the four we started."

George said, "Who cares? Anyway, talking about money. Are you ready to go with the final prospectus on Monday, Dinky?"

"Sure. Have you read it? Are there any problems?"

George said, "Come on Dinky, do you always have to be the perfect securities lawyer, even on the golf course?"

Dinky said, "No, I mean it George. I can't release it without your okay."

"What about Brad? Here he comes now. He's the responsible partner. Get his okay."

"He wasn't the responsible partner during the period covered by the prospectus and that partner's here — you."

George said, "Okay, I've read it and it's accurate. When do I sign?"

Dinky said, "At the closing. Good morning, Brad. We're just talking about Tensitron going final on Monday."

Brad said, "When did we decide that?"

George said, "Jack and I decided it in San Diego on Thursday, but I guess I forgot to tell you."

"You forgot to tell me?"

Brad saw Dinky made a quick movement to signal him to drop the subject. He shrugged and said, "When do we tee off?"

By the time they reached the third tee most of the small talk had been exhausted. Miles said, "Tell us about China, George."

"What do you want to know? The Chinese food is better here."

"How'd you get that great contract for Tensitron?"

George teed up, smiling, "Powerful negotiator ... runs in my family."

Miles said, "We got a government inquiry, George."

"Based on what?"

"Some lawyer in Chicago filed a complaint."

"Remember his name?"

Miles said, "I don't."

"Wouldn't happen to be Gold ... David Gold?"

"That's him."

"Sore loser, that's all. He was there and he lost."

"He says there was bribery."

"I'd say it too, if I were in his place."

"Says he has an informant."

"Yeah, who?"

"What's his name, Dinky?"

"I think it's Chang."

George swung, topped the ball and bit through his cigar.

They played the next two holes, but George played increasingly poorly.

They had to wait at the sixth tee. Miles said, "George, are you sure you don't know this Chang? Gold seemed pretty certain in his affidavit."

"Affidavit, schmavit. The name sounds vaguely familiar, but all those Chinese names sound the same. There was a Chang ... works for the University ... a Professor type Chemist."

"Chang was arrested yesterday, George. He implicated you and a man named Sen, who he says works for you."

"Everybody who's arrested always implicates someone else. It's part of their script." George said, as he nonchalantly practiced his swing.

Brad listened and watched all of this in amazement. He started to speak, but Dinky motioned him not to talk.

Miles said, "Chang was arrested trying to sell information to a Japanese industrial spy. It seems the Japanese have been keeping close tabs on Professor Fu's progress. Included in that information was a tape recording of you and this man Sen, arranging to set up a lab in Xiamen."

"Probably a fake tape ... they do it all the time."

"I recognized your voice, George."

"What the hell is this, Miles? Are you gonna take the word of a Chinese over your own partner's? I'm not gonna listen to any more of this shit. Count me out."

George started to walk away, when a golf cart with two men in it came toward them at top speed. It lurched to a halt in front of George.

Two men jumped out. George recognized one, but couldn't figure out from where. The man said, "George Chambers?"

"Yeah?"

My name's Williams. This is Toughy. We're Special Agents of the Federal Bureau of Investigation." He pulled out an ID billfold. "You're under arrest."

"What's the charge?" George asked, belligerently.

"There are so many, Mr. Chambers, I don't know where to start. But how about starting with violation of the Foreign Corrupt Practices Act?"

George said, "That's gonna be hard to prove, Mr. Williams. I was just doing what my client asked. I have documents to prove that."

The Agent said, "If you don't like that one, how about conspiracy to violate the reporting requirements of the Securities Act?"

George shrugged. "Hey, I'm not the responsible partner. There's the man you want on that one, Brad Talbert."

Miles shook his head in disgust. "Mr. Williams, he's going to stonewall this the whole way. There doesn't appear to be a chance for a quiet plea."

The Agent said, "We're not through with the charges yet, Mr. Dean. Put your hands behind your back, Mr. Chambers, while my partner affixes the cuffs."

George hesitated. The other agent quickly grabbed his wrists and put the handcuffs on.

Mr. Williams said, "You have the right to remain silent. Anything you say can and will be used against you in a court of law— "

George said, "You don't have to read me Miranda rights, I'm a fuckin' attorney."

The Agent said, "You sure are. I've read the files in this matter. You've fucked everybody—your client, your partners ... you're one of the most fuckin' attorneys it's ever been my pleasure to arrest."

The other agent hustled George into the waiting golf cart. Before they left, Mr. Williams said, "He'll cooperate. We also have an extradition request from China for our friend, the fuckin' attorney here. Seems they have a whole set of documents showing him as the top dog in a baby-kidnapping ring. That's a capital crime in China. It gets a quick bullet through the head. If he doesn't cooperate, we'll probably honor their request."

As the cart pulled away they could hear, "You have the right to remain silent. If you can't afford counsel ... " then the cart was gone.

Miles said, "Let's get out of here." The three of them piled in the cart and left the golf course.

They all sat silently in the golf cart. Even Dinky was quiet, as it jolted it's way across the course.

As they pulled up in front of the clubhouse, Brad said, "I assume you two know more about this than I do."

Before walking inside, Miles said, "I have to call Tim. He's standing by. Tell Brad what just happened, Dinky. Then bring him into the club-house. We all need a drink."

Brad said, "Was that scene real, Dinky ... not just another one of your jokes?"

"As the fly said to the swatter, I hope it doesn't ever get closer. It was real, alright."

"Why did they do it on the golf course?"

"I know. It pissed me off, too. I was three under par when they arrested him."

"Dinky, for Christ's sake, aren't you ever serious?"

Dinky pulled his golf shirt off over his head and said, "As serious as this, pardner."

Brad didn't know what he was looking at. It was some kind of contraption taped to Dinky's body.

Dinky pulled his shirt back down and said, "Property of the FBI."

"You or the machine?"

"Me, if I don't return their hidden transmitter to them. Come on inside. I know how to get the tape off."

Brad trudged into the clubhouse bar as Dinky was ordering, "Four strong, straight whiskies."

"There's only three of us."

As the bartender poured, Dinky pulled off his golf shirt, dipped a napkin in one of the whiskey glasses and said, "Rub this on the adhesive tape as I pull it off. It'll help to melt the glue and leave me with a little more skin."

The bartender said, "I'm sorry, sir, but we don't allow gentlemen in the clubhouse without a shirt."

Dinky leaned toward Brad and whispered, "That's the best straight line I've ever been given. Don't spoil it by saying anything."

Then he straightened up and loudly said, "I'm no gentleman, I'm a fuckin' lawyer."

Brad couldn't stop laughing. The whiskey helped.

Miles came into the bar holding a cell phone to his ear. He said, "I'm waiting for Tim to come on the line. He's finishing his shot."

The bartender said, "I'm sorry sir, but the club doesn't permit gentlemen to use cell phones in the restaurant or bar."

Dinky looked at Brad and said, "The same straight line twice in one day. I won't dignify it with a punch line a second time." They both laughed.

Miles just looked confused, but then spoke into the phone, "Tim, it's all over. Yep, they arrested him on the sixth tee. Are you planning to tell the partners tonight at dinner? ... Okay, see you then."

He switched off the phone and said, "Let's go sit in that corner booth, Brad, we owe you an explanation."

As they sat down, Miles said, "About a week ago I got a call from a chap I used to practice with at another firm. He was always sort of a political type. He's now at the Justice Department ... Deputy Assistant Attorney General. Anyway, he asked me to come to his office right away. He's a solid guy, so I knew it must be something important."

Miles signaled the bartender for another round. "When I got to his office he shut his door and held all his calls. He told me this incredible story about George in China. Anyway, he introduced me to Agent Williams, who's been working on this case for three months. Their problem is that George is a fox and they couldn't get proof. Then they got this breakthrough with a Chinese Ph.D. named Chang. They were afraid George might try to slip out of the U.S. if he knew they knew. So, they were conflicted. They wanted to see if George would hang himself."

The bartender brought the new round, showing obvious disdain for these non-gentlemen. Miles continued. "That same week, Dinky came to me with what he discovered in putting together the prospectus. We couldn't figure out how much you knew. After the FBI told us the story, it all seemed so obvious to us. We thought you must know what George was up to. Yet we felt you were as honest as they come. We wanted to talk to you. But, the FBI told us we couldn't, just in case you were in it with George. So, we honored that, but we didn't like it. Anyway, Brad, when you told me all your suspicions about George and China on the plane, I knew you couldn't be part of it. That's when I called Sheila and gave the prearranged code word for your being in the clear. That's when we felt free to include you in the rainmaking meeting.

Dinky said, "They'd been following George. They wanted to hold off arresting him. But, I didn't want the prospectus to get out, even by accident. It was materially incorrect. So, I agreed to have the transmitter strapped to me. Then I could use a conversation about the prospectus to push George into doing or saying something incriminating. As soon as George made a few blundering macro denials, which gave rise to probable cause, the Agents made the arrest. They were hiding out under the trees in the rough, listening to the transmission. That's when they swooped down on us."

Miles said, "Welcome back to the land of the living, Brad. It's really kind of funny when you think about it. George was sunk by Dr. Chang's sale of the same information to four countries. If Chang had been less greedy, we might be finishing the golf game with George and heading for real trouble."

Dinky said, "Chang's a great example. Comedians know we can always find comedy in what people do to themselves. You had some real examples today on the golf course."

Brad said, "You mean George's arrest?"

"Yep, that and Miles' golf game."

Miles laughed and said, "Come on, Dinky, save it for your comedy routine at the dinner tonight."

Brad said, "I see it in myself. I was the perfect dupe for George. I don't know whether to laugh or cry about being so withdrawn. Do you think I can ever overcome those childhood fears?"

Dinky said, "No problem. If you don't change, your partners will throw you out of the firm and Janet will divorce you. Your dog will probably bite you, too. But you're a smart guy … just stay the way you are. You'll be able to find another George to take advantage of you. So, what's to worry?"

-Finis -

Appendix

A Personal Message From The Author:

Would you like to find out what *your* rainmaking skills are? And then, perhaps work with us to improve those skills? I've spent the last 17 years counseling and placing lawyers in the country's top law firms using the techniques that are now available to my readers. Read the endorsements both in the book and online at my website, *www.mentoringpros.com* and learn what partners in leading law firms across the country say about my work.

How can you measure your rainmaking skills?

First answer the questions in the appendix at the end of the book by measuring your feelings about Brad's, Janet's and George's actions and re-actions in the book's story. The questions are about your reaction to their actions. They are not tests of knowledge, intelligence or comprehension. Just answer with your feelings about their actions.

We'll send you a computer-based confidential diagnostic analysis of your answers highlighting your rainmaking strengths and weaknesses. Tell us how you would like us to send you the analysis of your answers.

The cost is per analysis is $85, if taken on our website, or $115 if submitted on a paper form (via mail or fax).

Processing is easy. You can go online to our website, enter your answers, give us your credit card information. Both your answers and our analysis of them will be processed immediately and confidentially displayed on the site, to be printed out if you want. You can also send the answers, together with a check made payable to Associates Publishers, at the address on page 175. You can fax your answers and your credit card information to 561-865-2155. Indicate whether you want the analysis returned by either fax or mail. If by mail, look for your confidential envelope within 10 days.

HOW CAN YOU IMPROVE YOUR SKILLS?

Personal Counseling

You can elect to have personal rainmaking counseling. The mentor will be expert in rainmaking by experience and/or training. This can be done in person, by telephone or on the web, depending on your location and/or preference.

Online Group Counseling

You can join one of our web-enabled live, anonymous, interactive group meetings. You can use either your actual name or a "pen name" for anominity. Sessions are archived for those who cannot attend the web-based meetings. Sessions are held for twelve consecutive weeks for 1-hour each.

I would appreciate it if you would visit our web site, and let me know if you enjoyed, or didn't enjoy, the book, would like additional information or would like to be put on the mailing list for my next Interactive Adventure Novel at www.mentoringpros.com.

It's that easy. You can answer the questions anonomously at the website, or you can fax or mail your answers to us.

OUR THREE-STEP PROCESS:

We offer this three-step process:

First, answer the questions at the end of this book. You need only answer as to how you *feel* about the questions posed. The questions are about your reaction to the actions taken by the characters in this novel.

After you tell us where you would like us to send you the analysis of your answers about you as a rainmaker, you will receive a computer based confidential diagnostic analysis of answers. This will relate to you as a rainmaker. This report will highlight strengths or weaknesses. The cost is $85, which can be paid by check or credit card. If your firm has a contract with us, just use that code number instead of payment. The turnaround time is about one week by any method except live on the web, which is substantially simultaneous.

The reader may, thereafter, elect to have personal rainmaking counseling with a mentor. The mentor will be expert in rainmaking by experience and/or training. This can be done in person, by telephone or on the web, depending on the reader's location and preference. The cost is hourly and varies by the type of service and is shown on our website.

The reader may also join one of our web based 12 week 1-hour live interactive group meetings. These are anonymous and confidential, since any participant can use a "pen name." This means that the participant's identity is unknown to the others. This anonymity from all other participants can be retained for all of the sessions, if desired. These meetings on the web are held weekly at a date and time set by consensus. The cost for these sessions varies according to a number of factors and is shown on our website.

We can be reached in the following ways:

Our address is:

Associates Publishers

7491 N. Federal Highway, Suite C-5

Boca Raton, FL 33487

Our website is: www.mentoringpros.com

Our telephone and fax is: 561-865-2155 (in the eastern time zone) the number is the same for both voice and fax.

ANSWERING THE QUESTIONS

The purpose of these questions is to identify your impediments to having successful rainmaking relationships. There are no right or wrong answers. Respond, giving your instinctive reaction, feeling or answer. There are no "trick" questions, but each one deserves thought. All the questions are important and must be answered to give the test validity. If you're not certain about a given answer, just put down the answer that makes you feel the least uncomfortable. The questions are all answered in the same way. They are multiple-choice with a quantified ranking of answers.

The only context is that of the information disclosed in the novel. You can either answer the questions after reading the chapter, or after reading the entire novel. There is no other information available to assist you with your answer. Just do your instinctive best.

Each group of multiple-choice questions is based on the quoted parts of one chapter. That quoted part is repeated immediately above each group of questions. The numbers at the end of each quote, i.e.: (12/4), are the page and paragraph where the quote begins. All questions are answered in the same standard –5 to +5 ranking system, to reflect your total disagreement (-5), your total agreement (+5) or anything in between. Any other responses are not acceptable. Thus, if your feeling is slight, use 1, if moderate, use 2, if substantial, use 3, if very strong, use 4 and if complete, use 5. Enter your rankings in the space before each question.

CHAPTER 1 QUESTIONS

1(A) My reaction, when George said the following, is shown in the rankings below.

"Are you kidding? The guy's so out of it he doesn't even have the guts to ask a client for business. He's just a great grinder and that's all I use him for. I bring it in and he grinds it out. We're a great team. Only I make five times what he does." (14/8)

____ 1) If George originated the business, then, all other things being equal, Brad deserved to make substantially less than George.

____ 2) George is an oppressor.

____ 3) That's just the way it works in most firms.

____ 4) It's called survival of the fittest.

____ 5) The quality of work is important, but totally unimportant compared to securing it.

1(B) My reaction, when Janet said the following, is shown in the rankings below.

Through his pain he felt Janet's arms around his shoulders, hugging him. He felt her tears on his face. He heard her whisper, "Are you thinking about it again? Don't do it to yourself. Get some help Brad. I can tell when you do it. I can feel your body getting tense." (18/1)

____ 6) Brad needs too much coddling.

____ 7) Janet hooks into this.

____ 8) Brad's unfortunate to have someone like Janet, giving him a shoulder to cry on.

____ 9) Brad needs someone to shake some sense into him.

____ 10) Brad just feels sorry for himself.

1(C) My reaction, when Brad said the following, is shown in the rankings below.

"You've lived through all the other times I tried ... three different therapy groups and two therapists. But it's so hard for me. My record with these guys sucks. I've quit them all. I know why I quit, and I know I shouldn't quit, but I can't seem to do anything about it." (18/4)

_____ 11) Brad just has a different problem than most people in a position requiring selling.

_____ 12) Everybody should have a supportive spouse like Janet.

_____ 13) I saw this as another appropriate challenge for therapy.

_____ 14) Brad seems to acknowledge his need for treatment.

_____ 15) At least Brad is open about his problems, which is good.

1(D) My reaction, when Brad said the following, is shown in the rankings below.

"Miles reminds me of the headmaster. He's one of the most important partners in the firm and he's Chairman of our department. His client base is a hell of a lot bigger than George's. I think he likes me and I like him too. I do some work for him sometimes. What a class act he is. But I still get scared when I think of telling him. It isn't rational, Janet, and I know it." (19/7)

_____ 16) Brad should have confided in Miles.

_____ 17) Miles could have stepped in earlier and stopped George's overreaching with Brad.

_____ 18) Brad shows some ability to trust in being so certain Miles likes him.

_____ 19) The comparison made between Miles and the headmaster was perceptive.

_____ 20) Brad has good business reason to be concerned about telling Miles.

1(E) My reaction, when Brad thought the following, is shown in the rankings below.

Then he thought back to his childhood ... to the town where his family lived ... the town where his relatives found him a bastard embarrassment ... the town where he was sent to far away private schools ... those schools where he never was part of the crowd of boys ... where his lack of pocket money and cheap clothes marked him as an outsider ... to his mother who he longed for but seldom saw ... to his father who he never met ... where he was abandoned ... to the school where other boys'

parents would come ... but never his ... where he was abandoned ... to
his unsuccessful attempts to make friends ... where he was so lonely ...
where he was abandoned ... (17/11)

___ 21) This is a literary dramatic device, rather than reflecting real feelings.
___ 22) By the time someone has Brad's education, he should
have overcome these feelings.
___ 23) Brad needs to stop feeling sorry for himself.
___ 24) Brad never should have entered a field like the practice of law with these serious emotional problems.
___ 25) We all have our problems. Abandonment is just another one.

CHAPTER 3 QUESTIONS

3(A) My reaction, when Janet said the following, is shown in
the rankings below.

He was relieved to see Janet become less tense. "Isn't there some kind
of support group? You know, 'Attorneys Anonymous' ... like a twelve
step group for lawyers who can't build their own book of business?" (32/1)

___ 26) That's a great idea.
___ 27) I'd join a group like that in a flash.
___ 28) I agree with Brad. People wouldn't tend to join.
___ 29) If there were such a group, it could work.
___ 30) If there's enough pain, most people will eventually
get help and change.

3(B) My reaction, when Brad thought the following, is shown
in the rankings below.

Brad could feel the perspiration on his forehead, as he thought, *I like
Jack. He's a great guy ... almost too great. But I never know what to say.
Once we've covered the business, I always feel like I want to escape back to
the office. I could force it into a quick phone conversation the way I usually do, but I know that's not the right thing to do. I can't really tell him I
don't have any time all day. Maybe I could make it a short lunch by having
sandwiches brought into our conference room. I'll get my secretary to interrupt after about thirty minutes with an urgent message.* (33/10)

___ 31) I know the feeling well. I'm like that myself, and/or I've seen people like that.

___ 32) Brad's feelings are extreme, but lots of people suffer from varying degrees of this type of withdrawal.

___ 33) Jack Mann probably sensed Brad's discomfort, but he needs to work with Brad.

___ 34) Brad is right on the edge of being dysfunctional.

___ 35) Jack Mann is probably not happy with Brad's behavior.

3(C) My reaction, when Brad thought the following, is shown in the rankings below.

Brad thought about what George would do if he got that same call. He had been in George's office lots of times when those client calls came in and he patiently sat through George's side of the conversation. He pictured George on the phone. "Jack, what a pleasure to hear from you. You're in Washington. That's great. Are you free for dinner? Oh, too bad. Can you make it for lunch? Good. I'll have to cancel something, but I'm sure it'll be okay. There's nothing I'd like to do more than have lunch with you. Why don't we meet at the Cosmos club at noon? Wonderful ... (33/12)

___ 36) How naïve Brad is to not understand the need to make people feel good.

___ 37) I wish I could be as smooth as George.

___ 38) Brad should be emulating George's style.

___ 39) Whether George is a phony or not, he knows how to handle clients.

___ 40) This is called either good interpersonal skills, or being a phony— depending on George's sincerity.

3(D) My reaction, when Miles said the following, is shown in the rankings below.

Miles didn't wait for Brad's usual excuse. "I've covered this a number of times in departmental meetings, Brad. Try to look at it from the client's perspective. He calls the main number. He gets the switchboard. He asks for you. They ask him whose calling, 'cause you want your calls screened. God forbid a mere client should get right through to you. Then he gets your secretary, who intercepts all your calls at your request. Then he asks for you again. She won't even give him the courtesy of answering his question, again at your request ... 'cause you want to have another personal screen of your calls. So instead of answering him, she asks him again who's calling. Then he gives his name again. Then she still doesn't tell him whether you're in, she puts him on hold while she waits for you to answer on the intercom. Then he waits until you're finished with whatever you're doing. Then finally he gets through to the great Brad Talbert. And what greeting does he get after all that? The great Brad Talbert doesn't even say hello. All he says is 'Brad Talbert'. By this time he's really pissed. Only the fact that he's temporarily dependent on this firm keeps him from telling you to shove it." (34/8)

___ 41) Miles didn't recognize the distracting pressure of having to concentrate on lots of matters.

___ 42) Lots of law firms have this double screening on calls. So what?

___ 43) Without this screening, lawyers would be constantly interrupted.

___ 44) My own firm and my secretary do this.

___ 45) Miles can afford to take this kind of time with his clients. He doesn't have to produce paper like Brad.

3(E) My reaction, when Brad thought the following, is shown in the rankings below.

At noon, while Brad and Jack Mann sat in the conference room having their roast beef sandwiches, Brad thought, *I sure do admire this guy. He's built Tensitron from nothing in five years. Now he's got over a hundred million in profitable sales and he's a decent guy, too. But how the hell can he be fooled by phonies like George? Is it possible even self-confident people like Jack need reassurance?* (35/10)

___ 46) If Brad admires Jack Mann so much, why can't he say so?

___ 47) Some people just don't need self reassurance like the Jack Manns of the world.

___ 48) If Brad can't deal with a longer time with Jack, he should schedule it just as he did.

___ 49) If Brad doesn't solve this problem, he'll continue to be a low compensated partner.

____ 50) If I were Jack Mann, I'd terminate with Brad after being treated like this.

CHAPTER 4 QUESTIONS

4(A) My reaction, when Brad heard the following, is shown in the rankings below.

Brad thought, the Managing Partner and my Department Chairman … I wonder what I screwed up. He waited for what seemed like another five minutes. Then he heard Miles' voice on a speakerphone. "Brad, this is Miles. I'm in Tim Long's office. There's only the two of us here and the door is closed, so feel free to be open." (41/9)

____ 51) On a call like this, most people wonder what they did wrong.
____ 52) Suspecting it had something to do with George would be a sign of good self-esteem.
____ 53) When Miles said, "feel free to be open", it's not the time to be guarded.
____ 54) Brad created his own problem by not knowing more about what George was doing in China.
____ 55) This sounds like a caring organization.

4(B) My reaction, when Brad said the following, is shown in the rankings below.

As Brad walked down the hall, Miles said, "Remember Brad, no word of this to anyone. Now, let's get you started on some other matters. Given what happened, George may not be able to return for awhile. First, I have a client coming in for lunch today. Can you join us?"

Brad was so surprised he could hardly get out his "Sure." In six years George had hardly ever invited him to have lunch with a client. It was almost always: prepare the paperwork and then make yourself scarce. (44/2)

____ 56) George's extreme pattern of keeping Brad away from his clients, is understandable. People steal clients.
____ 57) If George had client paranoia, then Brad was lucky in finding a home.
____ 58) Making oneself scarce is not necessarily detrimental to developing client skills.

_____ 59) Miles' luncheon invitation to Brad reflects Miles' lack of sophistication about his client relationships.

_____ 60) I'd never terminate the relationship with anyone just because he consistently refused to have me talk to clients for which I had done work.

4(C) My reaction, when Miles said the following, is shown in the rankings below.

"You don't seem very sociable. I mean if you're not talking business or law, you just sit there. You should do something about that. It makes people uncomfortable, Brad. They think you don't want to relate to them as human beings, only as a source of billing hours."

"It's hard for me, Miles. I was always told as a kid to be seen not heard and I don't have much experience with clients, 'cause George handles all that stuff himself. Besides, it always seems so phony to me." Then he quickly added. "I don't mean you seem phony Miles." (44/11)

_____ 61) Brad's "just sitting there" reflects how incredibly difficult it is to change interpersonal behavior.

_____ 62) Fear of saying the wrong thing creates unsociable people like Brad.

_____ 63) Fear of rejection can create them as well.

_____ 64) "Be seen, not heard" can be a destructive childhood message.

_____ 65) Affability can seem phony, depending on the perception of the observer.

4(D) My reaction, when Miles said the following, is shown in the rankings below.

"Either you like me or you put up a great front. You aren't silent with me. I'm your boss, but we're friends. You talk to me, but you don't talk to clients. You're just a pleasant computer with them, but still a computer. And you don't seem programmed for anything but law or business." (45/3)

_____ 66) He was reflecting his own uncertainty about Brad's sincerity.

_____ 67) Being a "pleasant computer" with clients is a compliment.

___ 68) Another compliment is not being "programmed for anything but law or business".

___ 69) Brad isn't silent with Miles because he feels Miles' acceptance.

___ 70) Brad doesn't understand the effect his silence has on other people.

4(E) My reaction, when Miles said the following, is shown in the rankings below.

"Okay, here it is. We're lucky. You and I both have lives that most of the rest of the world only dreams about. We get to meet and deal with the best of the best. The only people who can afford this firm's billing rates are those who are themselves successful. They're bright, articulate, positive ambitious and have chosen us. Remember, we can't choose them."

Brad thought about that a moment and said, "That's true Miles, but there's a lot of slime buckets with money and I guess we get our share." (45/7)

___ 71) Every professional should be able to take this view of his job.

___ 72) Miles could just as easily see clients as tough ruthless competitors who claw their way to the top.

___ 73) This is an example of looking at the same glass half full instead of half empty.

___ 74) This is another example of our realities flowing from our perceptions.

___ 75) Brad's comment about "slime buckets" is a good example of perception to reality.

CHAPTER 6 QUESTIONS

6(A) My reaction, when Brad thought the following, is shown in the rankings below.

Brad thought, *I hate these things. I never know what to say. They're just a bunch of people, bullshitting each other and I always end up eating too much, 'cause I get so nervous.* But he said, "I appreciate what you're trying to do for me Miles, but there's no way I can get Janet to go at this late hour. She'd have to get dressed, find a babysitter and get into the city. It's impossible." With a sigh of relief, he thought, *thank God for wife excuses.* (61/1)

____ 76) For someone in professional services to not like receptions is like a captain of a cruise ship not liking passengers.

____ 77) Of course all these social events result in people mostly bullshitting each other, but that's the game.

____ 78) Brad gets nervous, but so is everybody at these receptions.

____ 79) How fortunate for Brad that Janet and Miles tricked him into going.

____ 80) If Brad already knows he eats too much, he should be able to overcome it.

6(B) My reaction, when Brad thought and Tim said the following, is shown in the rankings below.

As Brad waited in line for his turn, he felt the nausea rising. He thought, *I hate this stupid, goddamn small talk, these phony people, and the same idiots who populate all these parties. Damn Janet, why does she get me into these things?* Then he saw her, wearing a strapless brilliant blue evening gown, in a group of about three men and two women. He thought, *God, she's beautiful.*

He was staring at her when he heard Tim say, "Well, Brad Talbert, this is an occasion. Didn't you have anything else on your schedule Brad, or were you just in the neighborhood? Come on in and see how the other half lives." (62/8)

____ 81) If I had Brad's outlook, I'd hate being at the reception too.

____ 82) The idea that Brad had nausea at being there is too exaggerated.

____ 83) Tim, the managing partner's sarcastic greeting should be enough for any partner to be deeply concerned.

____ 84) Having a beautiful wife like Janet doesn't hurt at these receptions.

____ 85) Tim's comment "Come on in and see how the other half lives", is just a joking statement — not to be taken seriously.

6(C) My reaction, when Janet thought the following, is shown in the rankings below.

Brad shrugged and wandered off. Janet watched him as he moved around the room. She thought, *he seems like a marshmallow floating on the water. He just wanders from group to group ... he never joins in ... he doesn't smile ... he just stands there nervously eating ... eating ... well, I guess it's better than drinking ... now he's ended up with two of his other wallflower buddies from the firm ... the three of them talking to each other ... what a waste ... they hardly have a client between them ...* (63/2)

____ 86) Everybody wanders from group to group at these receptions. Brad's behavior is no different. ·

____ 87) Nervous compulsive eating is common. Nobody much notices.

____ 88) These receptions are an opportunity to meet with colleagues. Brad's behavior is normal.

____ 89) The three of them are probably talking about how to get clients.

____ 90) So, Brad's serious ... he doesn't smile — so what? It doesn't make any difference.

6(D) My reaction, when Janet said the following, is shown in the rankings below.

"My point is they're nervous habits ... just like wolfing down food is. If you've stopped grabbing your nuts and picking your nose you can stop anything else. You're not mining for buggers, or massaging your nuts, here 'cause your partners would be in a state of shock. At some level you know they'll put up with the other marginal stuff you do." (64/17)

____ 91) Janet's too gross to be at a reception like this.

____ 92) If Brad stopped his other habits (grabbin' and pickin') he should easily be able to stop the compulsive eating habit.

____ 93) I agree with Janet's conclusion that Brad probably made a subconscious decision as to which bad habit he'd retain.

____ 94) If Janet were my wife, my first priority would be to send her to a course on good manners.

____ 95) No partner of a prestigious law firm would be wolfing down food at a reception.

6(E) My reaction, when Dale said the following, is shown in the rankings below.

"He did say that. But he still thinks the Xiamen deal should be competitive. He's gonna file a complaint with State, Commerce and the International Trade Commission. In short, he's gonna raise hell. He's gonna ask for a full formal hearing on what's going on in China. He wants a full investigation, witnesses, subpoenas, an administrative law judge, the whole shot." (67/6)

___ 96) Given Brad's personality, his self defensive reaction should be to immediately go to the firm's senior management.

___ 97) Brad's in the clear. Why should he care what happens?

___ 98) A formal hearing isn't much of a threat to someone with Brad's emotional problems.

___ 99) Given George's complicity, anyone with a normal range of emotions would have confronted George soon after receiving the news.

___ 100) Brad will probably ignore the situation, which is an advantage of his reclusive personality.

CHAPTER 7 QUESTIONS

7(A) My reaction, when Art said and thought the following, is shown in the rankings below.

"Look Brad, those kind of questions answering questions may be cute and show how cagey you are in depositions, but in normal conversations, with people who care about you, they cut you off from mankind."

Then Art waited, he thought, *Can this decent man be brought back from the living dead? He's so far gone ... he's bright, presentable ... he's got it all ... except the most important thing ... the ability to deal with people ... maybe I'm jumping on him too soon ... after all we just got together.* (73/11)

___ 101) Brad's kind of indirect conversational responses are so common among the highly educated that they're expected rather than distancing.

___ 102) Brad's answering of questions with questions is his attempt to clarify.

___ 103) Art's suggestion that there are two modes of conversation depending on the circumstances is absurd.

___ 104) Art's thought that Brad is among the interpersonal "living dead" is too extreme.

___ 105) Art reserving judgement about Brad ("... after all we just got together.") is a sign of wisdom.

7(B) My reaction, when Brad thought the following, is shown in the rankings below.

Brad thought, *I hate this. I Goddamn hate this. If Janet weren't looking over my shoulder through Art's eyes, I'd tell this guy to stuff it. Who needs this shit? But, I better be careful. If I do that, I'll never hear the end of it.*

Brad sat without saying a word for another five minutes. (75/10)

___ 106) Brad permitting Janet to browbeat him into doing things he knows are not right is at the core of his problem.

___ 107) If I "hated" something, I'd be long gone, no matter what the circumstances.

___ 108) When Brad sat for five minutes without saying anything, it must have been very awkward.

___ 109) Brad's sitting for five minutes of silence in this setting shows the depth of his problem.

___ 110) When Brad thought, "Who needs this shit?" it showed his deep feelings in spite of his outward passivity.

7(C) My reaction, when Jim and Art said the following, is shown in the rankings below.

Jim said, "When I was in banking I saw the same thing. Good people who were fired or quit because they couldn't generate loans. They just didn't have the people skills."

Art said, "It's just as competitive when you're trying to establish a psychology practice. You'd think being a banker and having money available, or being a psychologist, would reduce the need to sell, but it's all the same." (77/2)

___ 111) There is a big difference between the people skills necessary to generate loans versus those for getting legal clients.

___ 112) These people skill differences are even more extreme when compared to establishing a psychology practice.

___ 113) The idea that there's a necessary behavior pattern required in all professions is spurious.

___ 114) Clients, customers or patients in any business or practice will tolerate negative behavior when demand is strong.

___ 115) That toleration on the public's part does a great disservice to the provider using it to engage in antisocial behavior.

7(D) My reaction, when Art and Brad said the following, is shown in the rankings below.

Art said, "When we get to the border don't say anything unless the Mexican Police ask you a question. There's usually only a couple of Mexican police. They hardly look up … just wave people through … Mexico's glad to have the gringo dollars."

"It sounds like intrigue."

"Nope, it's just the way you cross the border when you're a fugitive."

"I can't imagine what that's like to be a fugitive. It must be terrible."

Art said, "You should know what it feels like. You live your whole work life as a fugitive."

"I don't even know what you're talking about."

"I'm talking about being a fugitive from the mainstream of practice … just like I'm a fugitive from the U.S." (79/12)

___ 116) I consider this a politically incorrect slam at Mexico.

___ 117) This whole fugitive analogy is strained.

___ 118) Brad's not perceiving he's a fugitive himself is understandable.

___ 119) Art's reference to the "mainstream" means the interpersonal skills which are the most important part of any personal service relationship.

___ 120) They're even more important in getting clients than substantive legal skills.

7(E) My reaction, when Art and Brad said the following, is shown in the rankings below.

As they inched past the dead raccoon in the middle of the road, Art said, "That's another thing about being a fugitive. It's like driving this road. It's dangerous and you're always worried."

Brad said, "I'm not always worried."

"Well, if you aren't, you should be. My psychology background tells me that at some level you're worried, no matter what you say."

"Are you always worried?"

Art said, "Sure, it only takes one slip and I'm in big trouble ... same for you. And that's not all."

Brad looked at the dead raccoon as the car passed it, and said, "I'm sure glad there's more. I was concerned this verbal beating might actually end."

"No such luck, Brad. You're like me in another way. Neither one of us can do what we want. I'm stuck in Tecate and you're stuck at your firm —" (82/6)

_____ 121) I can't agree with Art's fugitive theory, creating constant worry.

_____ 122) People know when they don't fit in and that creates the worry.

_____ 123) Art's comment, "It only takes one slip ..." is overly dramatic.

_____ 124) The very fact that Brad considers the conversation a "verbal beating," instead of being helpful, is indicative of how serious his problem is.

_____ 125) Art's comment that Brad is "stuck at" his firm is unrealistic.

CHAPTER 8 QUESTIONS

8(A) My reaction, when Art and Brad said the following, is shown in the rankings below.

"Wait? This may be the only car through here all night."

"But it might be the Border Patrol."

"So what?"

"They'll want all kinds of papers I don't have."

Brad said, "Well whoever it was, they're gone now. Look, Art, we can't stay here all night 'cause you're afraid of the Border Patrol. It's cold and I don't mind admitting, it's damn scary too. Supposing some coyotes come around." (84/12)

___ 126) Art's caution about the Border Patrol is analogous to Brad's caution about everybody.

___ 127) Art's fear creating his willingness to risk a cold, dangerous night in the wild isn't analogous to Brad's fears creating his alienation from his society.

___ 128) The Border Patrol represents to Brad anyone who might challenge him.

___ 129) Brad's comments are strained and they're not indicative of the fears with which they both live.

___ 130) The momentary passing of the Border Patrol is illustrative of those moments in life when people need to reach out for help, rather than sink back into their habit patterns.

8(B) My reaction, when Art and Brad said the following, is shown in the rankings below.

"Look, Brad, it all has to do with how you feel about yourself ... which I gather is crappy. So, you didn't have a mother or father to nurture you. Are you going to let it ruin your life?"

Brad was silent for a long time, then said, "Why am I sitting in a disabled car on a lonely mountain creek listening to someone tell me about my crappy self image?"

"'Cause you want a father figure to recreate a lost childhood?"

Brad laughed. "Isn't there any way to turn off your therapist?"

"Sure, but you'd be indicted for murder. How quickly you change. Wasn't it only this morning you told me how happy you were to see me?"

"That was coerced."

"Maybe so, but that's your problem. It had to be forced out of you. Brad, you're no different than anybody else. Everybody plays to the parents in their mind. You're still trying to please them." (83/16)

___ 131) Art's first question is right on point.

___ 132) Most everybody has childhood problems. They need only dismiss them.

___ 133) It's about time someone talked to Brad about his "crappy self-image."

___ 134) Art's comment that "Everybody plays to the parents in their mind" is a typical psychologist's business-getting statement.

___ 135) That's the problem with psychologists — they want to see issues in the most benign behavior, even Brad's.

8(C) My reaction, when Art and Brad said the following, is shown in the rankings below.

"Americans don't sneak across. It's the Mexicans who are in prison."

"So are we just gonna sit here all night?"

"We might as well, the Border doesn't open again 'til six A.M. But the border to your prison's never closed, Brad. You can get out anytime."

"It's a good thing you don't charge by the hour."

"I would if I thought it would do any good. In spite of what you think, I'm not the best thing in your life, Janet is. Do you know why?"

Brad said, "As amazed as you may be, I wasn't sitting here in your crashed car, freezing in this creek and thinking you're the best thing that ever happened to me and I know why Janet is."

"It's not why you think. It's because your relationship with her shows there's hope for you. It's good. It's healthy. And yet she's your best critic. That's an emotionally healthy intimate relationship."

"Thanks … I think."

"It shows you're able to overcome the lack of any nurturing when you were growing up." (86/14)

___ 136) Art's comment that Brad's healthy relationship with Janet held hope for Brad was incorrect. Skills in business and personal relationships are too different.

___ 137) Art's reason about Brad being able to overcome a lack of nurturing is equally erroneous.

___ 138) Art's comparison of the Mexican Border being closed to Brad's self-imposed prison is accurate.

___ 139) I'm not sure Brad can get out of his prison anytime.

___ 140) In this quoted portion, Brad is comparable to the Mexicans.

8(D) My reaction, when Art and Brad said the following, is shown in the rankings below.

"Brad, George is scared. He's got to be afraid of you."

"Afraid of me?"

192 ~ MAKING RAIN

"Sure, you're here with 'his' client. He's on the other side of the world, in the hospital. The sicker someone's personality is, the more likely they are to act the opposite of how they feel. So the more afraid George is, the tougher he's gonna get."

"So, what do I do about it?"

"Just ride it out for the moment and take care of yourself. That's your gift from George. He's forcing you to take care of yourself. You've kept something good through all this that could be your salvation." (88/20)

___ 141) Art's idea that George is afraid of Brad is ridiculous.

___ 142) To demonstrate how silly it is, one has only to remind oneself of how inept Brad is.

___ 143) Art's thought that George's fear of Brad has resulted in a gift to Brad is equally silly.

___ 144) Being forced to suffer can be a great gift.

___ 145) George's absence and impending return give Brad both the breathing space and threat for motivation.

8(E) My reaction, when Art and Brad said the following, is shown in the rankings below.

Art ignored the comment. "You have the office pressures, but you don't bring it home. Janet's told me about how loving you are. And that's what it takes. Just think if that female cat killed the coyote and then didn't let her mate have first licks. It's the culture and she conforms. The kittens do too."

"Thanks, Art."

"But it's not all good."

"I suspected that."

"The price you pay is that you don't really compete. As a result, your family, someday, may actually go hungry. The challenge is not to bring a competitive work personality into a loving home relationship. You don't know that challenge 'cause you don't compete." (89/8)

___ 146) Art's point about Brad continuing to be loving at home in the face of severe pressure was well taken.

___ 147) The mountain lion analogy about conforming to the culture is illustrative of the one bright spot in Brad's possible recovery.

___ 148) Brad just competes in his own way.
___ 149) Brad has too many internal emotional pressures to try to compete for business too.
___ 150) Brad is a far more complex personality than most people.

PERSONAL MAKING RAIN ANSWER SHEET

Using a pencil or pen, fill-in the oval corresponding to your answer. Use only one oval per question. Each of the 150 questions must be answered. There are no right or wrong answers. This is not a test. Just answer as best you can, based on your feelings. This will enable us to give you the most accurate analysis.

These pages may either be torn out of, or copied from, the book. You have the additional choice of answering online at www.mentoringpros.com.

The strength of your feelings is shown by the numbered oval you fill; i.e., 1= slight, 2= moderate, 3= substantial, 4= very strong, and 5= complete; either disagreement (-) or agreement (+).

Please note that the copyright has been released on this Personal Making Rain Answer Sheet when used for this purpose.

ANSWER SHEET

Chapter	Questions	Disagree					Agree				
		-5	-4	-3	-2	-1	+1	+2	+3	+4	+5
1(A)	1	◯	◯	◯	◯	◯	◯	◯	◯	◯	◯
	2	◯	◯	◯	◯	◯	◯	◯	◯	◯	◯
	3	◯	◯	◯	◯	◯	◯	◯	◯	◯	◯
	4	◯	◯	◯	◯	◯	◯	◯	◯	◯	◯
	5	◯	◯	◯	◯	◯	◯	◯	◯	◯	◯
1(B)	6	◯	◯	◯	◯	◯	◯	◯	◯	◯	◯
	7	◯	◯	◯	◯	◯	◯	◯	◯	◯	◯
	8	◯	◯	◯	◯	◯	◯	◯	◯	◯	◯
	9	◯	◯	◯	◯	◯	◯	◯	◯	◯	◯
	10	◯	◯	◯	◯	◯	◯	◯	◯	◯	◯
1(C)	11	◯	◯	◯	◯	◯	◯	◯	◯	◯	◯
	12	◯	◯	◯	◯	◯	◯	◯	◯	◯	◯
	13	◯	◯	◯	◯	◯	◯	◯	◯	◯	◯
	14	◯	◯	◯	◯	◯	◯	◯	◯	◯	◯
	15	◯	◯	◯	◯	◯	◯	◯	◯	◯	◯
1(D)	16	◯	◯	◯	◯	◯	◯	◯	◯	◯	◯
	17	◯	◯	◯	◯	◯	◯	◯	◯	◯	◯
	18	◯	◯	◯	◯	◯	◯	◯	◯	◯	◯
	19	◯	◯	◯	◯	◯	◯	◯	◯	◯	◯
	20	◯	◯	◯	◯	◯	◯	◯	◯	◯	◯
1(E)	21	◯	◯	◯	◯	◯	◯	◯	◯	◯	◯
	22	◯	◯	◯	◯	◯	◯	◯	◯	◯	◯
	23	◯	◯	◯	◯	◯	◯	◯	◯	◯	◯
	24	◯	◯	◯	◯	◯	◯	◯	◯	◯	◯
	25	◯	◯	◯	◯	◯	◯	◯	◯	◯	◯
3(A)	26	◯	◯	◯	◯	◯	◯	◯	◯	◯	◯
	27	◯	◯	◯	◯	◯	◯	◯	◯	◯	◯
	28	◯	◯	◯	◯	◯	◯	◯	◯	◯	◯
	29	◯	◯	◯	◯	◯	◯	◯	◯	◯	◯
	30	◯	◯	◯	◯	◯	◯	◯	◯	◯	◯

Chapter	Questions	Disagree					Agree				
		-5	-4	-3	-2	-1	+1	+2	+3	+4	+5
3(B)	31	◯	◯	◯	◯	◯	◯	◯	◯	◯	◯
	32	◯	◯	◯	◯	◯	◯	◯	◯	◯	◯
	33	◯	◯	◯	◯	◯	◯	◯	◯	◯	◯
	34	◯	◯	◯	◯	◯	◯	◯	◯	◯	◯
	35	◯	◯	◯	◯	◯	◯	◯	◯	◯	◯
3(C)	36	◯	◯	◯	◯	◯	◯	◯	◯	◯	◯
	37	◯	◯	◯	◯	◯	◯	◯	◯	◯	◯
	38	◯	◯	◯	◯	◯	◯	◯	◯	◯	◯
	38	◯	◯	◯	◯	◯	◯	◯	◯	◯	◯
	40	◯	◯	◯	◯	◯	◯	◯	◯	◯	◯
3(D)	41	◯	◯	◯	◯	◯	◯	◯	◯	◯	◯
	42	◯	◯	◯	◯	◯	◯	◯	◯	◯	◯
	43	◯	◯	◯	◯	◯	◯	◯	◯	◯	◯
	44	◯	◯	◯	◯	◯	◯	◯	◯	◯	◯
	45	◯	◯	◯	◯	◯	◯	◯	◯	◯	◯
3(E)	46	◯	◯	◯	◯	◯	◯	◯	◯	◯	◯
	47	◯	◯	◯	◯	◯	◯	◯	◯	◯	◯
	48	◯	◯	◯	◯	◯	◯	◯	◯	◯	◯
	49	◯	◯	◯	◯	◯	◯	◯	◯	◯	◯
	50	◯	◯	◯	◯	◯	◯	◯	◯	◯	◯
4(A)	51	◯	◯	◯	◯	◯	◯	◯	◯	◯	◯
	52	◯	◯	◯	◯	◯	◯	◯	◯	◯	◯
	53	◯	◯	◯	◯	◯	◯	◯	◯	◯	◯
	54	◯	◯	◯	◯	◯	◯	◯	◯	◯	◯
	55	◯	◯	◯	◯	◯	◯	◯	◯	◯	◯
4(B)	56	◯	◯	◯	◯	◯	◯	◯	◯	◯	◯
	57	◯	◯	◯	◯	◯	◯	◯	◯	◯	◯
	58	◯	◯	◯	◯	◯	+1	+2	+3	+4	◯
	59	◯	◯	◯	◯	◯	◯	◯	◯	◯	◯
	60	◯	◯	◯	◯	◯	◯	◯	◯	◯	◯

ANSWER SHEET

Chapter	Questions	Disagree					Agree				
		-5	-4	-3	-2	-1	+1	+2	+3	+4	+5
4(C)	61	○	○	○	○	○	○	○	○	○	○
	62	○	○	○	○	○	○	○	○	○	○
	63	○	○	○	○	○	○	○	○	○	○
	64	○	○	○	○	○	○	○	○	○	○
	65	○	○	○	○	○	○	○	○	○	○
4(D)	66	○	○	○	○	○	○	○	○	○	○
	67	○	○	○	○	○	○	○	○	○	○
	68	○	○	○	○	○	○	○	○	○	○
	69	○	○	○	○	○	○	○	○	○	○
	70	○	○	○	○	○	○	○	○	○	○
4(E)	71	○	○	○	○	○	○	○	○	○	○
	72	○	○	○	○	○	○	○	○	○	○
	73	○	○	○	○	○	○	○	○	○	○
	74	○	○	○	○	○	○	○	○	○	○
	75	○	○	○	○	○	○	○	○	○	○
6(A)	76	○	○	○	○	○	○	○	○	○	○
	77	○	○	○	○	○	○	○	○	○	○
	78	○	○	○	○	○	○	○	○	○	○
	79	○	○	○	○	○	○	○	○	○	○
	80	○	○	○	○	○	○	○	○	○	○
6(B)	81	○	○	○	○	○	○	○	○	○	○
	82	○	○	○	○	○	○	○	○	○	○
	83	○	○	○	○	○	○	○	○	○	○
	84	○	○	○	○	○	○	○	○	○	○
	85	○	○	○	○	○	○	○	○	○	○
6(C)	86	○	○	○	○	○	○	○	○	○	○
	87	○	○	○	○	○	○	○	○	○	○
	88	○	○	○	○	○	○	○	○	○	○
	89	○	○	○	○	○	○	○	○	○	○
	90	○	○	○	○	○	○	○	○	○	○

Chapter	Questions	Disagree					Agree				
		-5	-4	-3	-2	-1	+1	+2	+3	+4	+5
6(D)	91	○	○	○	○	○	○	○	○	○	○
	92	○	○	○	○	○	○	○	○	○	○
	93	○	○	○	○	○	○	○	○	○	○
	94	○	○	○	○	○	○	○	○	○	○
	95	○	○	○	○	○	○	○	○	○	○
6(E)	96	○	○	○	○	○	○	○	○	○	○
	97	○	○	○	○	○	○	○	○	○	○
	98	○	○	○	○	○	○	○	○	○	○
	99	○	○	○	○	○	○	○	○	○	○
	100	○	○	○	○	○	○	○	○	○	○
7(A)	101	○	○	○	○	○	○	○	○	○	○
	102	○	○	○	○	○	○	○	○	○	○
	103	○	○	○	○	○	○	○	○	○	○
	104	○	○	○	○	○	○	○	○	○	○
	105	○	○	○	○	○	○	○	○	○	○
7(B)	106	○	○	○	○	○	○	○	○	○	○
	107	○	○	○	○	○	○	○	○	○	○
	108	○	○	○	○	○	○	○	○	○	○
	109	○	○	○	○	○	○	○	○	○	○
	110	○	○	○	○	○	○	○	○	○	○
7(C)	111	○	○	○	○	○	○	○	○	○	○
	112	○	○	○	○	○	○	○	○	○	○
	113	○	○	○	○	○	○	○	○	○	○
	114	○	○	○	○	○	○	○	○	○	○
	115	○	○	○	○	○	○	○	○	○	○
7(D)	116	○	○	○	○	○	○	○	○	○	○
	117	○	○	○	○	○	○	○	○	○	○
	118	○	○	○	○	○	○	○	○	○	○
	119	○	○	○	○	○	○	○	○	○	○
	120	○	○	○	○	○	○	○	○	○	○

ANSWER SHEET

Chapter	Questions	Disagree					Agree				
		-5	-4	-3	-2	-1	+1	+2	+3	+4	+5
7(E)	121	○	○	○	○	○	○	○	○	○	○
	122	○	○	○	○	○	○	○	○	○	○
	123	○	○	○	○	○	○	○	○	○	○
	124	○	○	○	○	○	○	○	○	○	○
	125	○	○	○	○	○	○	○	○	○	○
8(A)	126	○	○	○	○	○	○	○	○	○	○
	127	○	○	○	○	○	○	○	○	○	○
	128	○	○	○	○	○	○	○	○	○	○
	129	○	○	○	○	○	○	○	○	○	○
	130	○	○	○	○	○	○	○	○	○	○
8(B)	131	○	○	○	○	○	○	○	○	○	○
	132	○	○	○	○	○	○	○	○	○	○
	133	○	○	○	○	○	○	○	○	○	○
	134	○	○	○	○	○	○	○	○	○	○
	135	○	○	○	○	○	○	○	○	○	○
8(C)	136	○	○	○	○	○	○	○	○	○	○
	137	○	○	○	○	○	○	○	○	○	○
	138	○	○	○	○	○	○	○	○	○	○
	139	○	○	○	○	○	○	○	○	○	○
	140	○	○	○	○	○	○	○	○	○	○
8(D)	141	○	○	○	○	○	○	○	○	○	○
	142	○	○	○	○	○	○	○	○	○	○
	143	○	○	○	○	○	○	○	○	○	○
	144	○	○	○	○	○	○	○	○	○	○
	145	○	○	○	○	○	○	○	○	○	○
8(E)	146	○	○	○	○	○	○	○	○	○	○
	147	○	○	○	○	○	○	○	○	○	○
	148	○	○	○	○	○	○	○	○	○	○
	149	○	○	○	○	○	○	○	○	○	○
	150	○	○	○	○	○	○	○	○	○	○

assured that your responses are kept *confidential.*

Let us know how you want your personal analysis delivered:

☐ U. S. Mail   ☐ Fax   Fax Number: _____

Name or ID _____

Address   _____

City _____State _____ Zip _____

PAYMENT

The cost for this analysis is $85, if taken on our website, or $115 if submitted on a paper form (via mail or fax). If your Firm has a contract with us simply insert your Firm's Contract Code here: _____ and either fax or mail your answers.

If your Firm does not have a contract with us, enclose a check to Associates Publishers for $115 and mail it to us at 7491 North Federal Highway, Suite C-5, Boca Raton, Fl 33487. You may also fax your completed questionnaire to us at 561-865-2155.

If you are responding from a non-contract firm, you can also pay by credit card by giving us:

Payment by: ☐ MasterCard   ☐ Visa

Name on Card _____

Credit Card Number _____

Expiration Date_____

Signature _____

If you liked this novel, and would like to pass one on to someone else, please check with your local bookstore, online bookseller, or provide the following information:

Name_____

Address   _____

City _____State _____ Zip _____

Making Rain _____ copies @ $12.95 each $_____

Florida residents, please add applicable sales tax $_____

Shipping: $3.20/first copy; $1.60 each additional copy $_____

Total enclosed $_____

For more than 5 copies, please contact the publisher for quantity rates. Send completed order form and your check or money order to:

> Associates Publishers
> 7491 N. Federal Highway, Suite C-5
> Boca Raton, FL 33487
>
> Telephone orders: (866) 620-3189 (toll free)
> e-mail: info@mentoringpros.com
> Telephone and fax: (561) 865-2155
> Web site: www.mentoringpros.com

International shipping is extra. Please contact us for the shipping rates to your location, if outside the United States.